GOLDEN
GIRL

ALISTAIR MACLEAN'S

GOLDEN GIRL

SIMON GANDOLFI

CHAPMANS

Chapmans Publishers Ltd
141–143 Drury Lane
London WC2B 5TB

BRITISH LIBRARY CATALOGUING IN PUBLICATION DATA
Gandolfi, Simon
Golden girl.
I. Title
823.914 [F]
ISBN 1-85592-008-5

First published by Chapmans 1992
Copyright © 1992 by Devoran Trustees Ltd

The right of Simon Gandolfi to be identified as
the author of this work has been asserted by him
in accordance with the Copyright, Designs and Patents Act
1988.

Phototypeset by Intype, London
Printed and bound in Great Britain by
Clays Ltd, St Ives plc

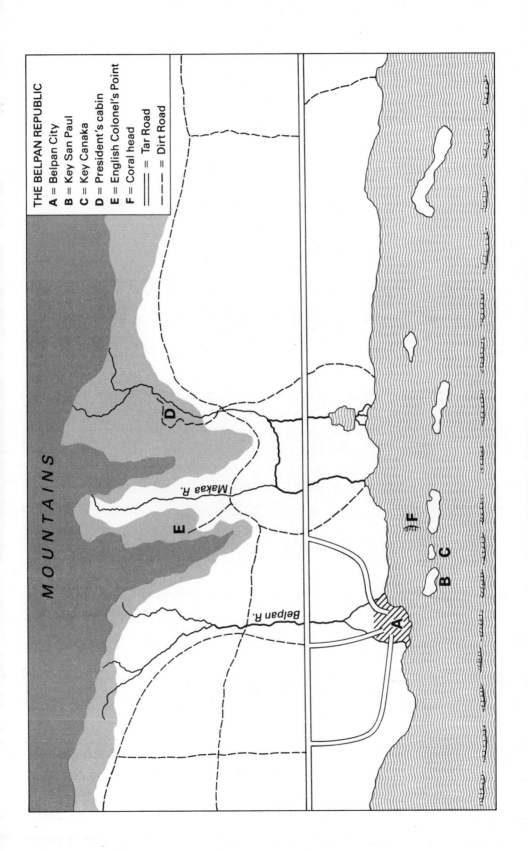

THE BELPAN REPUBLIC

A = Belpan City
B = Key San Paul
C = Key Canaka
D = President's cabin
E = English Colonel's Point
F = Coral head

——— = Tar Road
– – – = Dirt Road

MOUNTAINS

Belpan R.

Makaa R.

ACKNOWLEDGEMENTS

Though perhaps familiar geographically to those readers who have visited Belize, the Belpan Republic is an imaginary country. Those topographical similarities between the invented and the factual are accidental, or through paucity of imagination, and all characters in the book are fictional. I make these points because this book was written in Belize.

Belize is a country enviable for its racial, social, and political freedoms as much as for the beauty of its barrier reef and rainforest. Of the many Belizeans who gave me assistance and hospitality, I would like to thank in particular Lucy and Mick Fleming, together with their staff at Chaa Creek, for having provided me with the most perfect of studios. Where else in the world could I see and listen to more than one hundred different birds from the comfort of a wooden deck outside my room or while paddling gently down a river embraced by rainforest?

PROLOGUE

Pete Hendrik had been asleep on an air-mattress behind the cockpit. His alarm clock woke him. Both engines were running smoothly. Although he had set the alarm himself, he checked the time against his pilot's watch. Propping himself up on one elbow, he looked forward through the open cockpit door. The sky hadn't changed – bright stars, moonlight, and no cloud; the forecast had been correct.

Pete had started out co-piloting Air Force cargo in Korea. Now he was flying cocaine from Colombia into the US. Pete didn't like the stuff. He thought of himself as a booze man – always had been. Not continually, and never so it affected his flying, but he loved to party. But for the parties Pete might have flown for one of the straight outfits, Delta, TWA, and gone to work in a smart blue uniform with gold on his cap. But a straight outfit wouldn't have paid for his wives; Pete had been married six times and had eleven children, ranging from a four-year-old in kindergarten up to a 36-year-old lawyer working in the Public Defender's Office in Nebraska City. Wives were where Pete's money had gone and why he was flying for the Colombian Cocaine Cartel – wives and *perestroika*.

Between the Air Force and the Cartel he had flown mostly for Air America and other CIA-fronted airlines, recently in and out of Honduras flying drops to the Nicaraguan Contras. *Perestroika* had put him out of a job and threatened to make half the CIA redundant. Confrontation was out of fashion, as were the people who had fed off it.

At sixty-one he was too old to be sleeping crunched up on an air-mattress, Pete decided as he heaved himself up and tried to wriggle the stiffness out of his shoulders. He filled two mugs from the coffee thermos, black with extra sugar. Squeezing through the cockpit door, he checked the instruments before easing himself into the pilot's seat. Fuel flow fourteen gallons, course 358, altitude five hundred, oil pressure forty-five, revs at twenty-four hundred, EGT, all just fine. Fuel was down to an hour and ten minutes' flying time but that was as expected. Satisfied, he handed the spare mug of coffee to his young co-pilot.

Pete thought of the slim, dark, young co-pilot as The Kid and a club flyer. The Kid could hold altitude and fly a straight course, but Pete wouldn't have trusted his life to him landing on a strange strip in the dark with the marking lights only flashing for a few seconds. For Pete that sort of landing had been a way of life.

He didn't know how The Kid had got into this. True, he liked the powder, and perhaps he owed money on the street or higher up the ladder. Possibly he simply wanted to earn himself a stake. Pete didn't care. One flight was his own agreement, twenty thousand dollars. That would pay off the mortgage on his sixth wife's condo in Florida. Then all he'd have to find was food money for their boy – he thanked God that there was only one. And no more wives. He'd been too old for number six – his age rather than the partying was the reason she had given for throwing him out.

Pete didn't like cocaine and he didn't like Colombians. Airlines, even Air America, fired you if you messed up, but Colombians blew your head off or stuck a knife in your back. But they were efficient, he admitted as he checked the flight map. Load five hundred gallons of fuel in the cargo hold, fly low all the way over Mexico with the mountains protecting him from the radar, kick the coke out of the hold over the Texas desert, back to Belpan to refuel and straight on to Colombia. Thirty-six hours and twenty grand. Easy money.

Pete had never been to Belpan. It wasn't the sort of country anyone visited except by mistake – one hundred miles of narrow coastal strip, mostly swamp, a range of mountains cutting the strip off from the Central American hinterland, and a chain of sand-keys sheltered by a coral reef. Pete couldn't remember under what name, but up to the early sixties, Belpan had belonged to the British. Then they'd given it away. Pete's destination was a privately-owned strip on one of the keys, estimated time of arrival 0025 hours. One blue light at the touchdown point, three red lights marking the end of the strip. No trees on the approach so he could come in flat on the sea. Full moon. No wind. No sweat . . .

The Kid pointed down at a sand-fringed clump of palm trees and, with total confidence, jabbed the flight map. Pete neither believed nor disbelieved him. Way ahead and to the west he could see the scattered lights of what had to be Belpan City. Nowhere else in Belpan had that many lights. The broken foam-line of the reef lay below them. Ten minutes and they should be over San Paul Key, a further five minutes and the blue light would appear. Circle once and come in to land, those were Pete's instructions. Other than the occasional fisherman's hut, San Paul Key was the first inhabited island on the flight route: half a dozen small hotels lit by their own generators and fifty or so houses. The hotels shut down their generators at midnight so, given luck, everyone would be in bed.

Pete had a last go at wriggling the stiffness out of his shoulders before fastening his seat harness, then he reached for his spectacles. He didn't bother speaking to The Kid, merely gave him a nod and took over the controls. By the

9

time he'd got the feel of the plane and finished his coffee, San Paul Key lay ahead and a little to the left. Their outboards covered against the night dew, a half-dozen skiffs lay off the shore. There were lights on the beach and a crowd dancing. It looked the casual kind of party Pete liked. If he had been there and heard a plane fly over low on a heading for Key Canaka, he would have been sorely tempted to grab a skiff and race on over to check what the plane was doing that late at night. If any of the party-goers boated over to Key Canaka, Pete knew that the odds were on their getting themselves shot.

He had been shot at more times than he cared to count, and had done his share of shooting, but always in a war situation. Killing some half-drunk kid over a load of cocaine wasn't where Pete was at . . .

ONE

In celebration of the full moon, reggae music blared from a clapboard hotel on San Paul Key, largest of Belpan's offshore islands. The wind had dropped, bringing out clouds of the minute sandflies that plague the Caribbean. 'No Seeums' the flies are called in Belpan patois, and mosquito nets won't keep them out.

With sleep improbable, the hotel-keeper had built a fire of coconut husks on the beach and stood grilling lobsters over the ashes. His guests were mostly American college students or recently out of college. The reef is Belpan's main attraction; the primitive facilities of the hotels keep the young tourists' parents away. Rum retails at a dollar a bottle, and white rum mixed half and half with fresh orange juice is the national drink. The Gonjos from the Southern Province of the mainland grow marijuana. They are descendants of runaway slaves; they race dug-out sailing canoes, dance most nights, and are content to leave commerce and politics to the Latinos and Creoles.

A half-mile out, its slim varnished hulls barely visible from the beach, the fifty-foot sloop-rigged catamaran, *Golden Girl*, lay at anchor in the lee of the reef. A line held a fourteen-foot grey inflatable Zodiac dinghy to the catamaran's stern and a scarlet BMW R100 GS Enduro motor cycle hung in the after davits.

Golden Girl had been designed and built in cold-moulded marine ply by Rod MacAlpine-Downey as an ocean-racing machine. Speed and safety in a catamaran are products of lightness. The bows must be kept especially light to avoid their being driven down into the waves by a squall. On *Golden Girl* the bridge-deck joining the twin hulls ended three feet forrard of the central saloon. Forrard of this point the hulls were connected by inch-wide nylon webbing.

A man lolled on the webbing, watching the beach party through a pair of Zeiss binoculars. He had been born Patrick Mahoney. He had other names, but the one he could never use was his own, for to do so would have put men's lives at risk. Patrick Mahoney had been shot dead in an ambush in South Armagh – so the newspapers had reported, together with photographs of the burial in the Shannon churchyard with the rain beating down so that the faces of the mourners were indistinct in the grey winter light and, anyway, half hidden behind coat-collars and by dripping hat-brims pulled well down against the weather.

In Belpan, he went by the name of Trent, a name he had grown comfortable with. Thirty-five years old, he was dressed in dark blue cotton pyjama trousers and a dark blue T-shirt. His hair was long, black and slightly curling, and he wore a short thick beard so that even a trained observer would have found difficulty in describing his features. But his eyes were dark, almost black, and his body supple and strongly muscled. Perhaps a little incongruously, he wore a neckband of red coral beads. He had anchored out to escape the sandflies.

A light swell spilled over the reef, gently swaying the big catamaran. In retreat, the sea sucked at the coral, and the slurping and gurgling reminded Trent of his Irish grandfather sucking at his pint of Guinness, his false teeth safe

12

in his waistcoast pocket along with a heavy gold watch and a silver penknife. The teeth had been a bad fit.

The drone of a plane drew Trent's attention away from the beach. The plane was approaching low and from the south, on a course parallel to the coast. There were no commercial night flights into Belpan City, as Trent knew. Curious, he climbed the mast.

Seventy feet up, he should have seen the plane's navigation lights. He was familiar with aeroplanes. In the past he had waited on grass strips in the dark, listening through the engine roar for the threat of men closing in, the sudden splash of a searchlight pinning him in the sights of a Kalashnikov.

The approaching plane was twin-engined and slow. Trent pictured the chart. The only strip on the coast other than Belpan City Airport had been built by an American cosmetics billionaire on Key Canaka five miles north of San Paul Key. He lived there two weeks in the year in a big white bungalow on the reef side of the island. Belpan's President had a small wooden holiday house on the shore side. A grace-and-favour house, it would have been called in England, the billionaire playing the part of the Queen.

Climbing down the mast, Trent made his way to the sail-locker in the forward section of the port hull. All his fore-sails were stowed rolled and lashed with sewing cotton. He selected a lightweight ghoster and ran it up to the masthead where it hung in its cotton lashing like a long white sausage against the night sky.

Again to keep weight out of the bows, Trent preferred nylon anchor warp with only a few metres of chain attached to the anchor as protection against wear and to weight the angle of the anchor flat to the sea bed, thus helping the flukes dig in. To avoid the rattle of the anchor chain, Trent heaved in the warp till the chain showed. He made fast the end of the chain to the line on the dinghy, unshackled the chain from the nylon warp, and let the Zodiac drift clear.

A hard jerk on the portside sheet running back to the cockpit from the foot of the sail broke the ghoster free of its cotton lashings. Next to a spinnaker, the ghoster is the largest and lightest sail in a yacht's wardrobe. Out by the reef and away from the shelter of the islands there was just sufficient breeze to fill the sail. Trent listened to the soft ripple of the bows lifting to the water as the catamaran gained speed. *Golden Girl* drew two feet with her daggerboards up. There were no coral heads that shallow between his anchorage and Key Canaka so he had no need for the chart. He clipped sponge-rubber bands to the twin tillers and, leaving *Golden Girl* to sail herself, climbed back up the mast.

The plane had completed a full circle and was heading back now down its original track. Trent heard the pilot throttle right back as he came in to land, and thought he saw three red lights blink on Key Canaka. Then came a flash of brilliant white light that even at four miles' distance left a shadow across his vision. The plane's engines cut and he heard a series of thumps and snappings as if a heavy man had tumbled down a railway embankment into a bed of dry twigs and old cans.

To keep windage to a minimum the halyards for raising the sails ran inside *Golden Girl*'s aluminium mast and there was a small inspection panel at the masthead. Trent slid it open, hooked a finger round a waxed line and pulled out a Walther PPK with two spare magazines packed in a polythene bag.

When halfway between his anchorage and Key Canaka he heard a speedboat tear away towards the mainland. It took him an hour to reach the island. He dropped the sail, lowered a small kedge anchor overboard aft of the cockpit, being careful not to make a splash, paid out the stern line, and ran *Golden Girl* into the beach, holding her on the kedge so that the bows barely kissed the shingle. He dropped overboard and took a line ashore to a palm tree, clambered back on board and hauled the cat out ten feet.

He had feared the stink of petrol. It was there but very faint. The plane must have been low on fuel. Trent was wary of open ground, particularly at night. Walther in hand, heavy torch ready and a miniature camera in his pocket, he jogged round the airstrip in the shadow of the palm trees. The plane was at the far end of the strip, its nose thrust between two trees. Its wings had been ripped back by the treetrunks, braking the plane's speed and holding it on an even keel – the pilot had been lucky or extraordinarily skilful. Perhaps both, Trent thought.

He waited a further five minutes in the shadows, pistol hanging down by his side as he listened. Then he circled the front of the plane and saw the pilot, a dark shape behind the shattered windscreen. The freight door on the port side was open. Trent hauled himself in.

A fuel tank took up most of the room aft of the door and a row of steel canisters, each twice the size of a scuba diver's air bottles, were lashed to a reinforcing bar forward of the tank. Trent clambered over the usual refuse of a crash towards the cockpit. A dark young man lay crumpled in the cockpit door in a pool of blood. Trent presumed that he was the co-pilot. His torch showed a shard of glass buried deep in the young man's throat. The glass had severed the artery.

The crash had hurled the pilot forward over the control column, the impact crushing the top of his skull against the windscreen. Easing him back into his seat, Trent flashed the torch beam and found himself looking at a broad, tough face gone a little puffy at the jowls, a squashed nose, grey eyes bleached by sun and alcohol. What remained of a pugnacious crew-cut bristled beneath the gore. A bar-room brawler, Trent thought as he checked the pilot's scarred knuckles – into his sixties and too old for the role. He recognised the man, not as an individual, but as a type – one of the Good Ol' Boys. Oil-field pilots, survey work, Air America, and those small semi-official operations that the least savoury branches of the CIA dreamt up. Trent had entrusted his life to them often enough, and in his experience Good Ol' Boys didn't get to be Good Ol' Boys by making night landings with their safety harness undone.

Crouching forward over the dead man, he shone his torch over the blood-spattered windscreen. At the point of impact a small section of the glass had broken free. He snapped open his bosun's knife and levered the glass shards back, taking care to keep them free of the surrounding blood. A silver-grey flake stuck to one of the shards. Trent wiped his knife blade before scraping it free, then he found the pilot's navigation board and rubbed the flake along a clean section of the flight map. It left a grey line. The pilot's pockets were empty and there were no documents in the cockpit other than the flight maps which covered the Southern US, Mexico, and Central America.

The co-pilot's pockets were also empty. Trent had another look at the wound in the young man's throat. He photographed both men, then clambered back to the cargo hold and examined the steel canisters. There were fifteen of them in all, screw topped, and weighing around twenty kilos each. Trent opened one of the canisters, touched a damp fingertip to the white crystalline powder inside and rubbed it into his gum. The immediate numbing and the taste was all the evidence he needed. Five kilos of steel, the rest cocaine. Fifteen multiplied by fifteen, two hundred and twenty-five kilos. Three and a half million dollars wholesale, thirteen million dollars broken into grams and sold on the street. Trent closed the canister and used his T-shirt to wipe his fingerprints off the steel.

Dropping back to the ground, he examined the sand for footprints. His own showed clearly and that was all. Pistol ready, he circled a hundred yards back into the trees. Finally he cut the trail he'd expected. One man, heavily laden, had made two trips to and from the beach. The trails split fifty yards in front of the plane. Trent followed the left-hand trail. The footsteps ended one hundred yards inland from the end of the airstrip. Back-tracking, he followed the right-hand trail – same thing, except that this time it was sixty yards into the trees.

A cold bitter rage filled Trent as he walked back down the centre of the strip in search of the skid marks which would show where the plane had touched down. He paced the distance from the marks to the beach – one hundred and fifteen yards, a near perfect landing, as befitted the swan song of a Good Ol' Boy.

Eighty minutes later Trent picked up his anchor, dropped and stowed the sail and returned the Walther to its cache.

A companionway led off the cockpit into the big, light, airy saloon that spanned the bridge-deck. The chart table lay to port of the companionway. A big U-shaped settee upholstered in dusty blue filled the forward end of the saloon and half-circled the polished mahogany dining table supported by the mast-step. Steps led down into each hull from the saloon. Both hulls contained fore and aft cabins with double bunks, basins and private heads. A well-equip-ped galley separated the two cabins in the starboard hull. The same area in the port hull held a shower, large sink, worktop, and a store for Trent's photographic equipment. He developed and printed the film he had taken of the inside of the plane before dragging a sleeping bag up on deck.

Trent awoke to the approach of a fifty horse Johnston out-board motor. Johnstons, Mercuries and Yamahas were the makes of outboard imported into Belpan and Trent had soon learnt to recognise one from the others by its exhaust tone.

He opened one eye and squinted into the sun rising out of thin layers of dawn mist smoking off the steel-blue Carib-bean. Racing out of the sun came a white, twenty-foot, open lobster skiff. The boatman spun the wheel, cut power, and the skiff dropped off the plane and slid broadside towards *Golden Girl*. Its stern wave, trapped between the catamaran's twin hulls, jetted up, soaking both Trent and his sleeping-bag.

The boatman grabbed *Golden Girl*'s rail, holding the skiff clear of the catamaran's immaculate varnish. Mid-twenties and Latino, he was short and muscular with the barrel chest of a free-diver. Daily exposure to the sun had burnt his skin almost black, while sea salt had bleached the tips of his dark hair to yellow. Bright black eyes and a wide grin announced that he was pleased with himself, delighted by the world and all foreseeable futures.

Trent envied the young boatman his confidence. Wiping the salt out of his eyes, he said in Spanish, 'Carlos, one day you'll come at me out of the sun and I'll blow your head off.'

Trent's accent was Castilian and sounded a little over-precise given that it was coming out of a sleeping-bag at five in the morning off the coast of Central America.

The boatman called him a *maricon*: '*Venga*, let us earn our breakfast . . . '

With two hundred lobster-pots spread across the ocean floor, Carlos earned a great deal more than his breakfast. His expenses were minimal: no car, because there wasn't a road on Key San Paul and nowhere to go if there had been. A new pair of jeans, a pair of shorts, a couple of T-shirts and that was it for the six months of the fishing season. He owned two condos in Miami and was halfway through paying for a third. Trent helped him clear the pots, free-diving – lifting the pots would have doubled the time. They were finished by ten o'clock. Trent wanted to have a second look at Key Canaka in daylight but he didn't want to draw attention to himself by sailing over on *Golden Girl* so he asked if he could borrow the skiff, promising to drop it back at the Fishermen's Co-operative quay.

While Carlos unloaded lobster at the Co-op, Trent strolled over to Jimmy's Bar, which was the general meeting place on Key San Paul. On the way he had to step round four young Americans sitting in the middle of the path, seemingly discussing what to do with the day.

Jimmy was Creole, fifties, and beginning to put on weight through lack of exercise. Lobster-fishing had financed the construction of his bar and restaurant and he had added, above his boatshed, ten rooms with private bathrooms which occasionally worked. Both bar and restaurant thrived and he had imported a video player from the States on which he showed feature films pirated from Home Box Office by the mother-in-law of a cousin of his who had married a doctor and lived in southern California. The mother-in-law paid her bridge losses out of her commission.

In early middle age, Jimmy had switched track from island entrepreneur to beach-front philosopher. Trent found him seated in a deckchair under a palm tree in front of his bar. Some time earlier in the day Jimmy had begun rolling a cigarette from a pouch on his knee that didn't hold tobacco. He had licked four Rizla rice papers into a single sheet, then either run out of energy or been side-tracked by a fresh thought. Thinking was Jimmy's main occupation. His wife and four children took care of the rest.

Trent squatted down with his back to the wall and waited for Jimmy to return from wherever he was.

Finally Jimmy said, 'You hear a plane crash on Key Canaka las' night? They say it on de radio, nine o'clock.'

Trent said that he'd been out fishing.

'What you catch?' Jimmy asked.

'Lifting lobster with young Carlos,' Trent said.

Jimmy lost interest. On Key San Paul lobster was cheaper than chicken eggs and a lot easier to find. 'You get snapper, Trent Boy, you bring them by.'

Trent said he would. What fish he speared for the res-taurant, Jimmy credited against his bar bill.

Jimmy pointed at a wooden dock. 'The Presiden' down

there fishin' bonefish. Damn boatman forgot he mean' pick him up.'

Trent asked if the President was going out to Key Canaka and Jimmy nodded.

'I could run him over in young Carlos' skiff,' Trent said.

Jimmy fingered the weed in his tobacco pouch in an absent-minded way. Then he shook his head as if bothered by flies: 'I don' know, Trent Boy, but this man telling us the Presiden' playin' with the Colombianos.' He picked up a newspaper from the sand and dropped it in Trent's lap. The *Belpan Independent*, four pages of smudged newsprint but the best newspaper in Belpan. That and the *Belpan Times*. Trent had heard that both papers had changed hands over the past two months. He read the article, which was a classic of its kind – scurrilous supposition that built up into an accusation that the President was in the pay of Colombia's cocaine traffickers and was allowing them to refuel on Belpan's jungle airstrips and main highway.

The previous week a twin-engined De Havilland Otter, loaded with cocaine, had crashed into a culvert while making a night landing on an uncompleted stretch of new road in the unpopulated north of the country. Now there was this second crash on Key Canaka to add fresh fuel to the fire and Belpan was heading into Parliamentary and Presidential elections.

Trent handed the paper back to Jimmy and wandered down towards the dock. The four young Americans sitting in the path had become five and they had moved a couple of metres to keep in the shade.

One of them said, 'Hi,' which struck Trent as about right.

Belpan's President was in his late sixties. Creole, a good deal more black than white, he was tall and slim, though with a slight paunch, grey-haired and going bald on top. He wore long khaki pants and a shirt to match, round, steel-rimmed spectacles, feet in blue canvas pull-ons. He was casting for bonefish with a carbon rod, dropping the fly light as a feather on the still water where he could see the tails of the fish standing up like triangles as they drove through the shallows. Trent thought that the old man looked worried, but he could have been worried at not catching fish or because his boatman had forgotten to pick him up.

Trent considered Belpan the only nation in the world where the President's boatman would forget. It was also the only country he knew where the President could fish from the end of a public dock or wander down the sidewalks of the capital in search of a cab without need of a bodyguard.

A young woman in her late teens to early twenties sat on the dock watching. Paler-skinned than the President, she had the old man's slim figure without the paunch. Her lips were well-shaped and generous and her eyes were large. Her hair was pumped up by a red bandana into a bouffant Afro, and she wore cut-down jeans with a red halter-top to match the bandana. She was watching the President as if he were the most wonderful man in the world and it was her duty to protect him.

Trent strolled down the dock and said, 'Good morning, Mister President.'

The old man looked round in surprise, probably at being recognised by a foreigner.

'Trent, sir. Jimmy up at the bar said you might like a ride over to Key Canaka.'

'You're English – '

'British, sir,' Trent said.

The old man had a kind smile, warm and understanding, that reminded Trent of his own father. The initial tension that Trent had sensed in the President melted away: 'A Celt?'

'Yes, sir.'

'We are also racially very mixed, Mister Trent.' The old man looked down at the girl. 'My granddaughter read Politics and Economics at the LSE. Ah,' he said as a thirty-foot blue launch came round the point. 'Late but not forgotten. Most kind of you to offer your assistance . . . '

Trent suspected that the old man needed a great deal more assistance than a Recruitment Agency's offer of a new boatman.

Two

A twenty-mile strip of plush hotels, nightclubs, restaurants, condominiums, and private mansions, Cancun, in the Province of Quintana Roo, Mexico, was about as far, in tourist terms, as a man could get from Belpan's Keys. Sailing *Golden Girl* up from Belpan, Trent had encountered near-perfect wind and sea conditions. The voyage had taken twenty-four hours at an average of thirteen knots. With the catamaran safely moored in the marina, Trent had unloaded his BMW on to the dock before finding a last Sunday's copy of the *New York Times* and a sidewalk café that served freshly-ground coffee.

Over his newspaper, he watched a tall, lean, square-shouldered man in a fawn linen suit stroll towards him along the promenade. He wore an MCC tie and a Panama hat and was shod in highly-polished brown brogues that looked as if they had been made to measure. Cold grey eyes inspected Trent for a second – very pale grey indeed. The face matched the eyes: thick grey eyebrows, pale tight nostrils above the fiercely-clipped moustache, hard mouth and square chin all indelibly marked the face with that mixture of absolute social confidence and calm authority peculiar to the British Guards or Cavalry officer accustomed by birth as well as career to immediate and unquestioning obedience.

Because of his father, Trent had suffered the genial contempt of such men throughout his childhood.

Folding his paper, Trent crossed the promenade and took the first turn on the right. The street ended at the main dual carriageway leading from Cancun along the causeway to the Mexican mainland. The sun beat down on the black tar surface, the heat warping the light into shimmering waves. It was too hot for pedestrians and there were few cars. The Highway Department had planted acacias down the central strip and along the edges of the carriageway. Some of the trees had died, more had been eaten by goats. The remainder were stunted and offered insufficient shade for even the most hardened Maya peasant seeking a siesta.

Turning left, Trent watched the man in the linen suit approach on the far side of the carriageway. The heat waves cut the Englishman in half at the waist so that his legs appeared to strut independently of his upper body. Certain that no one was following the Englishman, Trent kept him in sight as the older man crossed back over the dual carriageway and turned up a side street towards the promenade. Trent quickened his pace, turning up the same street. The Englishman looked back over his shoulder and Trent dropped his newspaper. Stooping to retrieve it, he watched the Englishman turn into the side-entrance of the Hotel Rena Victoria, a twelve-floor concrete tower in pastel pink built cheaply for the bottom end of the package-holiday business – the owners had done a deal on the paint.

Rejoining the promenade, Trent turned into the hotel's main entrance. He rode the only one of three elevators in working order up to the rooftop bar and ordered a Corona beer from a half-asleep barman.

Ten minutes later he took the elevator down to the third floor and walked down the service stairs to the first. A slim Mexican in a red T-shirt busily slapped white paint on to the landing wall. Along the corridor a heavier Mexican in a green T-shirt knelt beside a toolbox, screwdriver in hand, pretending to examine an electrical outlet. In the time the fake electrician would have taken to drop the screwdriver and grab his gun out of the toolbox, Trent could have put three bullets in his head. Trent didn't know where the Englishman found them; like most desk men he knew, the Englishman was a le Carré addict, and in love with the theatrics of fieldwork. Trent was unable to resist shooting the Mexican with two fingers, and the man gave him a broad grin and a shrug. He blew the imaginary smoke away from his fingertips and walked down the corridor to Room 111. The door was unlocked.

Colonel Smith, Director of the EC's new anti-terrorist unit, stood a foot back from the window looking out through the gauze curtains which the years of neglect and parsimony had stained yellowish nicotine-brown. Glancing back over his shoulder, he pointed Trent towards one of the two easy chairs upholstered in custard-yellow plastic set each side of a plastic-veneered coffee table.

The same chipped and peeling veneer covered the desk and what the architect had probably marked on his plans as a vanity unit. The double bed sagged beneath a grubby white bedcover, the carpet was metallic-flecked Dralon tartan in three shades of brown and there was a stink of cheap cosmetics blended with stale tobacco.

In his Savile Row linen suit and MCC tie, the Colonel looked as incongruous as a sheeted Ku Klux Klansman thumbing a cab on a Harlem street corner. Trent knew the effect was deliberate and designed to irritate; he had given the whys a good deal of thought in the first years of his employment, only to decide that was the impact intended. The Colonel was a master in the manipulation of other men's emotions. Trent had known him all his life and had lived in the Colonel's London house from the age of twelve. Trent's father and Colonel Smith had served in the same Cavalry regiment – the Colonel with distinction while Trent senior had been permitted to resign his commission after the discovery of serious though incompetent fraud in his Squadron accounts – Cavalry regiments dislike scandal.

'So you think you've got a bad one,' the Colonel said quietly and without emotion apart from that almost hidden weariness which is the hallmark of men who bear continual responsibility for the security of their fellow citizens. All problems that came to Colonel Smith's desk were bad, differing only in degree.

'It's probably not our business,' Trent began carefully. 'Belpan's in the American sphere of interest and it's drugs – or it's meant to look like drugs.'

He waited for the Colonel to respond but the other man merely continued his inspection of the street, his silence a game he played with his subordinates, as Trent knew of old. 'First, a plane lands on the north–south Highway. None of the culverts has been bridged. Both pilots dead and a hundred kilos of cocaine on board.' Marijuana smugglers might have been too far into a drug-filled dream world to check out the Highway, but the cocaine trade was for professionals. 'I took a look,' Trent continued. 'The culvert was fifteen feet deep. Sheer sides. They didn't have a chance.'

Though considering himself reasonably imaginative, Trent hadn't found an excuse for visiting the morgue so he hadn't seen the bodies.

'Next, a plane carrying cocaine makes a night landing out on one of the keys where the President has a beach house. The strip is the right length but the touchdown marking light is placed one hundred yards in from the beach and the end-lights sixty yards into the trees. The pilot comes in to land and someone on the ground blinds him with a powerful strobe light. The pilot's a real pro.' Trent dropped on the coffee table the photograph he'd taken of the pilot. 'The Americans will have him on file. Somehow he got the plane between two trees. The wings took the speed off and he survived. So did the co-pilot.'

'Impressive.' The Colonel sounded about as impressed as a butcher offered a box of musty cod.

More games, Trent thought. Early in their working relationship, he had let the Colonel get to him. Now he didn't give a damn. 'If intentional, it was brilliant,' he said. 'I doubt if he was even stunned.'

Trent pictured the scene. The pilot knew he'd been set up and was a sitting target as long as he stayed in the plane. With his night vision destroyed by the strobe light, he hadn't much chance of making a run for it. But running was his only chance. As he hit the ground, someone smashed his skull in with a length of lead pipe.

'He had a lot of experience. One of the Good Ol' Boys,' Trent said, his anger for a moment breaking through. He banished the picture with a quick shake of his head. The Colonel came of a hard school where emotions were a useless and dangerous luxury detrimental to efficiency, and therefore strictly proscribed.

The killer had used the same pipe to smash the windscreen. 'I found a flake of lead on the glass. Whoever it was also slit the co-pilot's throat and stuck a piece of glass in the wound. Professional. Nothing complicated, but sufficient to fool the local police.'

'Did you inform them?' The Colonel's manner seemed a little too casual – as if interested rather than anxious, Trent thought.

Trent played a little silence of his own. The Colonel crossed to the coffee table and picked up the photograph, which Trent considered a point won.

'Of course you didn't.' The Colonel slipped the photograph into his leather wallet and returned to his inspection of the street. 'What else do you have?'

Trent shrugged. 'Dumps like Belpan are all the same. Every kid who comes home with a degree in Literature starts a newspaper. However there are two more or less serious papers. They've changed hands recently and they're

27

accusing the Government of being involved with drugs.' Trent paused. The Colonel disapproved of outside involvement, but there had been no other choice. 'Out on the Keys, it's hard to keep in touch,' Trent resumed. 'So I sailed into Belpan City and called a friend to run a check. The *Washington Post* picked up on the story. So did the *New York Times*, and there's been a couple of questions asked in the House of Representatives.' To Trent it was obvious. 'Someone's building a scenario.'

Colonel Smith turned to face him. The wry smile barely touching the corners of his mouth was denied by the sudden fatigue which shadowed his eyes. Trent suspected the fatigue.

A lorry rumbled up the street. Waiting for the noise to abate, the Colonel took a slim gold cigarette-case from his inside pocket, withdrew an oval Abdullah and lit it with a matching lighter. The case had been a gift from Trent's father – its use was a reminder to Trent, even if not deliberate, that the Colonel had been instrumental, through argument and by replacing the missing funds, in saving him from court martial. 'Damn fool would have gone to jail,' the Colonel had told Trent the year he finished school: 'Shock of it would have killed your mother.' Instead of which she had died in a car crash three weeks after his father's death.

Colonel Smith shut the cigarette case, 'Why didn't you put this in writing?'

Trent's thoughts went back to the pilot – the Good Ol' Boy – the stomach-tearing fear as the strobe blinded him, the shocked surprise filling his mind as he switched on the landing-lights and rammed the plane between the trees. The helpless rage at being set up, and not understanding why; and having no time to think of anything but how to get out, knowing that getting out wasn't going to help. Night blind as he jumped, knowing there'd be someone waiting on the ground and not wanting to know. Still somehow hoping, even when he knew that there wasn't any hope . . .

28

Trent wondered what the Colonel would think of a top agent identifying with a cocaine smuggler. If he remained a top agent? Or had he been put out to grass? Did the Colonel believe that he had been burnt out by three years of living under cover in Ireland – burnt out by the daily fear as he inched his way into the confidence of the terrorist cell, his nerve finally shattered by the ambush?

He said, 'Seven months in the Caribbean and the papers to a fifty-foot catamaran is a lot of money for a new identity.'

'Is that a complaint?'

'Let's call it a suspicion.'

'You always were suspicious, even as a boy,' the Colonel said coldly, and, as an afterthought: 'Why the devil do you have to wear those damned beads round your neck?'

Suspicion had kept Trent alive. So had the throwing-knife held between his shoulder-blades by the beads. He couldn't escape the pilot – that jump out of the plane, night blind and panicked. Nor could he escape the similarities between the pilot's death and the manner of his own betrayal in Ireland.

'Four people have been killed by a pro. I'm paid to be out on a limb. Keeping me blindfolded is plain stupid.'

The Colonel gave a dry sniff of pretended mirth. 'We've been dabbing your scent here and there,' he admitted.

So that was it! Trent had thought that he was free of the fear that had become his constant companion through the last year in Ireland. It was the fear of there being no one he could trust or depend upon, of being sacrificed to a greater good in which he no longer had any faith. He knew that his fear and loss of faith made him dispensable. And so the fear fed on itself – the fear of being set up because he had become dispensable.

'Bait.' His grin was practised and casual, the mirth in his eyes mocking both the Colonel and himself. He knew it was well acted, and he was rewarded by the barest hint of irritation in the Colonel's voice.

'If you enjoy thinking of yourself as a worm.' Colonel Smith stubbed his cigarette out in the Corona ashtray on the vanity unit. Then, coming to a decision, he faced Trent, looking him in the eye for the first time. 'We're rather hoping someone may suggest you do a little gun-running. Take them up on the offer. Make sure they pay well. And remember,' he warned, 'you'll have to account for the money.'

As Trent's father had been unable to do. Points to the Colonel, Trent thought as the older man looked at his watch.

'I'm expecting an American. You'll be working with him. The Americans are good – very good,' the Colonel insisted in dismissal of a natural prejudice against the *nouveau riche* senior partner in the Atlantic Alliance in any way influencing his judgment. He was of that generation in the British Intelligence community which would never forgive the Americans for having frozen them out after the Philby affair. But the Colonel had never been frozen out. On the contrary, his close relationship with Langley had been an essential foundation of his power-base and Trent, until his posting to Ireland, had been the active tool of that relationship. But it was an arrangement about which Trent had developed serious doubts even prior to his Irish mission.

'I'd like a little more information.'

'Damn it, I don't have any,' the Colonel snapped, his anger suddenly in the open. 'It's not our operation. Damned EC Commissioners. We're doing someone a favour.' He jammed his hands in his pockets as if to keep from throttling someone. Too old for new masters, he glared down at Trent as though he were to blame for their transferred allegiance to the EC – Trent's generation, the pan-Europeans. 'The gun-running may or not be connected . . . information from a different source,' he added, for a moment revealing to

30

Trent the complications of working under different, if not conflicting, flags. 'Keep it under your hat. You report direct to the American, no one else. The fellow's called Caspar – wretched name. He was with the Agency. Now he's DEA.'

Trent had hoped that his move to the EC had ended his direct involvement with the Americans. Memories crowded in of the missions he had undertaken for them at the Colonel's command. Wet jobs, the Americans called those assignments. Wet because of the blood.

But once you were in there was no way out – or no way out that he had found. The only friends you had were within the secret world because they alone knew and understood what you did. Only with them could you share your feelings and experiences, and without them you were condemned to isolation.

And, above all, he remained in the Colonel's debt; the Colonel had saved his father from jail and his mother from the social hell that marriage to a common criminal would have brought upon her.

The Colonel, prior to their meeting, would have charted Trent's thoughts and reactions as carefully as Trent plotted his course through the coral reefs before weighing anchor. Trent was aware of this but there was now a deeper level to his thoughts, hidden from the older man; thoughts that must remain concealed. He smiled, as lazily as any holiday-maker in Cancun arranging a date: 'I meet Caspar here?'

'Down south,' the Colonel said. 'Bacalar. Restaurant called the Cenote Azul. Lunch there tomorrow, then go to the fort. Sightseeing. Caspar will be there at three o'clock.'

Which was one plus, Trent thought. Meeting anyone in Cancun with the Colonel, and with the two clowns outside for protection, would be about as secret as broadcasting over Radio Moscow's foreign service.

The Colonel had used Trent as bait often in the past. It was a role Trent disliked because the action was out of his control – but at least on previous occasions he had known who or what he was meant to catch. He was an unhappy man as he rode his BMW from Cancun south to Bacalar.

Bacalar is three hundred and sixty kilometres from Cancun, the road dead straight with thick bush on both sides. Apart from the turn-offs to Chichen-Itza and Mérida, the only side-roads dead-end at one or other of the dozen or so beach resorts financed by optimistic investors – optimistic given Mexico's talent for expropriation. Tailing Trent from the front and rear would have been as easy as following an elephant giving children rides round a small municipal zoo.

One of the phenomena of the coastal strip of Quintana Roo Province are the caves carved out of the soft limestone by millennia of water seepage. The roofs of some of these caves have collapsed, so forming lakes or ponds of an extraordinary clarity, the depths painted a brilliant copper sulphate blue by the sky's refraction in the lime water.

As befitted its name, the Cenote Azul restaurant at Bacalar stood on the lip of one of these open ponds. The rough wooden tables were shaded by half a dozen trees growing up through loose thatch. The chairs were as crude as the tables while the menu was a mix of fresh seafood and a variety of wild game that would have sent the more fanatical and unreasoning of First World conservationists into paroxysms of hate and horror.

Trent had met various of these conservationists resident in Belpan, many of them funded by grants which permitted them to enjoy a lifestyle beyond the purses of all but a very few Belpanese. Their aim seemed to be the imprisoning of the local inhabitants in a zoo where the men would be castrated and the women made sterile, thereby creating of Belpan a paradise of the eco-tourists of the First World. The sterilisation programme would lead eventually to a shortage of waiters and maidservants but that was looking forward to a time when the conservationists would have retired to the air-conditioned comfort of three-car life at a

Mid-Western university. Trent supposed that the conservationists irritated him because he risked his life defending a system which they considered evil. He recognised society as imperfect but it was the best on offer.

Meanwhile, and despite the conservationists, the Cenote Azul's patrons were having a good time. Trent was the only foreigner – Bacalar was too far off the track to be popular with the Cancun crowd.

The older their generation, the less flesh the Mexicans showed: grandfathers in black suit trousers and long-sleeved shirts; grandmothers in long-sleeved blouses, skirts, stockings and high heels. With the middle-aged the sleeves were short and some wore shorts. The young, in bikinis and swimming trunks, were in and out of the pool between sipping margaritas.

It was noon, too early for the serious luncheon that would stretch on into the late afternoon; but every table was spread with *antojitos*: plates of tiny shrimp, conch, *ceviche*, baby squid. Trent ordered wild boar because the price would irritate the Colonel – on the keys he never saw meat. He drank a fresh lime juice while waiting to be served.

The boar came and was tender and full of taste. He looked up from his plate at a sudden hush. A party of six stood by the bar. The three men were a little too rough and loud for the Cenote Azul, the women too brassy. The men dragged two tables together next to where Trent sat and shouted for tequila. One of them asked Trent if he was American and Trent said British. 'British good,' said the man, and poured three inches of tequila into a glass for him.

'*Gracias, Señor*,' Trent said, and '*Salud*,' as he sipped the tequila. Refusing might have led to a fight.

The three women were shedding clothes; all were amply busted and wide-hipped with a slight roll of flesh bulging at the top of their bikini briefs. They giggled a lot as they teetered on over-high heels to the pool edge.

33

The man who had poured the tequila leered at Trent: 'You like Mexican women, yes?' He had spoken loudly and there were other parties listening.

If Trent admitted to liking Mexican women he would be insulting their purity, but if he said that he didn't he would be denying their charm and beauty.

He stood up, and said in a voice loud enough to carry across the restaurant, '*Dons y Donnas*, may a humble Irish tourist say that Mexico is the most varied and most beautiful of countries and its people the most hospitable and polite. It would be a great honour if you would accept my thanks for the most perfect of holidays by allowing me to purchase for you all a drink.'

He said Irish because the Irish were Catholic and the sufferers of a colonial power's abuse – facts that earned them a popular kinship with Latin Americans who believed that most of their misfortunes were the product of the United States' Protestant élite.

'Bravo,' a man called from the back, prompting a round of applause as Trent crossed to the bar both to order drinks and surreptitiously to pay his bill. Slipping out the back, he kicked the motor cycle alive with a minimum of throttle and rode quietly away. He would be early for his rendezvous with Caspar at the fort, but that was what he had intended.

The fortress at Bacalar was a five-pointed star of stone battlements enclosed within a moat and surrounded by palm and mango trees. Cannon thrust their black snouts out at the incredible blue of the lagoon below the low hill on which the fortress stood. A stone bridge crossed the moat to the two narrow doorways into the courtyard. The doorways were barred by iron gates.

A clump of oleanders grew by the edge of the parking lot close to a big mango tree, only a dozen yards from the bridge. Trent parked the BMW in the shade of the tree but at an angle so that it would be seen by anyone coming up the road. He wrapped the chain round the treetrunk and through both wheels and the frame before walking over the bridge to where an old janitor slept between the gates, sharing the shade with an almost empty bottle of tequila. Siesta time, and there were no tourists.

One of the gates was open, a brass padlock hanging on the latch. Trent slipped the padlock into his pocket. Entering the flagstoned courtyard without waking the janitor, he climbed to the parapets from where he could view the inside of the fort. Not liking what he saw, he walked round the outside of the building in search of a tree that grew within reach of the walls but there weren't any, and it was a long hard drop into the moat from the fortifications with no escape other than by ladder.

Returning to the motor cycle for his own padlock, he hid in the oleanders, waiting. He imagined the Colonel leafing through a tourist brochure of the Yucatan. Chichen-Itza? Too many tourists to be certain of an identification and security. Tulum? The same. So on south with the Colonel failing to find anything to catch his fancy until he came to Bacalar, with its fort built by the Spanish in 1633 – nothing better than a fortress to please an old military man. Add a few lines lauding the Cenote Azul and the Colonel must have been humming pleasurably to himself as he sought for a sarcasm appropriate to Trent's expected expense account. Trent would have his own sarcasm ready. The fort had one entrance. Put a guard on the gates and you had the perfect killing field.

They came, as he had expected – the three men from the restaurant. The driver parked their VW Jetta beside Trent's BMW. In their place, he would have disabled the motor cycle but they were too confident. He could tell by the shape of their hands in their pockets that they carried knives, which again showed over-confidence. Knives were good at close quarters when backed by surprise but they were useless out in the open and against a gun. Trent knew.

For fifteen years he had practised almost daily with the small, matt-black throwing-knife in its shammy-leather sheath that hung down the back of his neck on his neckband of red coral.

Two of the men went into the fort, the third stayed by the entrance. Trent waited three minutes. Then he came across the ten metres of tarred car park and over the bridge as silently as a cat. He took the man from the back, hand over his mouth to choke the scream, a jab at the pressure-point on the side of the neck. No unnecessary damage. He was connected to the three men by the scene in the res-taurant and getting jailed in Mexico was a lot easier for a foreigner than finding a decent steak. With *Golden Girl* moored in the marina at Cancun, he couldn't slip across the border into Belize.

He laid the man down and swung the iron gate shut, locking it with the padlock from his motor cycle. Opening the Jetta's hood, he prised the contact off the breaker points. As he rode off, he could hear the two men inside the fort yelling and hammering on the gate. He pulled off the road short of the intersection with the main highway. The confrontation had been far too easy for his peace of mind.

The Colonel had said three o'clock. A white Bronco turned up the fort road at five minutes to three. The driver was alone and had to be American: florid face, heavy jowls, a day's growth of to-hell-with-you stubble, cigar clamped between his teeth, Raybans, Budweiser beer can T-shirt, and a nylon-mesh baseball cap promoting a Florida golf course.

Trent stepped out of the bushes and flagged him down: 'Caspar?'

The Drug Enforcement Agency Agent said, 'You're meant to be up at the fort.'

'I didn't like it,' Trent said. 'Drive back up the Cancun highway. Kilometre forty-five, there's a thatch shack that sells cold beer and tacos. Park round the back. I'll be right on your tail.'

The DEA man said, 'The beer had better be cold and I *mean* cold.'

They sat at a table made out of planks discarded from a building site. A crudely thatched *palapa* shaded them from the sun but not from the heat; only air-conditioning could have done that. But the beer was cold.

Caspar drank, sweated, and waited while Trent sipped a club soda. They wanted to know what each other knew of what was going on, but the command structure had been complicated.

The Colonel had instructed Trent to report to the DEA Agent and work with him – which didn't mean work *for* the American. Trent had never worked for anyone but the Colonel in years. And even then, according to the Colonel's repeated complaints, Trent had been working for himself half the time. Trent's answer was that he came out alive.

Caspar was big and remained tough despite the beer-gut spilling over a tooled leather belt. Outwardly he was in there with the pilot who'd been murdered on Key Canaka – one of the Good Ol' Boys. But it was a front. Take his Raybans off and there were a pair of steel-blue eyes, cold as ice. Caspar was used to giving orders, not taking them.

Trent had worked with his like too often prior to being posted to Ireland to doubt the man's energy, intelligence and organisational ability in the field. Caspar was the sort of man capable of charging a Powerwagon over a mountain track as ruthlessly and effectively as he could train and direct a group of jungle mercenaries. He and his like had kept Trent's back safe. They had got him in and they had got him out. And they had never let him down. Never a hesitation, never a delay while reporting back to Langley for guidelines from some committee or other, as was the case with Caspar's British counterparts.

37

Finally Trent said, 'The Colonel will have told you what I know,' which both knew meant that the Colonel would have told Caspar what he wanted Caspar to know of Trent's initial report.

Caspar spat a piece of cigar in the dirt and said, 'I pulled your file. You've been a son of a bitch to work with from way back but the file says you get the job done.'

'Thanks.'

Caspar laughed. 'Go drown yourself. Beats me how a one-man mayhem machine like you can work for that prissy bastard.'

'He has his good points,' Trent said.

'Yeah, well he's your boss.' He flicked fingers for a fresh beer: 'Want a drink, or are you sticking with water?'

'I'm on two wheels,' Trent said, and the DEA Agent shrugged.

'Please yourself.'

'The Colonel told me to report to you.'

'Meaning you'll tell me what you want me to know.'

Trent saw no point in lying, and said nothing.

'But you want me to watch your back.'

'That would certainly help,' Trent said and, because it was true, added, 'I have a feeling you'd be good at that.'

Caspar grinned: 'I've never had any complaints – except when Washington screwed up – and even then I got my men home.'

'I believe you.'

'Good. So I'll give you a number and a radio frequency. There'll be a permanent on both. You want a meet, it's 10 a.m. or 10 p.m. Trent's some kind of a British river, right?'

Trent nodded.

'So River's a.m. and Stream's p.m. Day after tomorrow's today. Three days' time is tomorrow, and so on. Simple but it works. Any problems?'

'None.'

'Just don't come near the goddam Embassy,' the DEA

Agent warned. 'I'm strictly advisory capacity. Action's out. They see you, they'll have me back home sweeping streets.'

'I wouldn't want that to happen,' Trent said. Nor did he want to be left alone, out on a limb – particularly when he wasn't sure which tree the branch was growing on.

If advisory was the way Caspar wanted to play it, Trent knew that he would have to go outside for help. His habit of doing so infuriated the Colonel but that had never stopped him. Contacts, and how and when to use them, were the essentials that kept Trent alive. But he was with a new organisation now, perhaps less able to repay favours, and many of his old contacts were either out of date or compromised by the new relationship between the US and USSR. Cold War warriors were out of fashion.

THREE

Trent browsed the cheap shelves of a toyshop in downtown Cancun and bought a Taiwanese army tank for five thousand pesos. Battery operated, the tank shot sparks. A five-year-old would have destroyed it in ten minutes. He picked up a packet of boiled sweets at the cash desk and wandered on down the road to a phone booth at an intersection. He left the door open to the traffic, put two sweets in his mouth, and turned on the tank before dialling. The phone connected with an answering-machine.

Holding the tank close to the mouthpiece, he said, 'Hi, I'm down at Cancun. Four Swedish broads into having a good time – I need help. Why don't you fly on down? I'll look for you at the airport tomorrow.' He put the phone down, certain that the traffic, the toy tank and the sweets would delay a voice-print identification for twenty-four hours. Back on the sidewalk, he gave the tank to a six-year-old Maya boy who was too surprised to say *gracias*.

The American flew in on the morning American Airlines flight from Dallas. He was slim, but with strong shoulders, a quarter of an inch short of the six-foot mark, medium-length blond hair, eyes hidden behind a pair of round Amari sunglasses. He walked looser-limbed than a North European – confident carriage, but not arrogant.

He wore off-white linen shorts that came halfway down his kneecaps, a blue-on-white check Aertex sports shirt, Indian sandals, and a planter's Panama hat. For jewellery he wore a slim gold watch on a washable linen strap. He carried a leather briefcase about an inch thick that reeked of money and a blue Yardby tapestry Gladstone bag with the Beaufort elephant design woven on its side. The slimness of the briefcase stated that he was too important to carry more than the minimum of paperwork, the Yardby Gladstone spoke of taste and solid wealth. If he hadn't known better, Trent would have placed him as East Coast Old Money or a society coke dealer – possibly both.

The American hired a VW at the Budget desk. Trent rode out of the parking lot ahead of him and maintained his lead for the first half-mile. Then he let the man overtake. A further half-mile and the American backtracked at a roundabout, took the next left and left again, hit a second roundabout and backtracked for the second time. He took a right, drove two hundred yards, and parked.

Trent did a U-turn and pulled into the shade of a flame tree from where he watched the American lock the VW and stroll back fifty yards to an open-air café, briefcase in hand. The case would be wired and the clock running. Trent would have preferred the American to have left it in the VW. Chaining the BMW to the flame tree, he strolled over to the café and sat down beside the American.

'Thanks for coming.'

'My pleasure.' The American folded his sunglasses and slipped them into his briefcase to turn the electronics on and laid it on the table between them. He didn't try fooling Trent. 'We could have a difficult situation here so I'd like you to outline briefly who you're with and why you called me.'

'The European Economic Community's Anti-Terrorist Unit,' Trent said. 'I've been out in the Caribbean building a new identity since transferring seven months back. The

Unit's new, and I'm new to it, so I don't have any official contacts and I don't know the parameters. I've run into a scenario which I don't like and there are bits of it which I don't understand. This is a US sphere of influence. If I was with my old organisation I'd know what channels to use. I've worked with Langley. It's on the record. Here I'm working with a man from the DEA, Caspar. Used to be with the Agency.'

'You've made a report?' the American asked.

'Yes, and a bad mistake. My Control went outside for protection and surveillance. One of that team must have set me up. Mexicans. I need to know who they are and who they came from.'

'Ask your Control.'

'Reporting to him nearly got me killed; anyway, he's back in Brussels.'

'Caspar?'

'He's advisory only, which means he's a one-shot backup. Use him too soon and I'm on my own . . . and I'm not sure that this is the same scenario.'

'Why me?'

'We met at a conference on international terrorism. In the elevator,' Trent added, still unsure as to whether that meeting had been accidental or deliberate. 'We had a couple of drinks. Our ideas seemed to mesh. We exchanged telephone numbers.'

'When was the conference?'

'Frankfurt, a little over a year ago.'

'Before your transfer.'

'Correct.'

'And you call me the first time you get in a jam?'

'Who else would you have me call?'

'In your shoes? Hell, I'd've called me last week.' He grinned and held out his hand: 'Steve . . .'

In Frankfurt he'd been Robert in a grey flannel suit.

'Trent,' Trent said.

*

42

Steve ran the VW up a driveway into a four-car carport alongside a pale blue Ford and a white Cherokee jeep with the hood down, canvas seat-covers, outsize crash-bars, and a pile of diving gear in the back.

They had driven across town without talking. As Steve led Trent in through the back door, he said, 'I need to go through our man down here. Matter of politeness. There'll be a Mex with him.'

Trent noted that Steve had left the briefcase in the VW so the meeting was going to be off the record.

The living-room opened on to a back garden hedged with hibiscus and shaded by half a dozen acacias. The furniture had the leftover look typical of a safehouse. There were two men in the room. The Agency's local man stood over by the picture-window. He had the unformed features of a nondescript high-school student, perhaps a little too nervous at having to take an exam – mid-thirties, medium height, medium fat. He wore a freshly ironed blue-striped seersucker suit over a white tennis shirt as if unable to decide whether to be formal or casual.

In contrast to the American, the Mexican lolled in an armchair as if nothing was going to happen for the next twenty years. He was big, very big, and in peak condition – around the six-foot-six mark, Trent guessed – broad Mayan fetures and thick black hair that hadn't met a brush or comb since his first Communion. He sported a white T-shirt with the warning in red letters, TRESPASSERS WILL BE VIOLATED, scrawled across his massive chest. The sleeves had been cut out of the T-shirt to allow his biceps to get through. Glow-gold palm trees decorated black-swim pants that threatened to split if he moved a muscle, and he wore rubber flip-flops the size of a diver's fins.

The over-age high-school student nodded a greeting to Steve and said to Trent, 'I'm Dick, this here's Pepito. Good friend of mine.'

Trent doubted the description. 'Nice to meet you.'

43

Dick crossed the room to stand by the Mexican's chair to emphasise that he and the big man were on the same side. 'I'm in charge of the Agency down here,' he told Trent. 'Steve called me from Washington to set up this meeting so I pulled your record off the computer. You've earned yourself quite a reputation as a rental hit-man. That's not something we necessarily like.'

It was a description Trent didn't care for but he remained silent. The Mexican smiled for something to do. Had he been a smoker, he'd have lit a cigarette.

'Easy, Dick,' said Steve.

'Easy!' The anxiety Trent had sensed in Dick exploded. 'There's no authorisation for this meet. Getting me involved, you're putting my goddam job on the line.'

Steve crossed the room and put an arm round Dick's shoulders in that way Americans have of forcing intimacy into a relationship before the intimacy exists. 'Maybe you'd feel more comfortable if we left you out.'

'Too goddam right I'd feel more comfortable,' Dick said.

'Then why don't we do that?' Steve suggested. 'You put in a report on the meeting?'

'What do you think? I'm crazy?' Dick demanded.

'Fine, so that's the way we'll play it,' Steve said. 'Some-one asks, tell them you lent me the house. Have a good day, Dick, and remember, I owe you.'

'Too damn right, I'll remember.' Dick looked over at the Mexican. 'Want to go eat?'

The Mexican went on smiling.

Dick looked a little embarrassed. 'Yeah, so I'll see you around.'

Steve saw him to the door, smiling and patting him on the back. He waited for the Ford to back down the drive before turning to Trent.

'I'm sorry about that. We're having a little difficulty back in Washington.' A lift of his eyebrows said that Trent was an adult and should know the score. 'The Russian threat's over so there's Congressmen wanting to know what the Agency did when the Russians *were* a threat. Pick through the records. Find themselves a few heads to chop. Make themselves a reputation on TV.

'The stuff's there to pick over,' Steve said, as if Trent might have difficulty believing him. 'Maybe it started in the Kennedy era – so he was a saint except for the sex thing – but he was a little hot-headed, and he was young, and in a hurry. *"Negotiations don't work, call the Agency, have the man taken out."* The people who did the taking out got themselves a lot of support from the top and a lot of power within the Agency.

'There were others saying, *"Hey, wait a minute, maybe that's not the way."* I'm not talking Constitution here, I'm talking smarts.' He gave Trent a grin that was meant to show that they were allies and that they trusted each other and were sharing deep secrets. 'Then along comes *perego*god-damned*stroika* and it's a whole new ball game, right? The taker-outers are out of fashion and are trying to save their backsides. Burying stuff fast as a squirrel buries nuts in the fall.

'We've got people inside the Agency taking sides. And there are people like Dick who are someplace in the middle. Nice wife, three kids, Company housing, pension, health insurance, reasonable career prospects.' Steve shrugged his understanding of Dick's position: 'Know what I mean? Kids that like to camp in the woods but won't go out of the tent when it's dark. You walk in with your reputation and that makes Dick a little nervous. The Colonel's a true-blue Cold War warrior and you're his boy out on loan half the year to the real heavies back at Langley; and here I'm saying, Hey, wait a minute, Dick, I met the man in an elevator and he's *all right*. He's been in Ireland, had himself a religious experience – like Saint Paul falling off his horse on the track to Damascus.' He grinned some more. 'Jesus! I mean, now *I'm* thinking, right? and *I'm* nervous.'

45

Trent had a feeling that he was meant to return the grin and say that he understood – but what he understood was that he was in the middle of something which he didn't understand and didn't like.

The Mexican seemed to have gone to sleep.

'I've always worked in the field,' Trent said.

'Meaning you don't care for office politics.' Steve's smile was a trifle sad: 'No offence but from where I stand that makes you sound a little like Dick. What we have here is a situation where we've got some people believing that all you have to do is change the top man in any country in the world and a local problem will go away. Others of us think that makes the problem worse in the long run.

'We need to *be* the good guys rather than *say* we're the good guys. Stop playing *realpolitik*, start playing co-operation. Stop trying to buy the top *honchos* and start helping the ordinary people. We're the experts. We write the reports. Maybe it's time we pushed a little. So it takes time and a lot of persuasion. It's not a morality thing,' he assured Trent as if it not being a morality thing made it all right. 'The other way's been tried and it doesn't work.'

He nodded at the dormant Mexican. 'Pepito and you and I are in the terrorist business. We catch a few people, get someone to shoot them for us, maybe shoot them ourselves. So we create a fresh lot of martyrs and make ourselves a fresh lot of terrorists. Or we can try doing something about what causes the terrorism. I'm not saying we stop catching the sons of bitches, what I'm talking here is additional long-term priorities.

'Now that's pretty much what you said about Ireland, which is why I gave you a number to call.'

Trent said, 'Yes,' because it *was* what he'd said and he agreed with Steve's view – which didn't mean that he trusted the American or wanted to be part of a power-play within the Intelligence community, which was what Steve was proposing in a roundabout way. If it wasn't a trap. And it could

46

be an either/or situation, dependent on the outcome, the American making the decision on which way to jump, and Trent finding himself out on a limb.

'Yes,' he said again because Steve and the Mexican weren't saying anything. 'Yes' was reasonably safe. And because he needed help, he added, 'I agree.'

'Well that's fine,' Steve said with a brilliant smile. 'Pepito and I are bachelors so we've chosen to play around a little at this and that,' he continued as if he were talking sense rather than coded gobbledegook. 'Sometimes Dick will know, sometimes he won't. Kind of depends on what we're doing whether we tell him or not. I have to get home but Pepito will show you around. Cancun's his backyard. You need more help, holler. You want the heavy brigade in, wave a yellow handkerchief so they don't shoot your back-side off.' He tossed Trent a bright yellow silk square. 'See you around . . . '

Steve hadn't said who the heavy brigade were. All far too neat and tidy, Trent thought. He walked down the hall to the front door and watched the VW leave.

Pepito opened one eye as Trent returned to the living-room. After a while he opened the second eye, smiled, pushed himself out of the armchair, and shambled out of the back door. A double tap of his fingers on the hood of the jeep brought a Doberman slinking out of the hibiscus. The dog leapt into the back of the jeep. Pepito pointed Trent to the spare seat and started the engine. Reversing out on to the road, he drove Trent back to his motor cycle without having to ask where it was parked, and jabbed a finger in the direction of the marina.

Riding the BMW in Pepito's wake, Trent watched the big man pretend to shoot a slim but well-muscled Mexican beach-boy loafing at the head of the marina dock leading to the *Golden Girl*. Pepito parked his jeep at the foot of the gangplank. A second beach-boy lay sunning himself on

Golden Girl's cabin top. His swimsuit could have stood in for a stripper's G-string but a big beach towel covered his right hand.

Trent presumed that the towel covered a gun. He hadn't thought of himself as seriously at risk but Pepito obviously did or he wouldn't have placed the catamaran under Care and Protection.

Alongside *Golden Girl* lay a twenty-eight-foot dive-boat powered by two one-hundred horsepower Mercurys. Pepito shouldered diving gear on to it, took an electronic detector from his shoulder purse, and singing to himself to prompt any voice-activated microphones, he swept the dive-boat from bow to stern. He started both motors before beckoning Trent on board. 'We are going diving, Señor,' he said in an impressively deep voice.

Trent said that he had guessed as much and added that he had been wondering whether they were going to communicate finally by writing on slates one hundred feet below the surface of the Caribbean.

'To be careful is to survive, Señor,' the Mexican said. 'Gringos!' He spat over the side. 'They give to their politics the seriousness a Mexican only gives to making love.'

Someone he could trust, Trent thought as he watched Pepito con the dive-boat out to sea. 'I need help,' he said. 'There's a lot happening round me and I don't know what it is or who is behind whatever it is.' The two Mexican bodyguards protecting Colonel Smith at the Rena Victoria Hotel were his only lead.

'Little fish show where the big fish feed,' the Mexican agreed, grinning his confidence. 'We will find them, Señor.'

Eleven o'clock at night and Cancun was jumping. Bars blasted music at the tourists patrolling the sidewalk; discos flashed neon *Come hither and bring your cash* signs. Toy-boys and toy-girls twitched their backsides in ritual semaphore, dope peddlers loafed under the flamboyant trees. The big Mexican cruised the street as if he owned the place. They were seven in the jeep: Pepito, Trent, four Swedish women in their early twenties, and the Doberman.

The four Swedes were there as an unspoken warning to Trent that Pepito had listened to a recording of the message with which Trent had summoned Steve. The Mexican had spotted the girls sunning themselves topless on the beach out at Isla Mujeres where he and Trent had gone diving. Running the boat into the shore, Pepito had strolled up the beach and corralled them like a shepherd penning lambs. What had chiefly impressed Trent was the Mexican's ability to divine the women's nationality through his binoculars at a hundred yards.

They had dined at a restaurant serving a sophisticated development of traditional Mayan food – grilled lobster-tails as a first course, followed by wild turkey cooked in a black sauce made from burnt peppers, with mango sorbet for dessert. Margaritas with everything – at least, the Swedes were drinking margaritas. Trent and Pepito had been drinking bar-girl style, margaritas with the alcohol left out.

Now they were searching for the two Mexicans who had guarded the Colonel's meeting with Trent at the Rena Victoria Hotel. 'The men have been paid. They will be out on the town,' Pepito had said. 'That is the way here in Cancun, Señor.'

So far they had hit a dozen bars and three discos. The margaritas were beginning to melt the Swedes out of the last of their few inhibitions. One of them sat on the jeep's hood with her arms flung back over the top of the wind-screen, her skirts up, and her shirt open to the navel. A second sat side-saddle on Pepito's lap, the third on Trent. The fourth sat on a pad of folded towels between the two men, her arms round their necks. From the way she kept on looking across at Pepito, Trent was certain that the young lady on his own lap considered herself the loser of the party.

As one more confirmation of Pepito's status in Cancun, two policemen on foot patrol saluted smartly as the big Mexican pulled over and parked the jeep up against a No Parking sign outside the Clarissa Disco. The girl who had been sitting on Trent's knee manipulated herself under one of the Mexican's arms which left Trent with the girl on the hood and the one who'd been in the middle. He laughed because the girls were laughing – he wasn't as good at it as Pepito, whose deep rumble rolled ahead of them into the strobe-lit disco like the prelude to a tropical storm. The music was the kind that people danced to on their own. Blacks and Latinos were good at it, but the Caucasians looked awkward.

Pepito pointed over the top of the crowd. Trent couldn't see who or what he was pointing at. The Mexican put his hands on Trent's waist and lifted him close to the ceiling as if he were light as a sack of loosely-packed goose down. Pepito had been pointing to the Mexican who had acted bodyguard while pretending to fix the electrical outlet outside the Colonel's hotel room.

Trent showed Pepito a thumb up. The Mexican lowered Trent to the dance floor and strode through the dancers as if they didn't exist. He returned with the fake electrician slung over his shoulder like a side of pork in an abattoir – except that the fake electrician wasn't dead but merely looked as if he expected to be dead.

Pepito dumped the man in the back of the jeep. The Doberman lay on top of him with its jaws an inch from his throat. Two of the Swedish girls had followed them out of the disco. They looked uncertain as to what their role had become, but Pepito grinned happily and spread hands nearly as big as baseball gloves: 'My apologies, Señoritas, first a little business. Then *mucho* pleasure.'

Trent had got into the jeep. Pepito lifted one of the girls

50

on to Trent's lap before she could give him an argument. The other he kissed on both cheeks and on the lips, handing her on to the folded towels packed between the seats. Patting the Doberman, he eased his bulk in behind the wheel and beckoned a policeman over. The policeman ran into the disco and came back with fresh margaritas for the girls in half-litre vacuum tankards. The police saluted. The girls giggled, reassured by this – which proved their ignorance of Latin American policemen.

'It is sensible to have witnesses,' Pepito shouted happily at Trent in Spanish in explanation of his bringing the girls along. 'Foreigners are the best witnesses. They can make truthful statements from the safety of their own country while our own people are easily persuaded to give the account preferred by those with the greatest power.'

Back across the causeway, Pepito drove into the courtyard behind Cancun's central police station. Removing the prisoner from his Doberman, Pepito marched him in through the back door. Fifteen minutes later he reappeared looking pleased with himself.

Returning to the tourist strip, he made a quick bar stop for fresh margaritas, then followed the seafront dual carriageway round to where the hotels gave way to the houses of the super-rich. Pulling in to the kerb, he switched off the lights before reversing into the trees. The jeep faced a pair of iron gates on the far side of the carriageway.

'Now you will see the Cancun version of *Miami Vice* played live especially for you, Señoritas,' said Pepito. He pointed to a palm tree to the left of the jeep. 'Sit there and sip your margaritas, Señoritas. Ten minutes and we will go to my own house where we will swim under the moon.'

'It's a new moon and it's already set,' Trent pointed out.

'Romance is not of necessity truthful, Señor Trent,' Pepito chided. He pointed to the gates: 'The home of the man who supplied your Colonel with the two bodyguards. Don Roberto Fleming. Born London, England, February

2nd, 1922, as Robert Charles Richard French. Diabetic. Exempted military service. Graduated in Modern Languages, 1943. Joined MI6. Latin American desk, special interests Chile, Guatemala, Argentina, Uruguay. Took early retirement in 1974. Since retirement has acted for various insurance companies as negotiator in kidnappings throughout Latin America. Adviser to various multi-nationals on personal security. Supplies personal security personnel and equipment through a privately owned corporation registered in the Cayman Islands, PSLA Inc. Rich, old, vicious, and dangerously well-connected.'

'Why early retirement?' Trent asked.

'Conflict of interest, Señor. Many conflicts of interest.'

'Freelancing?'

'Both for governments and in the private sector, Señor.'

'If he's that good why did he supply a couple of lousy amateurs?' And why, Trent wondered, had three heavies been set on him in Bacalar? Or would-be heavies – any agent of his experience could have killed the three of them before they even *thought* of getting out of their car.

'That is a question we should ask of Don Roberto, Señor.' Pepito waved a piece of paper. 'Warrant to question in the attempted murder of a foreign tourist. You are the tourist, Señor.' Pepito smiled his satisfaction: 'Fortunately I, too, am well connected. My cousin, Ricardo, is a judge. I had arranged that he should wait for our arrival at the police station.'

Trent was about to get out of the jeep but Pepito restrained him.

'If we ring the bell, Señor, Don Roberto will telephone Mexico City. Ricardo is a young judge,' Pepito explained with a touch of sadness: 'Amongst his senor colleagues there are those who consider Ricardo somewhat adventurous.'

Trent suspected that it was a family trait.

'If you would be kind enough to hold this for me, Señor . . . ' He passed Trent a tiny Smith & Wesson ·38 hammerless revolver, then fastened his seat belt; Trent did the same. Pepito stuck the jeep in first gear, waved at the Swedish girls, and put his foot flat on the accelerator. They were doing twenty when they hit the centre division of the road, forty when they hit the gates.

The jeep smashed the gates out of their concrete posts and rolled on over them. The drive led round a gentle curve to a fake Spanish Colonial mansion. A flight of wide steps mounted to big double doors of carved wood. The steps were shallow, as befitted Don Roberto's age and reported frailty. The jeep continued to accelerate up the steps. The crash-bars burst the doors and Pepito skidded the jeep to a halt in a big hall floored in pink marble.

Trent unclipped his safety belt and hit the marble. The big Mexican was out the other side, a massive ·44 Magnum enveloped in his right hand.

A thirty-foot drawing-room opened to the right. The heavy Spanish furniture was genuine, and so were the eighteenth-century portraits of English country squires and their wives, though the names under the portraits were fake. A Bechstein grand stood in the window, silver-framed photographs covering its satin top. Don Roberto was absent.

More portraits decorated the dining-room to the left of the hall. The refectory table and high-backed chairs were early Colonial and worth a fortune.

The library was full of books that looked as if they were read. The desk was a superb piece of eighteenth-century English walnut and the chairs were club leather. A small but beautiful scene of a London stretch of the Thames by Canaletto glowed in a period frame above the unnecessary fireplace. The wall-safe was open and Don Roberto was dead. He lay by the safe on a red Bokhara rug amidst a greal deal of blood which had welled from his throat. The blood was dry, but the air-conditioning had kept the body fresh.

Don Roberto was a small, thin man with a long nose,

short grey hair, clipped moustache, thin lips and ears that lay very close to his skull. He wore a cashmere dressing-gown over his striped silk pyjamas as protection against the chill of the air-conditioning, and red velvet slippers decorated with gold braid coats of arms. Trent had known him as Richard Fallon. He had acted as Trent's contact between the Colonel and the men from Langley, though, according to Pepito, Don Roberto had left Government employ in 1974. Trent hadn't seen him since being posted to Ireland in 1987.

Crouching beside the corpse, Pepito first lifted the eyelids then raised the right arm to test the elbow joint: 'Some time last night?'

'Probably.'

Both men knew how Don Roberto had been killed. It was an unusual way. Trent reached down the back of his neck for his throwing-knife. The Mexican slid the blade into the wound in Don Roberto's throat. The fit was perfect. He looked up at Trent: 'An unpleasantness, Señor.'

'Yes.'

'You were alone last night.'

'Yes.'

'I was not questioning you,' Pepito chided. Rising, he slowly surveyed the room. 'Your fingerprints are here, Señor . . .'

'Yes,' Trent said. A glass, book, piece of paper – unrecognisable because he had no idea as to why he had been set up or who had done it; and therefore no ability to divine from which period of his past the planted evidence came. The two-man bodyguard team had led him to Don Roberto. They, in turn, were connected to the three thugs at the Cenote Azul – further links forged to connect him to the murder. For a moment the image of the pilot returned to haunt him. The Good Ol' Boy, blinded by strobe lights, jumping into the night . . .

He said, 'Yes, yes, yes, yes,' and smiled at the Mexican,

deliberately freeing himself of the pilot, and forcing himself into speech. 'I'm sorry, Pepito, I sound like a moron, but I don't understand what the hell's going on. I'm a field agent, for Christ's sake. And I'm in a new organisation. I'm not important enough for someone to kill a man simply to set me up. Maybe in the past – but even then . . . ' He couldn't believe it: 'No, it simply doesn't make sense . . . '

'To you,' Pepito corrected. 'It makes sense to whoever killed Don Roberto. As I told you, Señor, Don Roberto was a cultivator of powerful friends. They will be angry.'

'With me,' Trent said.

'And also with me, Señor,' Pepito said with no smile at all. 'If I attempt to protect you, our joint activities today will be construed as evidence of friendship. True, I could produce as witness to your innocence my man who watched you last night; but that he is in my employ would tarnish his evidence. Now perhaps you understand the necessity for Swedish señoritas. Had you enjoyed, in reality, the company of those four of whom you boasted to the American, you would have an alibi that I would be forced to defend. As it is . . . ' He shrugged shoulders strong enough to carry a bull: 'It would be a kindness, Señor, if you would point your pistol at me and reclaim your knife. Then perhaps you would force me to drive you and the señoritas back to your boat. The tip of Isla Mujeres would be a suitable point at which to maroon us.'

'And I sail back to Belpan and await a warrant for my extradition,' Trent said.

Again the Mexican shrugged: 'The killer must be careful in disclosing his evidence against you, Señor, or I may discover his identity. From my end, that is our hope. Your hope is to stay alive long enough for this thing to break into the open so that we may see what it is.'

Or run, Trent thought. But he could guess at Don Roberto's friends. Evidence of their power and influence lay in the wealth Don Roberto had accumulated. For Trent to hide himself from their dogs would be as impossible as hiding Mount Everest from the Sherpas of Nepal; this much he already knew as he walked back through to the drawing-room.

The photographs stood in ranks of influence on the grand piano: bankers, corporate heads, heads of government, cabinet members, minor royalty, the aristocracy . . . and a tall, fair, moustached young army officer in the dress uniform of a British Lancer Regiment lolling in confident indolence at the feet of a young woman in evening dress seated on a grass bank at Glyndebourne.

There was a slight tremble in Trent's fingers as he took the photograph from its frame. He turned to find Pepito watching him from the doorway. 'My mother,' Trent said.

FOUR

Pepito had advised Trent to return to Belpan and wait for affairs to break into the open. Trent knew that Pepito was right, but he was an activist and found waiting both frustrating and unnerving.

While sailing back from Cancun to San Paul Key he had put down on paper what he knew in the hope that a pattern would appear. To simplify his thoughts he had listed them under two headings: first there was that which directly affected Belpan.

Fact One: Someone was building a scenario, its purpose being to discredit Belpan's Government and its President.

Fact Two: Colonel Smith expected gun-runners.

Add the two together and the answer Trent found most obvious was a coup d'état. In terms of force required, a coup would be easy enough to carry out. Belpan had little crime, no enemies, nothing worth stealing, and no territorial ambitions. As a result, the police force was rudimentary and inexperienced while the Belpan Defence Force was primarily a supplier of honour guards for the rare visitor of sufficient importance to warrant ceremony.

But a coup took more than force. There had to be some political acceptance both inside the country and, more importantly, outside, because since the end of the Cold War military take-overs were met increasingly by an immediate freeze of foreign aid. Belpan depended on foreign aid for its survival.

And there had to be a reason for a coup. As far as Trent could see, there was no reason at all. Belpan's tax base was less than that of a medium-sized European market town, which made running the country a financial nightmare. Because of the reef, there was no port; this precluded a military base. Anyway, with the Cold War over, the super-powers were closing bases. The cost of developing Belpan as a tax haven would be prohibitive and the competition in the Caribbean was already established. For the same reasons Trent was unable to visualise Belpan as a future gambling Mecca.

But, in ruling out a coup, Trent had to presume that the arms had a further destination and weren't connected to the drug scenario. And why the drug scenario? The money involved, the ruthlessness, and the organisation, were all far too great to be explained by the political opposition to the President wanting to discredit the Government prior to the coming election.

Next Trent had listed those facts appertaining to his own role.

He had been sent to Belpan by Colonel Smith as bait for gun-runners. Belpan was outside the EC's sphere of influence so the Colonel was doing someone a favour. The Colonel had built his career on doing favours for the CIA – but Trent's contact was with Caspar from the DEA.

This made sense to Trent. The end of the Cold War produced fresh priorities in the Intelligence community. Drugs and terrorism now came top of the list. In doing the DEA a favour, the Colonel was continuing his habit of laying down lines of influence.

The Colonel had summoned him to Cancun for the meeting at the Rena Victoria Hotel.

Don Roberto had supplied the Colonel's bodyguard.

The Colonel's bodyguard had led Trent and Pepito to Don Roberto.

Don Roberto had been killed with a similar knife to the one Trent carried.

Three men had mounted an incompetent attack on Trent at Bacalar.

The only reason Trent could imagine for the attack was to link him to Don Roberto's murder – this presumed that the three men were Don Roberto's hirelings. But who had persuaded or paid Don Roberto to supply the men, and what reason had he given him?

Don Roberto was a highly successful and influential free-lance in the Intelligence and Security business. Whoever had killed Don Roberto had known him or had a first-rate introduction because there were no signs of violence other than the knife wound and Don Roberto had given his staff time off.

Why had Don Roberto been killed? Presumably to keep his mouth shut. But about what?

Why had he been set up as Don Roberto's murderer? Trent knew that he was insufficiently important to be the target so there had to be linkage. The only linkage he could see was with Colonel Smith. Don Roberto had worked with the Colonel and had acted as cut-out between him and the CIA on the operations which Trent had undertaken on the Americans' behalf.

Was someone trying to discredit Smith through Trent? And, if so, what had pushed them to such ruthless lengths?

Which brought Trent to the American who had called himself Steve in Cancun and Robert in Frankfurt. Trent would have liked to know whether their meeting in Frank-furt had been deliberate on the American's part.

And, most of all, Trent would like to have known why the photograph he had taken from Don Roberto's house had been there in the first place. And why that particular picture? In all the years that Don Roberto had acted as his

Control when on loan to the CIA, the elderly Englishman had never mentioned Trent's mother.

Trent had come out of hospital after the ambush in Ireland with nothing left of his old life. Now the photograph was pinned to the saloon bulkhead on *Golden Girl*.

With nothing to do but wait, Trent had agreed to act as sail-master on one of Belpan's sand lighters in the regular Sunday race meeting. Forty-foot open sloops, gaff-rigged and shallow draught, the lighters were built to load river sand on the mainland for construction projects out on the keys. Trent was crewing for Baccy, a six-foot-four Seventh Day Adventist black Customs officer who captained Belpan's lone patrol boat when he wasn't racing sailboats. Seventh Day Adventists were the favoured race skippers – they didn't drink, which was more than could be said for the lighter crews.

The lighters employed moveable ballast made up of two-hundred-pound sacks of wet sand and crewing was hard work, particularly in a tacking race. Each time the lighter went about on to a new tack the ballast had to be shifted to the windward side of the boat. For fuel the crews ran on rum and fresh orange juice. Two Creole girls squeezed oranges in the bows while Baccy shouted at his crew as if they were galley slaves rather than a bunch of half-drunk amateurs trying to have Sunday fun. But Baccy never used a curse word, nor did he ever take the briar pipe out of his mouth despite having abandoned the tobacco habit on joining the church at the age of eighteen.

Maria Magdalena was Baccy's craft. Old Man Eddy was helming *Caribbean Queen*. The course was from Jimmy's dock on Key San Paul, round Key Canaka and back, with the local brewer's fifty-foot motor yacht acting as Committee boat. There were no rules to lighter racing and the need for a Committee boat was restricted to the brewer's generosity in distributing cases of beer and crates of white rum. The crews supplied their own oranges.

Maria Magdalena and *Caribbean Queen* cleared Key Canaka thirty metres apart with no more than a bowsprit between them. The finishing line was on a dead run and Baccy had his crew throw the ballast overboard. Then the crew got down to serious drinking. Trent spied the President and his granddaughter on the end of the dock below the President's beach house. Island gossip said the President was keeping clear of electioneering from fear that the rumours spread about his involvement with the Colombian cocaine trade would harm his party's performance at the polls.

With three hundred metres to the finish line, Baccy's *Maria Magdalena* was losing by a length to *Caribbean Queen*. Baccy might be a stalwart Christian but he hated to lose a sailboat race. He ordered those of his crew still in a fit state to swim to take to the sea. Trent dived overboard along with half a dozen crew and *Maria Magdalena* surged ahead.

Trent strolled up the path to Jimmy's Bar. Jimmy had been watching the race from his deckchair. He beckoned Trent over: 'Trent Boy, strangers askin' for you.' He jabbed a thumb over his shoulder at the interior. Trent walked round through the lean-to kitchen and stood in the doorway, from where he could see into the restaurant.

There were four of them: one thin, one fat and two nondescript. They were Latinos and in their mid-thirties to early forties. They wore the standard uniform of the well-to-do American out of office hours: Lacrosse sports shirts, tan cotton Oxfords, leather loafers. Their jewellery would have looked heavy on a Gringo: chunky wedding rings and Omega wristwatches in two tones of gold. And they wore silk socks that would have been frowned upon at the more establishment country clubs in the Hamptons. Cashmere sports jackets hung on the back of their chairs, insurance against an encounter with air-conditioning. Good quality hold-alls were stacked beside the table.

Businessmen, Trent thought, in the professions. Probably checking Belpan's investment potential. They would have alligator-hide wallets for their credit cards and carry photographs of their children. They had ordered halves of the local draught beer which they weren't in a hurry to finish. Quiet voices and Cuban cigars. Americans from the US and the same background would have been emphasising their masculinity by drinking large rums and making too much noise.

The thin one appeared to be the senior partner. Tall, he suffered the sunken chest of a consumptive, and had a hooked nose and eyes that, though hidden behind dark lids, were too big for his face – it was the starving poet look that enslaved self-sacrificial women. He had caught cold, or more likely, suffered from an allergy, Trent thought as he remarked the inflamed eyelids that shuttered the eyes and a nose drip that the thin man dipped into a linen handkerchief every half-a-minute – dip, dip, like a skinny waterbird feeding along the tideline.

The fat man was stocky and broad-faced, but the fat was a thin disguise cloaking the layered muscles of a retired athlete now restricted by his job to twice-weekly sessions at the health club. Calm and quiet, Trent picked him as the technical adviser along for the trip but without direct responsibility for the outcome.

The nondescripts were observers straight out of the nine-to-five banking bureaucracy: groomed to perfection, marvellously polite, and for sale to the highest bidder guaranteed to keep his mouth shut. Or her mouth shut, Trent corrected himself. Pleasurable prejudice, he thought, and smiled contentedly as he entered the bar. He nodded to Jimmy's son before strolling over to the men's table. He introduced himself with a slight bow to the tall man. 'Trent, Señores. You asked for me.'

The man unshuttered his eyes for a moment. They were dark eyes, but without warmth and used to obedience, as was the voice, low-pitched through years without need of recourse to argument. 'We wish to make an inspection of the reef, Señor.'

Trent waited, but the tall man had had his say. The fat man was there to arrange the details. He introduced himself: 'Gomez. Pedro Gomez.' English, it would have been John Smith. 'You have a catamaran. You can approach close to the beaches and also cross the reef where necessary.'

Personal experience or acquired knowledge, Trent wondered. A slight callus marked Gomez's right index finger. Trent imagined him holding a golf club but the callus didn't fit. He said, 'To be safe I require two feet of water under the hulls.'

'You are for hire?' Gomez asked.

The thin man's lids rose for a fraction of a second to show a look of quiet amusement which Trent answered with a slight shrug: 'Señor, whether a man is for hire depends on the circumstances.'

'Of which the amount is an important part,' Gomez suggested smoothly.

'And the difficulties,' Trent said. He found himself studying the thin man's hands. Long-fingered and skeletal, they remained totally at rest on the rough wood of the table top. As if waiting for a command to bring them to life, Trent thought. He had known an Irishman with similar hands; hands that had seemed to perform as separate entities from the man himself; acting on his behalf yet leaving his conscience free of responsibility for their actions. The Irishman had used a gun but a fountain pen could be equally dangerous.

'As a foreigner, Señor,' Trent said, 'the law forbids me to work. Given that I wish to stay in these waters I must be careful neither to give offence nor to provoke jealousy.'

'We wish to sleep on board and we wish to remain close to the reef. What other boat could take us?' the fat man asked. His Spanish was harsh and a little guttural. Trent couldn't place the accent.

'In comfort? None,' Trent said. 'Give me an hour.'

Fetching a bottle of rum and paper cups from the bar and a carrier bag of fresh oranges from the kitchen, Trent strolled over to the lobster Co-operative. He found half a dozen fishermen seated under the palm trees at the foot of the Co-operative quay. Squatting down, Trent poured rum and squeezed orange juice into the cups. He had grown familiar with the fishermen of Ireland's west coast. There they would have been complaining about the weather, the European Commission's new fishing controls and the imminence of bankruptcy. These men were discussing Florida investment property and the stupidity of the Co-operative repatriating their full US earnings to Belpan. A large part of their earnings went back again to the USA for investment; as a result they had to pay Belpan National Bank's transfer charges twice.

Listening to the conversation, Trent watched three frigate birds sailing the on-shore breeze beyond the quay. They were waiting for a lobster boat's arrival in expectation of being thrown a free dinner – less work than fishing on their own account; which about summed up life on the Keys, Trent thought. Sun, sleep, good booze, lackadaisical conversation, and a minimum of effort. The thump and fumes of the freezer plant's heavy diesel generator were the only unwelcome intrusion. Though not unwelcome to the fishermen, he reminded himself. He didn't want to think about the Latinos. But they were waiting and, into a pause, he mentioned that he'd met them over at Jimmy's.

The fishermen already knew of the four foreigners. News travelled faster than light on the small Key. The oldest of the fishermen, grey of head and wearing his false teeth on a string round his neck, spat in the sand and said, 'Trent, boy, you take them men, you make damn sure them pay cash money.'

Mad money to be hidden from Colonel Smith, Trent thought as the other fishermen nodded their approval of sound advice.

'An' you watch fo' dat Gilda woman, boy,' the old man warned, referring to the hurricane now hitting the southern end of the Caribbean. He looked up suspiciously at the northern sky, clear and tranquil. 'Dem radio men is always too damn late. Dat Gilda coming, de birds tell you. No messin', boy. You get up dem creeks an' lash up fast.'

There was a murmur of agreement from the other men. One of them told Trent to fetch a gas can over to the Co-operative quay to be filled at the Co-op's gas pump. Gas at the Co-op was tax-free. Trent thanked him and poured another round of rum. These men were wealthy and the rum was politeness rather than a bribe, particularly the effort of squeezing fresh orange juice. And he had his permission for the charter . . .

Back at Jimmy's, he nodded to Gomez from the covered terrace. The man came out. Trent turned with him and they walked in silence down through the palm trees to the beach and *Golden Girl*. The silence was deliberate on Trent's part and Gomez seemed content to wait.

For Trent it was a sizing-up process. Like a dog checking another dog's scent. Small dogs yapped, big dogs kept their own counsel. By the time they reached the catamaran Trent would have wagered the charter fee on one guess at the man's profession. He waded out to the craft and held her bows while Gomez shed shoes and socks and rolled up his Oxfords. He grasped the forestay in both hands as high up as he could reach and drew himself out of the water and on to the forward hull beam as smoothly as a dolphin breaking for air.

Trent had left an old man guarding the boat. Black Pete was asleep under the cockpit awning. Trent gave him a nod of thanks and a dollar, then stood aside to allow Gomez into the saloon: '*Mi casa es su casa, Señor.*' My home is

65

your home . . . The fat man's brief smile called Trent a liar, though without malice and Trent grinned. 'At a price, of course, and on a temporary basis.'

Gomez laughed softly. 'I may inspect the accommodation?'

'With pleasure.'

The fat man took his time. Trent had expected as much. Waiting in the cockpit, he watched a couple of tanned young Americans race each other in from the reef on sailboards. Gomez reappeared and pointed to the navigation electronics above the chart table on the port side of the main companionway into the saloon. 'Much equipment, Señor.'

'Toys,' Trent said. 'Christopher Columbus discovered America with a sextant and a chunk of lead tied to the end of a line.'

'America is a large target.'

Trent said, 'True,' and waited.

'And with your toys, Capitano Trent, how small a target can you hit?'

'Night or day, give or take a hundred feet, right on the spot.'

'Good toys.'

'Expensive,' Trent said.

Again that quick smile. 'So let us talk money, Capitano.'

Trent tapped the barometer. The needle remained steady at 29.9, one thousand and fourteen millibars. 'US dollars. One thousand a day, cash in advance,' he said. 'No receipt. Food and drink on me as long as you eat fish.'

Trent had been correct as to the alligator-skin wallet but there weren't any credit cards. Gomez slid three one-thousand dollar bills from the wallet. The bills were fresh from the mint. Trent said, *'Gracias, Señor,'* and folded the bills into his back pocket.

'De nada. We come on board tomorrow. Two o'clock.' Gomez held out his hand.

He had a good handshake, Trent thought, as they shook on the deal. He would have been happier if the Latin American had made at least a pretence at attempting to beat him down on the charter price.

'One rider to the deal,' he said. 'There's a hurricane down south. The weathermen say we're safe but if it even thinks of heading north, we run for shelter.'

Trent lay on the surface watching a barracuda. Despite the cotton T-shirt, he could feel the sun hot on his back. He held his spear gun out in front of him with the safety off and used his flippers to keep facing the fish. It was fair-sized, four feet long and weighing twenty-five to thirty pounds. Gunmetal-grey flank, big unblinking eye and the dark slash of a mouth, the fish looked what it was – a killing machine, more dangerous, in Trent's experience, than a shark. Sharks stayed outside the reef, while Trent knew Arab net fishermen in the Persian Gulf whose calf muscles had been ripped out by barracudas while they were standing on the coral with the water below their knees.

Trent had already warned his charter party back to the catamaran, keeping himself between them and the big fish. He thought that if he shot the barracuda behind the head, it would leap clear of the water with its jaws snapping. The open jaws of a big barracuda were enough to keep most people out of the water and his party hadn't shown themselves that keen over the past three days. He thought that they would be happier under the cockpit awning than they had been in the water. The icebox was packed with beer and he'd prepared a lobster salad that he'd left on ice. If his plan worked, he would have an hour or two to himself dawdling along the reef, which was a better way of spending the afternoon than acting as nanny to four Latinos. Though, as charterers went, they weren't bad. He hadn't had to tell them to take their shoes off before boarding at the Co-op quay and in three days of cruising they had washed the sand off their feet after each shore trip. They had listened carefully to his instructions on how to use the marine toilets – unblocking them was Trent's least favourite job. And, most importantly, none of them had ever sailed before, let alone on a big cat. Nor had they cared to learn and Trent hadn't tried teaching them.

The barracuda swam two complete circles with Trent watching. Part of the time it just hung there in the water, not even the tip of a fin moving. But it was edging closer to Trent, always a little closer. He doubted if the fish would attack, though, with barracudas, you could never be sure. A big one was the sea's equivalent of the savanna lion or jungle tiger. They were fearless because they were without enemies.

Hunter or hunted?

If the fish did attack and he missed with his spear, Trent knew that his chances of getting out of the water in one piece were nil. An eight-band spear gun took too long to load for the fisherman to have more than one shot. And if the fish went for his belly, he knew that he would be dead.

Knowing that the barracuda would dart forward the moment he fired, Trent aimed halfway down the jaw. The jerk of the rubber punched up Trent's arm and into the right side of his chest. For a moment he couldn't see through the train of bubbles left by the spear, which hit the fish dead centre and an inch behind the jaw hinge. It leapt high, jaws snapping, body arced so that Trent thought that he would hear its spine snap. The force of its leap dragged Trent breast high out of the water. The sun flashed on the chromed speartip and on the fish. Four leaps and it was dead. Jimmy's wife prided herself on her barracuda curry, which would make a change from lobster. Trent swam back to the catamaran dragging the fish behind him. He passed the gun up to Louis, the tallest of the Latinos, the one he thought of as their leader. Louis pulled the fish on board.

68

Trent suggested the Latinos came back into the water but they weren't keen. 'Then enjoy yourselves,' he told them. 'You don't mind, I'll fish for our supper?'

He spent a further two hours in the water. Most of that time he dived for red snapper along the edge of a break in the reef. A lot of big fish were heading out through the gap.

Between dives Trent considered his charter party. They had spent three days on the reef and had photographed every habitable key from every angle, one of the bank bureaucrats taking notes on a lawyer's pad. They had never drunk more than a couple of beers each, never raised their voices, and always complimented Trent on the fish he grilled each evening. That lunchtime they had told him their research was complete, but they had a day spare and were enjoying themselves. Gomez had produced another of his crisp thousand-dollar bills. Trent had told him to keep it; whether they had been on board or not, he would have spent the afternoon on the reef – having them along was a pleasure. That's what he'd told them, and now they were waiting. He had a feeling that they'd been waiting right from the start of the trip.

A thirty-pound tuna swam past, heading for the open sea. Trent let it go. Red and silver flashed thirty feet down. He drifted beyond a coral head jutting out from the gap's wall and took six deep breaths to hyperventilate his lungs before piking. Then he shot his legs up into the sky and slid down without a splash. At fifty feet he levelled out, slipped the safety off the spear gun, and swam slowly round the coral outcrop. The shoal of snapper were above him. He picked the largest, his spear taking it through the gut. Two kicks of his big flippers were sufficient to send him drifting back up towards the surface that quivered in the harsh sunlight like a sheet of liquid mercury. He unscrewed the speartip, slipped the fish off the shaft and fed it into his catch net. Two snapper per man made a good dinner. Towing the net, he swam slowly back to *Golden Girl*. The sea was an almost oily calm.

As always, Trent was impressed by the beauty of the big cat. It was a very different beauty from that of a 1930's Alden ketch or a clipper-bowed Herreshof schooner so admired by the traditionalists. Those yachts, with their flowing sheer, were the swans, *Golden Girl* was the barracuda, Trent thought as he recalled the big fish hardly stirring as it circled him. The same threat was present; even at anchor, the same promise of instant acceleration to a speed that the monohull sailor could only fantasise about.

Reaching the transom, he tied the catch net to the portside rudder. Pedro Gomez held out a hand for the spear gun. Trent passed it up along with his weightbelt, slipped off his flippers and mask, dropped them over the taffrail and pulled himself into the cockpit. Having rinsed and stowed the fishing gear in the after locker, he reached into the icebox for a cold beer.

The two bureaucrats lay drowsing on the port and starboard cockpit seats. Louis lolled at ease in one of the two deckchairs. Gomez sat on a bucket with his back to the companionway. A pistol had appeared in his hand, a 9mm Beretta 10-shot automatic. The pistol wasn't pointed at Trent. There was no need for pointing. As Trent had known it would, the callus on Gomez's index finger exactly fitted the trigger and upper edge of the trigger-guard. Hours of daily practice on the firing range had formed the callus. Gomez's slight smile was that of a man who believed that politeness demanded he act a little embarrassed at doing his job.

Trent was neither surprised nor, to his own amazement, frightened. But there was plenty of time for fear. 'Want a beer?' he asked.

'Not at this instant,' Gomez answered – one professional to another – no personal animosity.

Trent seated himself on the taffrail. Raising his beer can to Louis, he said, '*Salud,*' before drinking. 'With your knowledge of sailing, Señor Louis, have me shot and you'll float around out here the rest of your lives.'

It was a point Louis must have considered. He touched the ever present linen handkerchief to his nose. 'We wish you to do us a service.'

'Then point dollars,' Trent said. 'The more you point, the better I react.'

Louis snuffled amusement into his handkerchief. 'The gun is merely to assure you of our seriousness.'

'Consider me assured,' Trent said. He watched a distant flock of gulls wing their way towards the mainland. And the big fish were heading for deep water. Tongue out, as if licking the beer from his lips, Trent felt for the wind. Not even a breath . . .

'We wish to rendezvous with a ship,' Louis said.

'I've known that since the first day Gomez came on board and checked the Loran navigation worked. Are you leaving or are we making a pick-up?'

Louis sniffed. 'Pick-up. Twenty men.'

One and a half tons. 'Much baggage?'

'Seven hundred kilos.'

Trent said, 'Wind picks up, we'll need to tow half of it in the Zodiac.' The fourteen-foot inflatable dinghy would carry the weight and tow easily enough.

Louis carefully folded his handkerchief into a square and laid it on the deck beside his chair. His hands returned to lie parallel with each other on his knees. He examined them from beneath pink-rimmed lids – as if checking that they were his, Trent thought. His eyelids rose for a moment. Trent sensed that he was being inspected in the same way that Louis had examined his hands; as an abstract entity; a tool, at most; briefly useful, but, once used, to be discarded without further thought. It was a death sentence, Trent knew with absolute certainty, passed on him by a man who was both intelligent and psychopathic. Shades of Ireland, he thought: Colonel Smith and his power games that kept his minions in ignorance of the danger they were being manipulated into facing. Take a few months off. Relax. Get yourself a suntan. Establish a new identity. As a corpse . . .

Trent's thoughts went back to the photograph he had found on Don Roberto's piano. The young fair-haired Lancer officer lolling at his mother's feet, the look on the officer's neatly moustached face that of complacent owner-ship. And Trent too had been his possession. Not in day-to-day practice, perhaps, but by Trent's accepting his relationship to the Colonel as an inevitable part of his life. It had been his only relationship, a habit of natural loyalty founded in his childhood, further cemented by the dependence of the field officer on his Control, and never questioned in its foundations . . . perhaps because, in accepting the Colonel as his father-figure, he had been able to protect himself from the manner of his real father's death.

Damn them both, Trent thought, the British Colonel and the Latin American killer. And the killer was waiting for Trent's explanation. 'Catamarans are built for speed,' Trent said. Not for carrying weight. When hit by a squall, a conventional yacht heeled, thus spilling the wind from its sails. With a catamaran it was instant acceleration that dampened the force of the wind. 'Weigh her down and the first squall rips the mast out of her,' he warned. 'Tow the Zodiac and we sit Gomez on the taffrail with a machete. A squall hits, he cuts.'

Gomez grinned at the thought.

'But we lose the cargo,' Louis suggested coldly.

Trent shook his head. He had a thousand metres of nylon fishing-line on the marlin rod lashed to the port stay, three hundred kilos breaking-strain. 'We come up into the wind and collect the Zodiac.'

72

'So easy, Capitano?'

Trent raised his beer can. 'Easy, and you wouldn't have to pay so much.'

FIVE

The wind came in tiny puffs that hardly stirred the sea's surface. Despite the lack of wind, over the past hour a swell had built beyond the reef – a strange, almost oily swell that rose in long humps only to collapse back on itself as if exhausted by the effort. The heat was intense and the humidity so heavy that the setting sun seemed crushed into the mountains like a piece of squashed orange modelling clay.

The big fish had been making for deep water all afternoon and Trent hadn't seen a bird for the past hour. Seated portside of the cockpit, he pounded garlic, fresh ginger, black peppercorns, salt, and olive oil into a paste. He had already stowed the cockpit awning and set up the barbecue. One of the bureaucrats had cleaned the fish – Trent's fishing-knife had been confiscated by Pedro Gomez. Now the bureaucrats and Louis were below while Gomez, lazily watchful, sat on the saloon cabin top.

There was no hurry. The rendezvous was six miles out beyond the reef at 0100 hours. Say twenty minutes to transfer the men and cargo; two hours to the mainland and a further half-hour to reach the upriver disembarkation point. Although which river had been kept secret from Trent, he was certain that it would be the north fork of the Belpan where a bend would hide them from the road bridge. They would unload the cargo. Then Gomez would shoot him in the head. Gomez would neither dislike nor enjoy doing so. It was his job – like going to the office.

Trent held eight of the fresh thousand-dollar bills folded in the back pocket of his jeans; the original three for the charter augmented by a further five in payment for his agreeing to the rendezvous. Thoughts of the bills returning to Gomez's alligator-skin billfold were unpleasant, but less unpleasant than the thought of being shot in the head. Trent had wanted out for so long – out of the secrecy and isolation. These last few months of building a new identity had enabled him to relax for the first time in years. Now he was back at the sharp end.

Fear was useful as an adrenaline pump but dangerous if allowed to affect the ability to think clearly. So far Trent had managed to keep it under control but he could taste its sourness in the back of his throat and feel it in his stomach and up the back of his thighs – familiar tremblings imperceptible to an observer.

He wanted to check the barometer. To do so he would need Gomez's permission, and in asking he might arouse the Latino's suspicions. Anyway he knew what was coming. The when was important – the hurricane was a more accessible ally than either Caspar at the US Embassy or Steve back in Washington with his promise of the heavy brigade. Spooning the garlic and ginger paste into the snapper and over their skin, he dropped the first three fish on to the grill and called down to the other Latinos to bring plates and cutlery from the galley.

Eating dinner, Trent watched Louis run his knife down a fish's backbone, parting the flesh with the concentration and obsessively meticulous neatness of a surgeon. Louis was a man to whom error was unforgivable, in himself as much as in his associates or employees. Essential to Trent's possibilities of survival was that Louis should believe him ignorant of the death sentence already passed. Unsuspecting, Trent would be watched, certainly, but there might be a chance moment in which the Latinos relaxed or shifted their concentration.

Reaching for a beer from the icebox, Trent flipped the cap and asked casually, 'Why didn't you fly them in?'

He already knew the answer. The Latinos were used to flying their drug cargoes and knew that there was always the risk of someone, if only by accident, being on or near the airstrip. Smuggling drugs was a quick in-and-out operation. Land, refuel, and take off before anyone could get there. Now these men were involved in a long-term operation and total secrecy was essential to its outcome.

Louis looked at him, his red-rimmed eyelids lifting for a moment. The handkerchief appeared, the nose was dabbed. Then the tiniest flutter of thin fingers unfurling. 'We like the sea, Señor Capitano.'

But had no experience of it, Trent thought. This was their one mistake, this entering on unfamiliar territory – his territory. And because it was his territory, Trent retained hope, despite his fear of Louis; as he had retained hope back in Ireland under the inspection of the leader of the terrorist unit that he had infiltrated. The terrorist had hands identical to those of Louis and he had been a psychopath.

The wind puffs were stronger now, though no more frequent. Not squalls yet, but armed with sufficient force to drift *Golden Girl* to the length of her anchor warp, and there was a change to the sound of the swell on the reef, a growing harshness. Trent said, 'I'll need to get the sails ready.'

Neither stars nor cloud shadows marked the darkness stretching overhead and on down to meet the equal gloom of the ocean. The wind was irregular. The seas, long and oily-smooth, lifted *Golden Girl* without breaking on the light hulls, and left the barest traces of phosphorescence in

76

the twin wakes. Every ten minutes or so a larger swell came at them out of the darkness. These larger swells spilled the wind from the running genoa for a moment so that the big, light foresail snapped full again, the stays humming under the suddenly renewed tension.

Trent could sense the approach of these larger swells. He didn't know how – perhaps a different feel to the tiller or in the way the bows felt at the sea. It was a faculty common to all good sailors, the essential extra that enabled them to meet the seas whatever the conditions so that their craft ran straight rather than in the long zig-zags of the helmsman imprisoned by the compass and only reacting to the swing of its needle.

Trent hardly looked at the compass. It was there as confirmation of the course he sailed rather than as an ever-present guide, as were the slowly changing figures on the Loran's small screen on the bulkhead beside the companionway. He had no need to check the chart. Before raising the anchor, he had punched the rendezvous into the Loran's computer; now the radio navigation system gave *Golden Girl*'s position in relation to the rendezvous to within a hundred metres.

It was easy sailing but unpleasant, the threat always there in the darkness and in the thick feel of the night air. This despite the meteorological report and the barometer steady at 29.9. Pedro Gomez had sensed Trent's unease prior to their sailing. 'You can feel it?'

'What?' Trent had asked, still hopeful of subterfuge.

'The hurricane,' the Latino had stated flatly. 'You haven't wanted to look at the barometer in the last four hours.'

Trent had shrugged and the gunman had grinned at him, teeth flashing in the light from the saloon companionway: 'I like you, Trent. Not that it makes any difference.'

'Not that it makes any difference,' Trent had agreed.

Half an hour prior to Trent's calculated sailing time,

Louis had come on deck. 'Señor Capitano, you have a light rope?'

'How light?'

'Light enough for you to wear.' The eyelids lifted. Cold eyes. 'How sad it would be for us to lose you to the sea, Señor Capitano.'

So now Trent wore a fifty-foot leash of rope round his neck. Gomez had done the tying. His slight smile and a shrug had told Trent that this, too, wasn't personal, just part of the job . . .

With the leashing Trent had lost his last hope of escape. The fear was with him, still hidden, but unavoidable. Three hours to live. Three hours in which to think of all that he had missed. Love. Always love. The fantasy of living with a woman in a state of openness and trust. To have no secrets, no abnormal fears, no hidden agenda. To be like other people: gardening at the weekend, scent of freshly-mown grass, children playing on the lawn; wife in a cotton dress, long-legged, her smile sharing with him their private memories, future secured. Even the possibility of this birth-right had been stolen from him, though not by these Latinos. Colonel Smith had been the thief, with Trent's habit of loyalty as the accomplice; the Latinos were merely the instruments, Trent thought as he looked across at the thick shape of Pedro Gomez seated on the windward side of the cockpit.

Through the three days of their charter, Gomez was the only one of the four Latinos with whom Trent had formed the slightest relationship. He even found himself liking the gunman in an abstract way, despite Gomez's future role as his executioner. His liking for the man made him uncomfortably aware of the similarity in their jobs. Both of them were professionals, the only difference being that Trent was on the side of the law.

A heavy swell came at them out of the thick darkness. Trent met it with a slight movement of the tiller bar, and the big catamaran lifted smoothly. The sea slithered along the hulls with the sound of tearing paper as the yacht heeled to the slope of the wave, wind spilling for a moment, slap of canvas. A quick glance at the Loran indicator. One mile to the rendezvous. Two hours and fifty minutes to live. 'You are married, Gomez?'

'*Si, Señor.*' The gunman laughed contentedly. 'Three boys, three girls. One boy will be a lawyer, one will be an accountant, one will be a policeman . . . '

So much for female emancipation, Trent thought. 'You've got everything covered.'

Again Gomez laughed softly. 'The doctor remains to be born.'

'And obedient millionaires as husbands for your daughters.'

'But naturally . . . '

'Remember,' Trent warned, 'God is on our side. Unfortunately he believes that we improve with punishment.'

The fat man grinned, pistol held loosely in his lap. 'A depressing philosophy, Señor Capitano.'

'Don't doubt it,' Trent said. Two hours and forty five minutes to live . . .

The throaty rumble of twin diesel motors muttered at them out of the darkness. For a moment Trent allowed himself to believe in rescue. But there were no lights on the vessel. Up in the bows, one of the bureaucrats flashed a torch twice, waited five seconds and repeated the signal. A blue light above a green flashed in answer.

'Take the helm,' Trent told Gomez. 'Hold her steady while I drop the genoa.'

Careful not to hook his leash, Trent made his way forward. Waving the bureaucrat clear, he dropped the big foresail, furling and stowing it into its sailbag. The vessel was in sight now. White-hulled, she was a sleek ninety-foot Baglietto motor yacht. Two million dollars of Italy's finest craftsmanship. A thousand horsepower in each engine, she'd make thirty knots in calm water, Campari with soda sipped in the shade of the aluminium awning on the after-deck. Nothing but the best for the murderous pigs of the cocaine trade, Trent thought, anger and fear sour in his throat. Drug barons, the newspapers called them, giving the pigs a glamour in which to revel.

But the yacht would be a pounding hell if caught out in a rough sea. The skipper would be anxious to get the trans-fer over quickly, Trent knew as he made his way aft to the cockpit. Once unladen, the Baglietto had the power and speed to out-race the coming storm.

Easing *Golden Girl* up under mainsail, Trent watched the motor yacht roll gently in the swell. He was faced by a problem in seamanship. Though it wasn't a difficult test, it was sufficient to distract him temporarily from the fear. There were men on the afterdeck now. Two of them wore white uniform. The others were merely dark shapes. Louis had come up from the saloon. He stood leaning against the bulkhead, hands resting on the cabin top. A calculating machine, Trent thought. Louis, *El Jefe*, the Chief . . .

Trent's loathing for the man was suddenly unbearable. Unable to look at him, he turned to Gomez: 'I don't want the ship rolling on us. They'll have a stern ladder. We'll come stern-on and get a line on board. Load from the ladder.'

The gunman, nodding his understanding, called orders to the two bureaucrats now both in the bows.

Trent pinched *Golden Girl* a few degrees into the wind as the motor yacht rose to a swell which ran down her side in a flowing cascade of phosphorescence. Her stern rose with the sea, then dipped as the swell passed. Now it was *Golden Girl*'s turn to be lifted. Her bows rose level with the Baglietto's afterdeck.

'Throw,' Trent yelled. He saw one of the sailors catch the heaving line. Thrusting the helm hard over, he shot clear of the motor yacht's wind-shadow. A flick of the main sheet freed it from the cam cleat. 'Head down,' he warned Gomez as the boom swung. Then he was on to the cabin top and releasing the main halyard. The sail came down on the run. Trent gathered it and wrapped it with ties to the boom before going forward to raise the storm jib.

Broadside to the wind, *Golden Girl* was already drifting clear of the heavier motor yacht. 'Haul her in,' Trent ordered the bureaucrats. 'Slowly,' he warned and backed the tiny storm jib, making the sheet fast so that the breeze would hold them clear of the Baglietto's stern. There was a part of his mind filled almost to sickness with self-mockery, a bitter mockery grown out of the fear that was back with him now, mockery for the excellence of his seamanship. Two hours and thirty minutes of life left, why care what happened to *Golden Girl*? But he did care. And he cared that the sailors on the Baglietto should respect his ability.

The first specks of light rain fell on Trent's face as he looked up to see the motor yacht's captain studying him from over the brilliantly-varnished taffrail. Gold braid glowed on his peaked hat and epaulettes. The man was sixty years old, Trent judged, and no different to look at than any other skipper to the supra-wealthy – a tried and tested retainer on sixty thousand dollars a year, pension fund and the finest medical insurance. But this captain's bosses were different and that made the captain different. Pigs had piglets, Trent thought and called up, 'What do you make of the weather?'

'Barometer is steady,' was the reply. 'Nothing on the radio.'

And may you remain confident and get yourself drowned, Trent thought. A sailor stood beside the captain, behind them a dozen men in jungle fatigues and black berets. Jungle boots were looped round their necks and they carried weapons.

81

Kalashnikovs, Trent presumed. It was always Kalashnikovs.

'We'll take six of the men first as handlers, then the cargo,' he called. 'Let's get things moving.'

The men came down the stern ladder. Short, stocky *mestizos*, there was no pretence or possibility of disguise with these men as there was with his charter party. Killers, all of them, vicious hoodlums from the slums of Medellin, the cocaine trade's terrorists, bombers of bus stations, murderers of anyone who criticised their masters' rights to rule as self-appointed kings of Colombia.

And Trent had been correct as to the Kalashnikovs – one more failure for British exports.

Violence was a daily part of their lives, and the men paid Trent's leash as little attention as they would have spared for the commonplace of a bleeding corpse sprawled in the gutter back home. Leaving two of the men in the bows to receive the cargo, he positioned two more along the windward side deck. Then helped by the last two, he unlashed and lifted the inflatable dinghy overboard from the cabin top, making it fast fore and aft.

Back in the bows, he called up, 'Lower away,' and watched a metal ammunition box swing down. 'Keep it off the deck,' he ordered.

From behind him, Louis said, 'There are three sizes of boxes, Señor Capitano. Six of the small ones in the saloon and two each of the long boxes.'

Trent hadn't heard Louis come forrard. The sound of the Latino's voice, cold and quiet, brought back the fear that he had forgotten for a moment. Turning to face Louis, he said, 'I warned you. The cargo goes in the Zodiac or we'll be carrying too much weight.'

Louis, without any expression, said, 'Put three men in the Zodiac.'

His own fear clammying his T-shirt, Trent imagined the long terror the men would suffer, men with no experience of the sea set adrift in the pitch dark and drizzle with the swell building and the rising thunder of surf breaking on the reef ahead. But with Louis discussion was alien territory and deadly dangerous: 'They're your men. I'll give them a torch.'

Louis unhooded his eyes. A venomous snake's eyes. His voice was soft as the hiss of a snake. 'They have no need of a torch, Señor Capitano.'

In case, panicked, they should wave the beam. 'As you say,' Trent said and turned back to organise the loading. Ammunition for the Kalashnikovs and Beretta automatics, grenades, half a dozen hand-held rocket launchers and their missiles.

Next came the men's leader, Mario. He was short, slim, and light on his feet. His eyes were small and wide-set, bright like a ferret's. A knife scar showed pale on his left cheek. He spoke with a slight lisp and greeted Louis with respect but without subservience. As with his men, Belpan Defence Force shoulder flashes were sewn to his fatigues. The others followed, all of the same murderous breed, twenty killers to be let loose on the tiny defenceless country which Trent had learnt to love for its simplicity and innocence as much as for the variety of its natural beauty.

Three men to the Zodiac, two forward in each forecabin, four in the twin stern cabins, five in the saloon. He looked up to see the last of them swing a booted foot over the Baglietto's taffrail.

'Hold it right there,' Trent yelled.

The man peered down in mock confusion. 'Someone talking to me?'

'I'm talking to you. Get those boots off.'

The man giggled, high-pitched. 'Hey man, there a talking Gringo dog on a leash. You believe that?' he asked of his compatriots in film-world Hispanic-American, deliberately mocking. He swung his other leg over. Sitting up on the rail, he spat down at Trent, then tilted his head back and yapped like a Pekinese. 'Watch your backside, Gringo, back home we eat dog for dinner.' He jumped, boots striking the deck. As he landed, he skewered his heels deliberately into the pale teak. Two black streaks, shiny under the light rain falling steadily now, marked the wood. The man giggled. He was smaller than the others. Broad, high cheekbones and a mahogany skin underlined his Indian blood. He spat at Trent again and again giggled, black eyes crazed: 'Good dog, Gringo, you wanna wag your tail for Miguelito?'

Trent's self-control had been exhausted in holding down his fear. Blind rage took him. He hit hard. The man ducked, weaving to his left so that Trent's fist caught him high on the right cheek. He fell backwards, already rolling as he struck the trampoline between the hulls. Trent came after him, right foot driving at his crotch but hitting his thigh as he rolled again. The man was up like a cat, crouching, legs apart, the pale lights of the motor yacht shimmering on the knife in his hand, spittle foaming at the corners of his mouth, mad eyes.

Hands grabbed Trent from behind, pinning his arms to his sides. The man grinned, all teeth, and charged at Trent fast, the knife driving at his belly.

Then came Louis' voice, cold as dry ice, utterly controlled, utterly vicious: 'Drop it.'

The man stopped in mid-strike as if a steel door had been slammed in his face. His fingers opened, the knife bounced on the trampoline webbing and fell through into the sea. But his eyes remained on Trent, insane with hate. He spat frothy phlegm. 'I keel you, Gringo.' It was a promise as sure as a Lloyd's Insurance policy. 'Wait, Gringo. Wait. I keel you. I, Miguelito . . . '

Trent shook himself free of the hands that held him and turned his back on the man. The rage remained in him. His hands shook with it. No fear left now. 'Get that pig's boots off,' he told Louis. 'Get his boots off and get him below or I'll sail the lot of you straight into the reef.'

84

Louis dabbed his nose into his handkerchief. He must have a suitcase of handkerchiefs, Trent thought as he met the Latino's cold eyes studying him over the crisp white linen barricade.

'With the rope round your neck, you would die slowly, Señor Capitano.'

And while there was life there was hope. Except that Trent no longer had any hope. Two hours and twenty minutes to live . . .

Casting off the Zodiac, he led the laden inflatable aft, making the bow line fast to *Golden Girl*'s stern anchor cleat. The three men assigned to the inflatable waited in the cockpit. They watched him with unconcealed anxiety, wet already with the light rain. Soon they would be sea-wet and sea-sick. Trent considered showing one of them how to keep the bows of the Zodiac to the wind in case he had to cast them off but Louis was beside him.

'To delay us would be dangerous, Señor Capitano.'

Trent dug lifejackets out of the portside cockpit locker. While the men put them on, he led the fishing-line down from his marlin rod lashed to the after port stay. He made the line fast to the Zodiac's bow cleat and set the drag brake on the reel at two hundred kilos.

'Keep still, don't panic, and you'll be all right,' Trent told the three men as he handed them into the boat. With Louis watching, they nodded in dumb misery. 'We get hit by a squall, things will get busy,' he warned Louis and the hit squad's leader, Mario. 'The fewer men on deck, the better. They'll be in the way.' He had already planned the voyage in his head. 'Gomez I can use, he's learned a little – and one man at the mast.' To Mario, he said, 'One of your men who is quick on his feet and who understands ropes.'

While Louis ducked into the saloon, Trent made his way forward. He selected the number two jib, clipping the spring shackles to the forestay. Even in the light breeze a bigger sail would have made towing the Zodiac dangerously uncontrollable.

One of the soldiers had come up on to the cabin top. 'You know ropes?' Trent asked.

The man shrugged. '*Soy vaquero, Señor.*' A cowboy . . .

'Then watch,' Trent ordered. Dropping the storm jib, he raised the number two.

'Cast off,' he called up to the Baglietto's crewman. Quickly coiling the bow line, he raised the main, then back to the cockpit. Sheets in, he bore away from the motor yacht. The crewman waved, seaman to seaman, and Trent raised a hand in farewell. Two hours to live . . .

The jerk of the Zodiac's tow rope would have slewed *Golden Girl* broadside to the wind but Trent was ready with the jib sheet, hauling in hard to balance wind with tow. Once the Zodiac was in motion he was able to ease out the sheet. The big cat ran smoothly though sluggishly. 'Hold her steady,' he told Gomez and made his way on to the cabin top.

He showed the *vaquero* the main and jib halyards. 'I yell, you drop the sails,' Trent told him. 'Get the sails down fast and gathered on to the deck.'

Though clearly unhappy at the responsibility, the *vaquero* nodded his understanding.

The drag of the loaded inflatable had slowed the catamaran so that they were making a bare five knots. The swell had built steadily over the past half-hour. Ahead of them, Trent could hear the surf smashing on the reef, heavy now and threatening. The rain fell steadily. The wind remained light but the gusts were stronger and more frequent. Ten minutes to the gap in the reef, three-quarters of an hour to the mainland, twenty minutes upriver to the disembarkation point . . .

There was a tension in the air, as if they were sailing within a millimetre-thin glass bowl that was about to shatter.

At the moment of its shattering hell would implode on them from all directions.

Gomez felt it. He sat hunched by the stern cleat, knife ready to cut the Zodiac free. He had smoked one cigarette after the other, holding them cupped in his palm to protect them from the rain. Every half-minute or so, he peered over at the Loran navigation indicator – as if looking at it would make the numbers showing their position change more rapidly – then glanced up at the sky as if there was something to be divined in the matted darkness that could warn him of approaching doom.

'It is coming?' he asked for the fifth time since they had broken away from the Baglietto.

'Not yet,' Trent said. 'Maybe a couple of hours. Maybe longer. First there'll be squalls.'

And then one hit them, racing out of the darkness. The sound of it was buried by the thunder of the surf ahead and the white spume line was on them without warning.

As the wind struck the sails, Trent yelled, 'Cut,' and saw Gomez's knife flash as the big cat leaped forward, sails taut as an overheated drumskin, stays screaming with the power of it.

Then Gomez was on his feet; whether from fear or to do something, Trent didn't know. The leap of the big cata-maran unbalanced the gunman. He stumbled, arms flung wide. The fishing-line caught round his legs. The weight of the Zodiac plucked him out of the cockpit like a pip out of a ripe olive and he screamed with the terror of drowning as he struck the water.

'Drop the sails!' Trent yelled at the *vaquero* by the mast and slammed the helm hard over to bring *Golden Girl* into the wind. He jerked both sheets loose from their cam cleats and hit the sea in a flat dive. Ten strokes and he had Gomez by the back of the shirt. He had forgotten the leash. He thought the jerk would tear his head from his shoulders. He managed to get one hand on the leash, pulling with all his strength, his other locked in Gomez's shirt. The sea flooded his mouth and eyes, blinding and choking him, and the gunman's flailing arms threatened to knock him unconscious.

'Stop panicking!' he yelled. A swell lifted him and he saw men in the cockpit. The rope round his neck went slack. Gasping air into his lungs, he dived down, groping for the fishing-line looped and re-looped round Gomez's legs. He caught the line the Zodiac side of the gunman, wrapped it round his right wrist and kicked hard for the surface. Water filled his mouth as he fought for air. Salt seared his lungs and then the panicked Gomez flung his arms round Trent's neck, choking him and threatening to drag him back down.

Trent had no option. He brought his knee up hard into Gomez's stomach, driving the wind out of him. As the gunman jack-knifed, Trent hit him on the point of the jaw.

'Sorry,' he said, although Gomez was barely conscious.

Letting Gomez loose, Trent heaved a loop of his neck rope in and tied it to the fishing-line, leaving enough slack so that the strain was off Gomez's legs. He grabbed him, flipping him over on to his back so that the gunman's mouth and nostrils were clear of the sea. Then, ducking his head under, he tried to free Gomez's legs but the line was in and out of them like a cat's cradle.

Trent surfaced and yelled at the men in the cockpit to swim a lifejacket out to him. None of them seemed anxious to comply and Trent doubted his strength would last long enough to haul Gomez against the weight of the Zodiac.

The roar of the surf was closer. For a moment Trent thought of letting the whole damn lot of them go up on the reef. He could cut himself free on the coral. But he knew that it was a fantasy. The power of the swells breaking now would rip him to pieces in seconds. Better to live in hope – and better to be shot cleanly through the head than be smashed by the surf and stripped of his flesh by the knife-sharp coral.

He shouted at the men in the cockpit to make fast the rope that led to his neck. Floating Gomez up on to his shoulders, he held him there with his left hand while pulling steadily with his right. One-handed, and with both Gomez's weight and the weight of the laden Zodiac to drag, his progress was desperately slow. The reef was now less than a quarter of a mile away. As each swell lifted him, he could see the wall of foam ever closer.

A score more swells would do it . . .

Trent imagined *Golden Girl* picked up by the surf and flung tumbling and splintering into fragments. Bodies tossed, men screaming. The strain on his right arm was almost unbearable. He no longer had the strength to yell instructions to the men on the catamaran. And he had swallowed so much sea water he wanted to vomit. A part of himself longed to surrender, but he was close now, and hands reached for him. A swell swept him forward, and one of the uniformed terrorists caught his wrist. He gasped at the men to grab Gomez. Then he was into the cockpit.

The *vaquero* was still by the mast. 'Get the sails up,' Trent managed – no time to get his breath back with the reef now a bare two hundred yards on their beam. 'The big one first.'

The wind caught the sail. Trent sheeted it in and, as the sail drew, put the helm over to circle back towards the Zodiac. 'Someone pull in on the fishing-line,' he ordered. 'Not hard or you'll break it. All I need is to see the direction.'

As the slack came in, he got one of the uniformed men to cut the line away from Gomez's legs and retie it to the line on the rod.

'Keep reeling in,' he told the man. 'The rest of you get back below.'

Only then did he see the thin figure of Louis leaning against the saloon bulkhead. Trent had forgotten the Latino. The dark shapes of Mario's men ducked one by one into the saloon leaving only the man on the rod, the mast-man, and Gomez. Louis put a hand up to the boom to steady himself and crossed the cockpit to where Gomez lay on the cockpit sole like a beached grouper. Sea water leaked from his mouth, his breath gasped in jerky spasms. Louis looked down at him. 'We will be late, Señor Capitano.'

'We're alive,' Trent said.

Louis kicked Gomez in the belly and the gunman vomited. 'Time is important, Señor Capitano.'

Trent could no longer contain his loathing for the Latino. 'And you're a psychopath,' he said. 'Someone should have shut you in a hospital for the criminally insane and thrown away the key.'

The ever-waiting white handkerchief appeared. Louis sniffed into it, dabbing the end of his nose as precisely as a dentist drying a cavity. He tucked the handkerchief back into his sleeve. 'When you have a rope round your neck, Señor Capitano, it is a mistake to insult the holder of the rope,' he counselled without apparent emotion. 'Miguelito,' he called down into the saloon: 'Please sit with the Señor Capitano . . . '

With the wind drifting the laden Zodiac, Trent doubted his ability to pick the tow up before the men were on the reef. He could imagine them, lifejackets on, faces strained with a terror compounded by their helplessness. All their concentration would be on the great white wall of crashing surf ahead.

It was too dark to see the line, and Trent called to the man on the rod to keep it pointing at the Zodiac. He had set the brake on the reel at two hundred kilos, leaving a hundred as insurance against the line parting. Two hundred kilos of drag was enough to slow the drift of the Zodiac but nowhere near sufficient to haul the boat in to the catamaran. The line screamed out as Trent beat to windward off the reef. 'I'm going about,' he called to the *vaquero*. 'Watch the small sail. If it catches, free it.'

'*Si, Señor*,' came back the answer.

The man on the rod would be unable to reel in fast enough as they ran down on the Zodiac. 'Drop the rod and pull in by hand,' Trent told him. 'Fast but not hard or you'll snap the line. Get up in the bows. Shout the direction.'

Ahead of them the reef roared like a lion waiting to be fed. Four hundred yards, three hundred, two hundred, one hundred . . . Trent knew that the Zodiac was gone, the Zodiac and the three men.

Then the rod-man screamed, arm pointing straight ahead at the surf.

Trent shouted with all his force that he was going about. Thrusting the helm right over, he held the catamaran's bows directly into the wind and, looking aft, saw the madly waving arms of the terrified men outlined against the wall of white spray. The Zodiac was within fifty yards of annihilation. Thirty yards separated them from the catamaran.

Trent held the jib backed, sailing the cat stern on. A man was beside him, heaving rope ready. He had no time to see who the man was. Ten yards now. The rope dropped across the boat. He saw one of the men begin to haul on it. 'Make it fast,' he yelled but the man was too scared to understand.

'Tie it,' Trent yelled again but without time to watch if the man obeyed his instructions.

He let the jib sheet loose and heaved in on the main. The big cat started to swing on to the other tack but a swell caught her bow, slamming her back. Fifty yards to the reef. The thunder of it drowned his voice as he yelled at the rod-man up in the bows to hold the jib clear of the stays. The main filled and the big cat accelerated. Twenty yards from the reef . . .

He hadn't the speed yet to be sure *Golden Girl* would come about. Ten yards . . . Now! he thought and slammed the helm over. The cat shuddered as her bows bit into the swell. Up she came, the swell lifting her and lifting her, sails flapping crazily. Hold it, Trent warned himself. One second, two seconds, three . . .

Then *Golden Girl* was through the wind. Hard in on the sheets. The sails filled. He didn't bother with the Zodiac. There was nothing he could do – it was saved or not. He felt the tug of the tow rope. Only then did he dare look back over his shoulder. For a moment all he could see was the great wall of surf, dark at its roots like a dyed blonde. Then he recognised the darker mass of the dinghy against the white foam.

The tow held steady, but the weight of it was forcing him further and further off the wind. Another minute and he would be broadside to the swell.

'Watch yourselves,' he yelled, doubting if the men could hear. 'Going about.'

Over went the helm. Again the swell held the bows for an agonising moment. Trent saw a dark figure grab the jib foot, forcing the sail hard back into the breeze. The catamaran shook its bows against the swell, then she was through the wind and on to the other tack with the sails drawing sweetly. But they had lost ten yards in the manoeuvre, and the Zodiac was almost back into the surf. Trent glanced at the Loran. The gap in the reef lay two hundred yards ahead on the port bow. He needed more canvas, but he couldn't leave the helm. He glanced down at Gomez, still sprawled on the cockpit sole. No help there.

Beside him appeared the maniacal little knife-man, Miguelito, giggling like an over-excited schoolgirl at a birthday party. Trent saw him stuff white powder into his nose. The man snorted like a ploughhorse getting its breath after turning a long furrow. The powder left a white rim below his nostrils. 'Hey, little dog,' he giggled, looking at Trent out of crazed eyes. 'That baby beetch of a sail don' do you no good.'

What did he know about it? Trent thought, the rage

beating adrenaline into his bloodstream as if forced by a foot-pump.

Miguelito knuckled the white rims into his nostrils, a mass of white teeth gleaming. The high-pitched giggle drilled into Trent's brain as the crazy words came in the *mestizo*'s B-film American: 'Hey, leetle dog, you wan' help from Miguelito, jus' say the word.'

As if a homicidal maniac on cocaine could be of any help . . .

'Man, Miguelito know every dam' theeng. Better believe it!' The *mestizo* was on his feet, jigging a little dance in the cockpit. 'Where the sail, man? Tell Miguelito, he do good.'

Suddenly the backing of the jib connected in Trent's mind. However unbelievable, it had to have been the little *mestizo*. 'Portside sail-locker. Black bag with a white figure one painted on it.' A swell lurched the catamaran a further metre towards the reef. 'I'm going about,' he told Miguelito but the little man had danced his way forward.

The next swell lifted *Golden Girl*, and using the down slope for extra speed, Trent swung the helm over, holding the jib sheet tight till the bow came through the wind. The boom slammed over. He sheeted both sails hard in and glanced back to see the Zodiac lift high on the edge of a breaking swell. The tow rope sprang taut, plucking the dinghy clear as the swell broke, thundering forward on to the waiting coral.

Up in the bows the yellow mass of the number one genoa broke out of its bag. Miguelito scurried down the side deck, leading the port genoa sheet aft to the sheet winch.

'Hey, Miguelito do good, huh,' he giggled, with a little prance of his feet before scurrying forrard for the starboard sheet, and yapped dog-like as he jumped back into the cockpit, sheet ready. 'We haul the son a' beetch up that mast now, leetle dog. You ready?'

'Ready,' Trent said and watched the *mestizo* vault one-

93

handed on to the cabin top for a quick word with the *vaquero* at the mast.

The yellow genoa sped up the forestay, Trent switching sheets as the jib came down. The catamaran surged forward under the added power of the big sail. The Zodiac swung behind it. The gap in the reef showed as a dark stretch less than two hundred yards away on their port quarter. At any moment another squall might strike. Trent wiped the rain from his eyes as he tried to calculate speed and distance against the drift of the Zodiac. He required a minimum of fifty yards for safety.

'Going about,' he shouted and watched in amazement the crazed proficiency of the little cocaine addict leaping back into the cockpit to winch the genoa sheet in.

'Hey, leetle dog, you cut distance fine,' the *mestizo* giggled, thumbnailing white powder into his nose. 'You scare them like hell.'

'Better scared than dead,' Trent said. 'Where did you learn to handle a boat?'

'Miguelito sail with one gringo widow-lady, two months. Then she put Miguelito in jail. Bad time.' He giggled. 'Now *El Jefe* make Miguelito a present. Yeah, leetle dog, you the present.' He drew an imaginary knife across his throat. 'One dead gringo . . .'

Six

Trent had been correct in guessing their destination to be on the north fork of the Belpan River. Once into the shelter of the mangrove-bound estuary, he had taken the men off the Zodiac, ordering them below after stacking the dinghy's cargo along *Golden Girl*'s side decks. With the wind dead on their stern, he had changed the genoa for a much bigger and lighter cut. Main boomed out to port, genoa to starboard, they ghosted up the smooth waters of the river like a giant white butterfly as the first grey touch of dawn lightened the sky.

Along the banks the dark green tangle of mangrove had given way to tall jungle. The pale trunks of giant ramon trees rose out of the layered undergrowth of fan palms and creepers. Cotton trees shaded the bank. Cohune palms with nut pods that resembled huge wasp-nests stood sentry. Frangipani grew wild and rampant up a grey cliff of limestone above the south bank. The white star-flowers of wild coffee spattered the banks and the feathery ballerina skirts of kapok shimmered with raindrops.

Parrots should have been swooping, tree to tree, in search of breakfast; toucan, egret, cormorants, heron, trogons. But nothing moved, no sound disturbed the silence: no kingfisher flash of bright blue low over the water, no dawn fire-siren of cicadas. All was heavy with foreboding, and the rain fell steadily.

Requiem for a monk, Trent thought as he watched the cocaine-addicted *mestizo* squatting on the cabin top. For the past half-hour the little man had been giggling to himself as he stropped a Buck knife razor-sharp on the inside of his belt. Trent had no doubt that Miguelito would kill him and enjoy doing so – revenge for whatever had happened to him in a US jail and for the gringo widow-woman having put him there.

Gomez had recovered and sat beside Trent in the cockpit, solemn-faced. Hardly a word had passed between them but now the gunman looked up and said quietly, 'There is nothing that I can do.'

Trent didn't bother to answer. There wasn't an answer. They were professionals, they knew the rules of the game. But there remained an essential difference between them: their choice of masters. Whatever the pressures, Gomez had been free to make his choice.

Good or evil . . .

These were considered old-fashioned terms in a morally rudderless society, Trent thought with more sadness than bitterness. But they remained essential to him, perhaps because his life had so often been at stake. He would have liked to have known what Louis planned, if only to know in whose cause Colonel Smith had sacrificed his life and how much information Smith had kept hidden. Most of all Trent would have liked to know the power structure and the brains behind Louis. Whatever it was that these men planned, Trent remained certain that it was too sophisticated to have been plotted by the murderers of Colombia's drug trade.

Murderers . . .

It was important to Trent that he held to that word; as it had been important to him never to use the term 'Loyalist' when speaking of or reporting on the Protestant terrorists

96

in Northern Ireland. Accuracy of language was crucial when your life was at risk and each use of 'Loyalist', when applied to the Protestant equivalents of the IRA, had been to Trent, a Catholic himself by birth, an insult to the Catholic community of whom the vast majority were as opposed to the evils of terrorism as they were to the injustices of long-practised prejudice on which Irish terrorism bred.

Terrorism was an effect rather than a cause. Trent had learnt this lesson well in his fight against it. That this was true offered no excuse to the sick, evil, vicious minds that used it as a tool. In his years of infiltrating terrorist groups Trent had been forced to listen to every form of philosophical self-justification. Every word of it had been a lie and to this truth Trent remained as totally committed now, close to his own death, as he had been when plotting the downfall of the groups he had penetrated.

There had been moments during the past night when his fear had become almost uncontrollable. Now, with the dawn breaking and his death so close, he found himself strangely sanguine – almost as if he were an abstract entity observing, from another place, the last chapter of his life.

Louis came up from the saloon. The devil, Trent thought, and found himself smiling as he realised that continual fear had acted as a drug, lifting him free of reality in the same way that marathon runners broke through the pain barrier into an almost hallucinatory state of calm.

Louis examined Trent with less emotion than he would have given a sandwich. He dabbed his nose into one more spotlessly fresh handkerchief, folding it carefully back into his shirt-sleeve. 'When we round the next bend, bring your boat to the left bank, Señor Capitano.'

'Pray God someone shoots you,' Trent said.

Louis ignored him but Miguelito giggled happily, 'Hey, you one brave leetle dog, Gringo.'

They rounded the bend to see a landing-stage of rough piling and a mud track that led to the main highway and the bridge. Two Belpan Defence Force Land-Rovers and an army truck waited by the dock. The drivers had turned the vehicles back towards the highway to be ready to move the moment the men, weapons and ammunition were loaded. It was this detail of organisation that made Trent fear for the Belpan Republic. There was nothing he could do, no way of getting a message to Caspar at the US Embassy.

Easing the helm over, he slid *Golden Girl* into the bank. The *vaquero* dropped the sails while Miguelito threw a line to one of the waiting drivers.

'I could do with a cup of coffee,' Trent said to Gomez.

But Louis was on deck and Gomez shrugged his apologies: 'I must get the trucks loaded. Also I must ask you – '

'Be my guest,' Trent said and handed him the eight thousand dollars from his back pocket. He watched Gomez organise the transfer of the cargo. Gomez had earned his status through the calm weight of his personality as much as by his physical strength and the inevitable accuracy of his firepower. In the eyes of Louis, his near-drowning had been an act of self-emasculation, a loss of face tumbling him down the social scale to a level little higher than a peon's. Peons made sacrificial meat and the men smelt this on Gomez so that his command of them was tentative. Such were the risks of the gunman's trade.

They were not risks that Mario cared to take. The hit-squad's leader had kept below rather than find himself in confrontation with Louis or be seen by his men to be subservient to or afraid of the Latino leader.

Miguelito, on the other hand, had gained face the closer the men came to action – perhaps because he so obviously enjoyed killing, Trent thought as he watched Miguelito thumbnail more cocaine into his nostrils. Killing was about to be these men's business. Of that Trent was certain.

The *mestizo* looked up to see Trent watching him. 'You

wan' coffee? Sure, why not? Firs' we tie your han's, leetle dog.'

With Gomez watching, he bound Trent's wrists in front of him so that he could hold the coffee mug.

Mario followed the last of his uniformed men into the truck. The bureaucrats were in one Land-Rover; the other waited for Louis and Gomez. Miguelito had returned to his seat on the cabin top.

Though watched by Louis, Gomez held out his hand to Trent in an unspoken plea for absolution. 'Thank you for my life, Señor.'

'Be my guest.' Trent, as an outside observer, watched himself shake the gunman's hand within his own bound palms. He felt himself on the edge of hysterical laughter and fought to gain control. 'Nothing personal,' he said. Then, because fomenting distrust between the two men was all he could do, 'You get a chance, shoot him,' he advised with a nod at Louis: 'You don't, he'll kill you.'

He saw Louis' eyes flatten and felt the twitch of a nerve in Gomez's hands. He had condemned one of the men to death – which one was for the future.

Gomez dropped over the rail. Trent watched him walk very upright to the lead Land-Rover.

Louis sniffed into a handkerchief. His cold gaze rested on Trent for a moment. 'You have been most proficient, Señor Capitano.' He looked up at the *mestizo*. 'Dispose of him.'

'Sure, I take him in the jungle, *Jefe*.' The little man giggled in pleasurable anticipation and drew his knife as if across Trent's throat. 'I leave his body, big cat eat him.'

Louis indicated his approval with a slight wave of his handkerchief. 'When you're finished, join the roadblock at the bridge.'

With the vehicles gone, Miguelito swung down from the cabin top. 'You wan' a las' cup coffee, leetle dog?'

'Thanks,' Trent said, to delay his death, if only by a few minutes.

The *mestizo* dug his thumb into his cocaine pouch and cursed at finding only a few grains on the nail. 'Hey, we better go in the saloon, leetle dog. Too much rain out here an' Miguelito got to cut himself a leetle coke.'

He made fast the rope round Trent's neck to the handhold beside the companionway leading down to the head in the port hull. Trent sat on the saloon deck, holding his coffee mug cupped in his hands. Miguelito sat at the saloon table. He had taken a couple of square inches of rock cocaine from wherever he had hidden his supply and was chopping it with his knife on to Trent's shaving mirror. He didn't seem in any hurry: because Louis was no longer there, Trent presumed, and because his cocaine habit demanded a goodly supply ready cut; preparing more would be difficult once he was out in the rain.

'Hey, this Belpan one crazy place,' Miguelito remarked, head cocked to one side as he glanced over at Trent. 'They got a governmen' like they theenk this one real country excep' all they got is couple hun'red thousan' people.' He sliced a quarter-inch off the block and went back to chopping it into fine powder. 'Yeah, leetle dog. Crazy. And they got elections now so the politician' all over the damn place. No bodyguards. Nothing. Man, they real crazy. We goin' pick them like they ripe avocados.' Looking up from the mirror, he winked at Trent, saliva dribbling. 'Yeah, leetle dog – plop, plop, plop,' he giggled, and aped dropping ripe avocados into a basket.

'We goin' take these politician', leetle dog, an' we goin' put them in one beeg hole so they don' come back. Then Señor Louis goin' run this leetle country like it his *hacienda*. We goin' have planes landin' like flies goin' land on your body after Miguelito keel you. Yeah,' he said with satisfaction as he chopped another quarter-inch off the block. 'We get good and finish, ev'ry damn coke plane goin' fly via Belpan. That one beeg mountain coke, leetle dog.'

'That's a big operation for one man,' Trent said.

Miguelito lifted his eyebrows in amazement at Trent's stupidity: 'Hey, you think Louis the big *Jefe*? You one crazy gringo. Louis, he what you say? Groun' Operation; yeah, that the words.' The *mestizo* pronounced them again and with care, proud of his command of the language. 'Yeah, Groun' Operation . . . ' Thumbing cocaine into his nose, he giggled. 'Louis one crazy tough man, but he nothin'. We got bosses from all over, leetle dog. We got bosses from Colombia. We got Louis' Nicaraguanos. We even got one gringo boss no one ever see. He the brain, leetle dog. One smart mother.'

So Trent had been correct. But the information was useless to him. He pictured Belpan's President as he had last seen him, barefoot and casting for bonefish from the end of the dock out at San Paul Key. With no one to guard him, unless you counted his granddaughter . . . The other ministers, spread through their constituencies, would be as easy. But there was a piece missing from the scenario . . .

Trent put down his empty coffee mug. 'You really believe that the US and the UN are going to allow you to get away with this?'

'Belpan?' Miguelito giggled happily. 'You crazy, who you thin' geev a sheet? We the Belpan army, man, we got the uniforms, right?'

But it wasn't that easy, not any more. The end of the Cold War made the difference. The days of distant alliances based on a promise to support either Capitalism or Communism were over. The brain behind this operation had to know this.

'You wan' a try a line o' coke, leetle dog?' the *mestizo* offered with that cock of his head and a crazy grin. 'One hundre' per cent.'

Trent ignored the offer.

'Man, you don' know what good for you.' He scraped the cut cocaine into his pouch and stood up. He wore a pistol stuck in his belt and held his knife in his right hand. 'We goin' take a leetle walk now, leetle dog. You goin' give no trouble to Miguelito. Then Miguelito cut your throat good so you don' feel nothin'.'

He ordered Trent back from the handhold on the companionway so that he was safely out of range while untying the rope. Trent had a last look round the saloon.

'Yeah, leetle dog, nice boat,' Miguelito giggled. 'Adios . . . ' He followed Trent over the rail on to the dock, prodding him with the tip of his knife: 'We go jus' leetle way in the jungle, leetle dog.'

No path existed so that Trent had to force his way into a wall of vegetation. A knife-point poked into his back every few seconds, so he knew that the *mestizo* was close behind him. A clearing opened ahead, separated from Trent by a fan of palm fronds. As he parted them, he heard the familiar snuffling as Miguelito fed cocaine into his nose. Trent spun as he dropped, right leg kicking back. His foot hit home, sinking deep into the little man's belly. Miguelito buckled and Trent, as he hit the ground, kicked up hard with his left foot, catching him under the chin. The *mestizo* fell to his knees, but he still held the knife. Dropping Trent's neck rope, he scrabbled for the pistol in his belt.

Rolling and scrambling to his feet, Trent charged blindly across the clearing and into the undergrowth, holding up his bound hands to protect his eyes. Sharp leaves and thorns cut and tore at his arms and ripped his cheeks. Vines caught at his feet and at the rope round his neck. He tripped and fell into thick bush. Desperate with fear, he forced himself forward, crawling on knees and elbows under the low canopy. He could hear Miguelito cursing. Sweat blinded him. Ahead of him a rivulet trickled towards the river. He kicked his feet free of a vine and rolled into the water, the drag of the rope almost strangling him. Heading downstream, he saw a pool in front of him, more liquid mud than water. He plunged into it, and the mud closed over his head as he struggled for a footing. The feel of it plugging his nostrils added to his panic.

Panic was the enemy.

He commanded himself to think. His feet found bottom and he surfaced, hands up to smear the mud clear of his eyes. Then he saw the snake. It was three feet long, a greeny-brown ribbon with a yellow diamond on the throat. *Fer-de-lance*. Deadly . . .

Close behind him, the *mestizo* called, 'Hey, Gringo, you a bad leetle dog. Miguelito real angry!'

Trent turned his body slowly so that he could get his hands on the rope. The snake raised its head, hissing in fear or anger, tongue darting.

'Hey, Gringo, I can see you,' Miguelito sang as if teasing a child in a game of hide and seek.

The snake hissed.

The *mestizo* giggled. 'Miguelito goin' get you soon now, leetle dog.'

A mosquito landed on Trent's nose and bit him. The mud on his lips tasted of rotting vegetation and the stench of it was thick in his nostrils. He inched the rope in. The snake struck, fangs deep in the rope. Then it was gone, tail vanishing under the bushes through which he had crawled.

He heard the *mestizo* curse in fear as he saw the snake. 'Hey, Gringo, maybe I leave you here so you die slowly.'

More crashing of feet through bush, then the snuffling of cocaine – sniff, sniff. Then, as if talking to himself, 'Yeah, Gringo, that what I do. You die real slow in the jungle. Son of a beetch. Miguelito tell *El Jefe* you real dead meat.'

Trent suspected a trap. He heard Miguelito pushing his way through the bush to his left. Back to *Golden Girl*? Or would he join the men at the roadblock on the bridge? The quantity of cocaine the man forced up his nose must affect his judgment . . . but in what way? Trent wondered. Would he risk lying to Louis?

Trent had followed the rivulet down to the Belpan River, crawling the entire distance, squirming silently through the mud and rotting vegetation. Belly flat in the water, he inched his bound hands forward and drew his face clear of the undergrowth so that he could look upriver while remaining camouflaged by the overhang of a wild coffee bush. The rain had been falling now for more than four hours. The river had risen by almost two feet and the current, which had been almost imperceptible on their approach to the dock, was beginning to form foam-lipped eddies along the near bank.

Trent had hoped to be able to observe *Golden Girl* but the rivulet had led him downstream and the yacht lay upriver beyond the bend. Had Trent been Miguelito he would have lain in wait in the jungle by the catamaran. With the highway under observation, the yacht offered Trent his only hope of escape and, with access to the radio, he would be able to warn Caspar and the Belpanese and call in Steve's heavy brigade. But the *mestizo* was a gangster and his prime loyalty would be to himself. Safer to lie rather than confess his failure?

Neck rope coiled round his waist, Trent slithered into the river like a crocodile. Below the bend the water remained sufficiently shallow close to the bank for Trent to keep his footing. As he forced his way against the current, the water deepened. He tried to pull himself forward, branch to branch, but with his hands bound, he lost ground each time he grabbed for a fresh hold. He had either to swim to the far bank or return to the undergrowth. He pictured the topography.

The current had cut into a hillside on the upriver side of the bend so that he would be faced with a steep climb of some fifty feet. To be silent on the upriver descent as he approached the bridge would be impossible. If he swam the river, he would have to make his way upstream well beyond the yacht and within sight of the bridge or be swept back down by the current. But Louis had posted the roadblock to stop anyone with authority returning to Belpan City. His men would be watching the road rather than the river, plucking politicians into their net – as Miguelito had boasted – easily as plucking ripe advocados. Trent pushed off from the bank, swimming with his bound hands in an adaptation of sidestroke that was clumsy and inefficient.

Once out of the shelter of the bank he found the wind had strengthened. That, too, would make his escape more difficult. On the other hand, once clear of the river mouth, he could sail a clear reach for Key Canaka. He had to save the President from capture by Louis' men. Like a jigsaw, piece by piece, the picture was becoming clear. The President was the key. Leader of his country even before its independence, the President was alone in being known outside Belpan. Captured, he would be forced into giving credence to the coup. If he remained at liberty, he could authorise the calling in of outside help – hence, as insurance, the coup leader's attempt to destroy the President's reputation by connecting him to the cocaine trade.

From the outside of the bend, he saw *Golden Girl*. She lay as he had left her, moored fore and aft to the dock. But now, with the rise in river level, the dock was almost awash and the bow line bar-taut.

Face lapped by the water, Trent pushed his way upstream. The wind and the rain beating down on the river camouflaged his progress; he could see the bridge now and he waited, watching.

Louis' men had set their roadblock the far side of the bridge from Trent's observation point – upended ammunition boxes topped by poles cut from the jungle edge and a square white signboard on which Trent could see red letters made indecipherable by the angle of the board to his line of vision. The men wore rubber ponchos and had exchanged their black berets for jungle hats pulled well down against the rain so that he was unable to discern whether Miguelito was amongst their number.

He scooped mud on to his forehead and cheeks and kept close in under the dripping leaf canopy cloaking the bank. Shallows forced him to his knees, his progress desperately slow. The driver of a Toyota LandCruiser changed gear and drove slowly across the bridge to halt at the roadblock. Two of the men turned their backs to the wind and driving rain as they checked the driver's papers.

Seven in the morning. Sunday morning . . .

Only three roads led into Belpan City and Louis would have erected roadblocks on them all. Had they chosen a weekday for the coup, there would have been heavy traffic at this hour and news of the roadblocks would have spread quickly throughout the country, perhaps warning one of the ministers before he could be captured . . . one more example of exemplary planning.

Now upstream from *Golden Girl*, Trent looked back. Nothing moved on the bank nor on the catamaran. But if Miguelito was waiting, he would be well hidden. Trent counted the seconds as he watched a dead branch clear the bridge and float down towards the craft. Say four minutes to recross the river, two hundred yards of drift. For safety he would have to strike out for the far bank from a point less than fifty yards below the bridge and the current was gaining strength.

One of the men at the roadblock, bored, dropped a stick into the water and watched it float under the span. A second man joined him. They found fresh sticks. Though he couldn't hear them, Trent knew that they were setting up a race. Sure enough, they dropped their sticks at the same moment and ran across to the downriver side of the bridge to watch for the winner.

A third man joined them as they sought new sticks. Trent

waited until they made for the upriver side, then charged forward uncaring. He froze as they dropped their sticks and ran back. He could see their faces, and Miguelito wasn't one of them.

So it went on, Trent gaining ten yards each time and knowing that, while they continued racing, he had no chance of recrossing the river unseen.

Freeze and rush, freeze and rush. Half an hour, one hour . . .

Trent reached the point which he had marked but now the current was that much stronger and he needed to be at the bridge. No sign of Miguelito . . .

A Land-Rover Discovery followed an American Ford pick-up across the bridge. Trent took his chance, running in a low crouch for the protection of the span. Ten yards to go and he heard the driver of the Discovery accelerate away from the roadblock. Up on the bridge someone shouted. Trent dived belly flat into the protection of a bush sprouting from beside the concrete piling. Rolling on to his back, he lay still as a corpse with only his face breaking the surface.

He heard two men arguing, but with water lapping in his ears he couldn't make out the words. The men's footfalls were muted – jungle boots on concrete. The voices came to a halt directly above him. More argument. Then he heard the breaking of branches and a curse as one of the men leaped from the parapet on to the top of the bank, thirty feet above him. Trent held his breath, face under the muddy surface of the river. He gritted his teeth against the demand of his lungs to burst. Ten seconds, twenty, thirty . . .

Air escaped into his mouth. He could feel his cheeks bulging like hot balloons. He surfaced his nostrils, leaking the air out. Feet slithered in the mud halfway down the bank. A stone rolled free and splashed into the water no more than a yard from Trent's feet. Silence.

Then, hardly above a whisper, 'Hey, you there, leetle

dog?' A further slide of feet scrabbling for a foothold ac-
companied by a muffled giggle: 'Miguelito theenk he see you.'

That the *mestizo* kept his voice down was proof to Trent
that the little man, lying, had reported him dead. And
Miguelito couldn't see him from the bank. Not yet. To see
under the bridge, the *mestizo* would have to come right
down into the water.

Loosened by the rain, a chunk of the bank broke under
the little man's weight, and the caked earth tumbled into
the river. To Trent the splash was loud as a bomb. The
mestizo lost his footing, and Trent heard him slide, swear-
ing. Water fountained over the bush under which he lay
hidden as Miguelito hit the surface. Trent knew he was
finished; there was no way the *mestizo* could miss him now.
All the little man had to do was stand up and take one pace
forward, parting the branches. He heard the man up on the
bridge laughing. Miguelito shouted up a string of gutter-
Spanish abuse.

Then he said, 'Sheet,' softly, and Trent, forced to watch
from between the leaves, saw him shake the water out of
his pistol. He opened his jungle jacket and dried the magazine on the front of his sweatshirt.

'What are you doing down there? Fishing?' the man on
the bridge called down.

Miguelito yelled up that the man should do something
unmentionable to himself. He slapped the magazine into
his pistol-butt and took a step forward, his jungle boots
stirring the mud inches from Trent's feet. Pistol in hand, he
parted the leaves. Klaxons sounded from up the road. The
little man looked up. More klaxons beating a tattoo. 'Hey,
man, what the sheet goin' on?'

'Looks like a procession,' the man on the bridge yelled
down. 'Posters of some *cabrón* with a big moustache. Must
be a politico . . . '

Miguelito swore and released the branches. 'Man,
nothing here. I'm comin' up.'

'Yeah, hurry. And don't drown yourself.'

Klaxons beeped in rhythmic unison and a man's voice chanted over a megaphone the initials of the President's Party and the name of Belpan's Minister of Tourism and Transport: 'VOTE PP. VOTE GEORGE VICENTE BROWN.'

'George Vicente Brown goin' be one dead son of a beetch,' Miguelito swore as he struggled up the bank.

Trent was shaking. He tried to breathe slowly, calming himself as he waited. The electioneering procession was on the bridge, everyone shouting, klaxons blaring, and the PP chant repeated like a scratched disc. There had to be fifty trucks and cars.

Trent slid out from under the bush and took a deep breath. Hands out like a battering ram, he kicked underwater for the far bank, feeling the grab of the current. Twice he surfaced, filled his lungs, dived. Then he could see the catamaran. He looked back for a moment at the Minister's procession stalled at the roadblock. There was nothing he could do to save George Vicente Brown. Diving again, he kicked hard. By the time he surfaced, the current had swept him clear. The release from fear was almost unbearable. He wanted to roll on to his back and float, no further effort. He goaded himself by picturing the ageing President, grey-haired and frail. He had to reach Key Canaka before Louis' men got there. The rain beat down and the wind was picking up.

SEVEN

The river current swept Trent down between *Golden Girl's*
twin hulls. Grabbing at the Zodiac's tow line, he held himself against the river for a moment, getting his breath back.
Then he hauled himself up over the Zodiac's port tube and
rolled on to the floor slats. He had forgotten the rope
wrapped round his waist. Falling on it nearly winded him.
He longed for rest but knew that he had to keep moving,
and hauling on the line, he got his hands on to the taffrail
and vaulted into the cockpit.

He went directly to the radio above the navigation table.
Someone had ripped out the cables – more proof of attention to detail. Dropping down into the galley for a carving
knife, he cut the rope loose from his neck. Freeing his hands
was more difficult. He wedged the knife upright in the
cutlery drawer while jamming it shut with one knee. The
knife slipped twice, cutting into his wrists, but he managed.

Blood dripping, he raced back on deck and leaped ashore.
The dock was already a foot under water. He untied the
stern line, kneeling to lead it back round a pile to the
cockpit. Then he let go the bow line, jumped on board, and
ran aft to the cockpit. With the stern held, the current swept
Golden Girl's bows clear of the dock. Trent waited until
the catamaran was pointing downriver, then he let go the

stern line, pulling it in and coiling it down. He kept to the inside of the bends where the current was fastest and more powerful than the onshore wind. Sails would have been a hindrance. Where the river straightened, he took his chance to check the barometer. Pressure had dropped to 29.5, one thousand millibars.

Briefly he considered making for Belpan City and Caspar at the US Embassy but there was no certainty of the DEA Agent being there, and Louis would have men covering the city docks in case any of the Government returned from electioneering out on the Keys – that much *was* certain. As for reaching a telephone, given the meticulous organisation behind the coup, Trent was sure that the telephone exchange would be in Louis' hands and out of order, particularly for foreign calls, which put calling Steve in Washington out of the question. Trent didn't consider Colonel Smith.

It had to be Key Canaka. Whoever held the President held the hole card . . .

He heaved the Zodiac on board as the current swept *Golden Girl* round the final bend before the open sea. As he raised his binoculars to scan the coast, the wind struck him in the face. Already it had whipped the shallow water inside the reef into short seas, white-capped and capable of stopping the big cat in its tracks if he had tried sailing for the far point and Belpan City. Six miles on a reach to Key Canaka – and he was single-handed. Whatever the urgency, setting more than the number three jib and the mainsail would have been stupid. He raised the main, lashing the tiller bar, and ran forward to set the jib. The power in the sails lifted the yacht so that she left two long trails of dark blue in the spray. For a moment Trent gave way to the thrill of speed and power. But he had things to do.

With bungees holding the tiller arm, he heaved the heavy BMW inboard on the davits and manhandled it across the cockpit and into the saloon, lashing it to the mast support.

Next he unscrewed a foot-square drainage plate in the saloon deck.

Hurling the cushions aside, he lifted the settee locker lid clear. Pressing hard on the top inch of the panel at the back of the locker, he pushed sideways. The panel dropped. Behind it, held by padded spring clips, lay two 12-gauge single barrel Greener pump-action shotguns in their waterproof covers, eight cartridges to the magazine. Cartridge boxes were stacked in two layers. A cartridge belt and two bandoleers lay on top. Both belt and bandoleers were ready-laden with red Ely cartridges loaded with buckshot; one in the belly would blow a man apart.

Trent slung a bandoleer over his shoulder and grabbed both guns and two boxes of cartridges. Back in the cockpit, he checked the course, then fed cartridges into the magazine of one gun. He pumped a shot into the breech and laid the gun on the portside cockpit settee, covering it with his shirt weighted down against the wind with the coiled stern line.

Looking aft, he spotted a grey smudge a mile out from Belpan City. Through his binoculars he made out Belpan's one patrol boat with a great vee of spray at its bows. Baccy! Clearing the gap in the reef, the patrol boat drove into a wave and leapt half out of the water like a giant grey killer whale. Trent almost laughed with relief as he imagined the six-foot-four Customs officer at the wheel, empty pipe jammed between his teeth. Baccy was one man neither hurricane nor Louis would be able to stop.

He loaded the second Greener. Less than two miles to Key Canaka – get the President safe on board the patrol boat and contact the US Embassy by radio. He glanced over at the windspeed indicator. Force four and strengthening and *Golden Girl* was flying. Fourteen knots over the ground. Single-handed, and sailing faster than thirty millions of fully-crewed Twelve Metre competing for the America's Cup. But then he wasn't carrying tons of lead on a keel that had to be dragged through the water. Nor did he need to check the chart. *Golden Girl* drew twenty-two inches. He'd sailed these waters for six months and knew every reef and coral head shallow enough to be a threat.

With an eye on the speed indicator, he eased the main out an extra couple of inches and did the same for the jib. Fifteen knots. After the terror of the past twenty-four hours he was safe for the moment and in sight of victory. To hell with Louis and his Nicaraguans. To hell with Mario and his Colombians. To hell with the gringo brain behind the attempted take-over. And to hell with Colonel Smith. Head back, rain beating in his face, Trent laughed almost maniacally with the joy of freedom. He knew the feeling of old – operating outside the rules and hidden from the surveillance of his superiors.

He sailed past the President's beach house before coming over on to the other tack. He didn't bother with the dock or with a stern anchor but, dropping the sails, ran *Golden Girl* up on the sand. When he was ready, the wind would take him off the beach. He wore one bandoleer slung over his shoulder and carried a Greener. Jumping ashore with the bow line, he wrapped a clove hitch round the trunk of a palm. He avoided the path to the President's house, running in a low crouch, weaving between the trees, shotgun at the ready. There was no one on the terrace and the door was open. He scooped up a stone and leaping the steps to the terrace three at a time, he hurled it through the door and dived after it, hitting the living-room floor flat and rolling twice.

A woman screamed over to his right. The President's granddaughter. Her hands covered her mouth as if trying to hold the screams in. No one else. Greener covering the two doors leading to the rear of the house, he asked, 'You're alone?'

She nodded.

He checked anyway – two bedrooms, bathroom, kitchen – all empty. She hadn't moved. Her dark eyes watched him,

113

wide with fear so that the whites showed like two new moons. She wore her hair squeezed up into a ballooning Afro by the same red bandana that she had worn down on the dock the first time Trent had seen her. Black sleeveless T-shirt, black shorts, no shoes.

He thought of telling her that he was a friend but friends didn't dive in through the front door; they didn't have blood on their wrists nor cuts all over their faces; they didn't have a rope burn round their necks and they wore shirts, at least until they were properly introduced. Most of all they didn't carry guns and wear bandoleers. She needed an explanation.

'Trent,' he said. 'EC Anti-Terrorist Unit.' He added, 'British,' because EC clearly didn't mean anything to her. 'On secondment. Some people have mounted a coup d'état. Where's your grandfather?'

She wasn't going to tell him. He didn't blame her and he hadn't time to argue. 'You've no reason to trust me, but I'm probably the only person capable of saving the President. It's what I'm trained for.'

She hated what he was trained for. It was there in her eyes. CIA, MI6, *Deuxième Bureau* – these were the anti-heroes of every university student's political mythology. Particularly so when the student had read Politics and Economics at the LSE, came from the Third World, and had a dark skin. Student prejudice kept the KGB off the list, which made Trent mad or made him laugh, depending on the day of the week.

'Tell me one thing,' he said. 'Is he here on the key or is he safe?' She hesitated and he said, 'Please . . . '

'He's safe.'

'Thank God.' One last effort and he could rest. Wiping the back of his hand across his face, Trent showered sweat and rain on the varnished floorboards. 'The patrol boat's coming in the other side of the key. They've got a radio. Baccy, the bosun, knows me; we race lighters together,' he explained. 'I have a contact at the US Embassy.'

Mentioning the Embassy was a mistake. The US was demonology – the United Fruit Company, the assassination of Allende in Chile, the Contras . . .

He read the litany in her eyes. 'Stay here,' he said, 'I'll be back.'

He ran across the key, bandoleer slapping his chest, gun held at the port, and reached the beach in time to see Baccy ease the patrol boat in through a gap in the reef. To save time, Trent propped the gun against a palm, draping the bandoleer over the barrel, and ran out along the millionaire's dock. He hit the sea in a shallow dive, swimming out against the wind. Fifty yards out he stopped and trod water while getting his breath and watched the patrol boat drop anchor while still two hundred yards out. Normally Baccy would have come in closer but the wind was onshore and the storm couldn't be more than an hour away.

Half a dozen sailors were on the side deck. Trent waved and yelled, 'Baccy . . . ' A wave slapped him in the mouth. He coughed and shook salt out of his eyes. The sailors had run aft to the tender hanging in the stern davits. Despite the protection of the reef, there was sufficient sea running to make the patrol boat roll through sixty degrees. Lowering the tender took care and patience if they wanted to keep it in one piece. The man giving orders was short and fat. None of the men was black, none of them stood six-foot-four in bare feet, and none of them wore a pipe in his mouth.

Trent rolled over and swam for the beach. The sailors were dropping off the stern ladder into the tender as he reached the dock, and with the tender pitching in the steep lop, they were having a hard time. Trent sprinted up the dock and spotted the President's granddaughter. She was standing in the shade beside his shotgun. He needed the gun. He waved her back. Instead, she stepped out of the shade to meet him. He heard the fluttering of bullets before the fast slap-slap-slap of an automatic rifle. He hadn't played rugby football since leaving school but he tackled the girl as if he were a wing-threequarter playing for Ireland at Lansdowne Road. She kicked out at him as he covered her body with his but he held her tight and rolled with her into the protection of the trees.

'Keep on your belly,' he ordered as he grabbed the Greener. He didn't bother to look back to see whether the shots were coming from the patrol boat or from the tender. Both were equally unsteady platforms for a marksman but that didn't preclude one of them getting killed by a chance shot. 'I told you to stay at the house.' Then he realised that she hadn't recognised the slap of the rifle. Getting shot at wasn't included in the Politics and Economics degree at the LSE. More's the pity, he thought, given how many of the Third World's leaders came from that educational background.

'They're shooting at us, for Christ's sake! At least, they're shooting at me.'

Her next question would be 'Why?' so he gave the reason without waiting: 'If they have you, they have your grandfather. Because he loves you,' he added before she could ask. 'I've got to get you off the Key.'

He read in her face that she wouldn't leave under her own steam. Eyebrows knitted in support of her determination, she said: 'He told me to wait here. Belpan isn't a colony. You've got no right to order me around.'

'I don't happen to want to get killed.' He hadn't been able to keep the irritation out of his voice.

She bridled. 'That's your fault.'

'Lord God, forgive me.' Grabbing her by the arm, he yanked her to her feet. 'I can drag you or I can carry you – except that it would probably kill me.'

She recognised that he meant what he said. 'Don't push.'

'Then run,' he told her as he heard the tender's motor start.

*

116

Trent pushed *Golden Girl* off the beach, swinging the bows round before dragging himself on board. The wind was already driving them clear of the shore as he raised the sails. The barometer had fallen a further ten points to 28.5.

'We're going to get hit by a hurricane,' he told the girl as he dropped into the cockpit and took the helm. He grabbed lifejackets out of the port locker, tossing her one. 'Wear this. Something happens, don't bother swimming. Just relax. The wind will drive you onshore. Get into the trees and make for high ground.'

He rigged a lifeline fore and aft and clipped the safety line on the girl's lifejacket to it. He hadn't yet made up his mind where to head for but he needed shelter. He would have liked to have made a run for Mexico but he had work to do, and there wasn't a chance of their surviving that long a race against the hurricane. Belpan City was out, as was the Belpan River. Next north from the Belpan came the Makaa. Visualising the chart, he calculated the distance to the Makaa river mouth at about twelve miles. He changed course five degrees and looked aft to check for squalls. Whoever was skippering the patrol boat hadn't waited to pick up the tender. She rounded the key under full power, the spray bursting so high from her bows that Trent, through his binoculars, could barely make out the bridge. Thirty knots, Trent guessed. Ten minutes and *Golden Girl* would be in range of her bow cannon.

He had to think – but he was close to physical, mental and emotional exhaustion.

'They'll shoot, won't they,' she said.

He had been calculating the girl as a mathematical entry in the equation. The quiet flatness of her voice was mirrored by the fatalism he saw in her eyes. Rain streaked her cheeks so that he was unable to tell whether she was weeping. 'They won't harm you,' he said. 'They want you alive.'

She had already thought ahead. 'They'll ram us.'

'Probably. Or they may fire a warning shot.'

She nodded acceptance of her own thoughts: 'You'll hand me over . . . ' He thought it was an accusation but she met his eyes for a second: 'They'll kill you,' she said.

'You never know.'

'You do,' she said in that same quiet flat voice. 'That's what you said. It's what you're trained for.'

Instead of answering, he adjusted the jib.

'Who are they?'

'Cocaine trade. They want to use Belpan as a staging post.'

He saw that she couldn't believe him. He could have slipped the bungees over the tiller arm. Instead he told her to take the helm. Having something to do was better than sitting doing nothing other than wait for the first shell. He pointed to a slight gap in the mountains thirty miles inland. 'That's your heading.'

She protested. 'I never have . . . '

'Slow and easy,' he told her. 'Concentrate and don't over-react.'

He ducked into the saloon. The barometer had dropped like a plumb weight. He ran parallel rules over the chart and tapped latitude and longitude into the Loran. He watched the girl for a minute before calling to her to bring their heading a little to port. 'Hold her there.'

Making his way forward, he dragged sailbags out until he found the huge, feather-light balloon spinnaker. Because of the vast size of it and the difficulty of controlling it when sailing single-handed, the spinnaker wasn't a sail he used much and it was right at the bottom at the aft end of the sail-locker. His plan was certainly crazy and almost definitely doomed to failure but it was his only option. Re-stowing the rest of the sails gave him time to get the details straight in his head.

Shaking the spinnaker out of its bag, he curled it on to the trampoline while checking the cotton lashings that held it rolled. He hanked the head of the spinnaker to the spare forehalyard so that the sail would set outside the jib. Next he led the spinnaker sheets aft to the cockpit and made them fast to the stern cleats with plenty of slack.

The girl was too involved with the helm to watch him.

He said, 'You're a natural,' and she almost smiled at the compliment. Encouraged, he went on, 'The President introduced you as his granddaughter but he didn't give you a name.'

'Mariana,' she said.

'Nice.' He thought it about the stupidest remark he'd ever made – and so did she by the look on her face.

He looked aft. The sea, rather than dipping to the horizon, curled up like the lip of a dish. For a moment Trent thought that there was something wrong with his eyes. Then he realised that for the first time he was looking into the front of a hurricane. The patrol boat had gained a mile on them. Two sailors were on the foredeck manning the cannon. With the vessel bucking through the short waves like an unbroken horse, Trent hoped that they wouldn't fire a warning shot. Unless the men were experienced, it could go anywhere. He checked his bearings on the Loran. He wanted to take another look at the chart but he hadn't time.

He said to Mariana, 'I'll take her for a few minutes. Keep your hands on the helm so you keep the feel of her.'

Trent shifted course a couple of degrees to port without adjusting the sails and *Golden Girl* lost a knot in speed. He held her there for two minutes, then paid off a further two degrees, again without adjusting the sails. A spit of white sand showed in the far distance. The roar of the patrol boat's huge petrol engines thrummed in his ears and he glanced back over his shoulder. *Golden Girl*'s lead was down to a quarter of a mile. He checked his bearings again and pointed to the sand-spit.

'That's your course, Mariana. I'm going to try something. It probably won't work but it might. If it does, we'll almost certainly lose the mast, but we won't sink.'

Mariana didn't look up so the smile Trent gave her was a waste of time and he couldn't think of anything else to say, or nothing that would make any difference. So he said, 'Right, I'll leave you to it,' and vaulted on to the cabin top.

The sea was such a mess that it took him a few moments to be sure of the reef. The last time he'd dived off it, the coral heads had been awash. Now, with the tide driven high by the approaching storm, it was hardly visible. But it was there all right, dead ahead – a bar, knife-sharp and deadly. If they hit it, it would rip the bottom out of *Golden Girl* in less than a second.

Trent grabbed the spinnaker halyard. He looked back. Their lead over the patrol boat was down to two hundred yards. He could see the separate strands of spray thrown aside by the bows and make out the shadow of the helmsman in the wheelhouse. The reef was less than fifty yards. Caught between the rock and the hard stuff . . .

He glanced down at Mariana, throwing her a fresh smile that was meant to be encouraging but she was looking straight ahead, eyes fixed on the sand-spit. She was gripping the tiller arm so tightly that the blood had been driven out of her knuckles. Trent thought of calling at her to relax but he knew that it would be as pointless as trying another smile.

He checked the reef. Thirty yards and he could see the shark's teeth of coral waiting to devour them. 'Hold her steady,' he yelled to Mariana and heaved the spinnaker flying to the masthead.

The vast red sail burst free of its lashings, the wind filling it so that it bowed forward in a great scarlet curve on which was painted in brilliant gold the portrait of the Golden Girl herself, bubble-curled, lips pouting – Marilyn Monroe.

'Do it for me,' Trent prayed to the film star. He could feel it happening, the lift of the sail, loose-set, acting as a vast kite. The hulls were almost clear of the water, mast bowing like an archer's longbow. Then they were over the coral, clear of it.

'Fly,' he yelled at the Golden Girl and let the spinnaker halyard go. As the sail whipped free of the masthead, he leaped back into the cockpit to loose the spinnaker sheets. Entwined snakes of gold and scarlet streamed through each other as the sail, rolling and writhing, fled away on the wind.

Trent looked back straight into the bows of the patrol boat. For a second he could see every detail of the men's faces at the bow cannon. Then came the terrifying crash as the coral tore the ship's bottom out. He saw the gun shield cut the sailors almost in half, their torn bodies somersaulting high against the great mauve bar of the approaching hurricane. For a second the boat seemed to be frozen as if in a frame of news film. Then the ship tore herself away from the reef, back broken, thirty feet of bow section diving free. The dark hole of the ship's innards gaped for a moment. Then came the thunder of the fuel tanks exploding. Brilliant against the storm bank, flames streaked with ruby leaped to devour the sky as the heat of the explosion blasted the catamaran. Trent swept Mariana to the cockpit sole, sheltering her with his body as jagged fragments rained on them. A shard of steel plate knifed through *Golden Girl*'s mainsail, cutting the portside shrouds as if they were string. The mast quivered and bowed as Trent dived for the main and jib sheets, whipping them clear of the cam cleats. Leaping on to the cabin top, he dropped the sails. Without bothering to bag it, he stuffed the jib down into the sail-locker and lashed the main to the boom. Only then did he look back at Mariana.

He wasn't surprised at the horror he read in her eyes. But he had expected it to be directed by concern for the dead rather than against him as the perpetrator of their demise.

'You murdered them,' she said. Her judgment was

121

absolute, no hope in plea-bargaining. And Trent couldn't be bothered. He watched the first squall race towards them, the rain compressed into a curtain above the white line of wave caps. About twenty minutes and the hurricane would have them in its grasp.

The Makaa River was two miles now on a dead run. Looping a line over the crosstrees, he set the storm jib, sheeting it out to port in hope of putting the greater strain on the starboard stays.

A fresh squall came at them. The wind spun the sea into feathers of spume, the rain solid as it struck Mariana in the face. She flinched with the force of it. She hadn't moved from the cockpit sole, but crouched there looking aft as if mesmerised by the towering storm front.

'When it hits,' Trent said, 'we're going to lose the mast. You'll be safer below.'

Mariana didn't answer.

'Please . . . ' he said, and again she didn't answer.

They could see now that the front was concave. The summit of it curled forward like a giant wave at the point of breaking. As with a wave, the crest of the front was shredded into wisps – dragon tongues that licked out, desperate to taste their prey before devouring it. Lightning played across the front almost continually, and thunder rolled over the catamaran. Trent knew that Mariana was waiting for the hurricane to fall on them. That when it did, she believed that they would be obliterated totally, like midges slapped into nothingness by a giant. Tiny midges. Infinitesimal . . . The terror bound her chest so that her breath came in the short, dry, painful gasps of a dying asthmatic.

Trent knew that he should do something. He had read in Victorian novels of mothers smacking their hysterical daughters across the face. He had kneed Gomez in the stomach to break the gunman out of the panic of drowning. But that had been in the immediacy of action and as much to save himself as to save Gomez. He thought that he should touch her, offer her comfort. But he was trained in action rather than in comfort. He told himself that it wasn't difficult – to lay a hand gently on her shoulder and draw her into the protection of his own body. He would do it when the next squall hit.

The thick rumbling roar of thunder enveloped them. Lightning lit Mariana's face. Then the squall was on them. The force of it lifted *Golden Girl*'s stern and for a moment Trent feared that she would bury her bows in the sea and pitch-pole. He shifted the helm so that the storm jib lifted the bows, the catamaran lunging forward on to the wave top, surfing the squall front. Then the squall fled ahead of them, leaving the craft shuddering in its wake.

Trent hadn't touched the girl. The rain was so heavy now that he was unable to see the expression on her face. The vast curling crest of the hurricane reared over them, and its face stretched from horizon to horizon. Lightning flowed over it continually, and the thunder was incessant. He had to shout to make himself heard: 'Mariana, look . . . '

But he was trying to stop her looking, or wanted to stop her looking. The image of the Victorian mother slapping her daughter haunted him. Incensed by his own inadequacy, he heard himself yell at her in desperation, 'Mariana, have you read Jane Austen . . . ?'

EIGHT

Have you read Jane Austen? The insanity or inanity of Trent's shouted enquiry snapped Mariana out of her trance. Thunder shook the catamaran as she looked up at him, rain almost blinding her. He pointed at the deck between his legs and she scrabbled over on her haunches to sit there partially protected.

The sea had become a green-black pool spread with foam less than a hundred feet in circumference in which Trent steered by instinct. He could no longer read their position on the Loran let alone see the coast and the mouth of the Makaa River which remained his goal. Even the lightning was filtered into changes in density of darkness by the weight of rain cascading out of the cloud-front. The wind had steadied, not the calm before the storm, but the bunching of a tiger's muscles as it gathered itself to pounce.

Trent believed that they were less than two miles from the river mouth. In final preparation for the storm, he closed the cockpit drains. The wind hit. It came screeching out of the darkness, and not even the thunder could drown the scream of its menace. Trent let go jib sheet and halyard; the heavy canvas flashed free, disappearing into the rain curtain as if lighter than tissue paper. The seas smashed into his back, wind and water clubbed him off the seat on to the cockpit sole. He wrapped his legs round Mariana, an arm across her chest, his other hand on the tiller arm. In seconds the cockpit was full to the coamings. Waves crashed over their heads and burst through the open saloon door. The weight of the water forced *Golden Girl* down, as Trent had planned, so that she was little more than awash. There was no possibility now that she could capsize: built with positive buoyancy, she was incapable of sinking.

Waves smashed over Trent and Mariana almost continuously. Thunder rolled over and round them from every direction so that Trent had the sense of being in the interior of an enormous drum on which giants beat from all sides. Lightning spiked and zig-zagged. The wind screamed incessantly.

The lashings holding the Zodiac snapped, and the inflatable spun away like a Frisbee. The top section of the mast snapped at the crosstrees as if it were less substantial than a toothpick. A moment later the main section sheared at the mastfoot. The spar crashed down across the cabin top in a tangle of twisted stays and halyards. Unable to break them free, waves thrashed the jagged tubes of aluminium over the foredeck. At any moment they might come sweeping back into the cockpit, impaling Trent or Mariana.

'We have to get into the saloon,' Trent shouted in Mariana's ear. He couldn't tell if she had heard.

Gripping her in his arms, he rolled over on top of her and thrust with his feet against the stern locker, shooting them forward across the cockpit. Waves washed over them, driving Mariana out of his arms as he grabbed for the side of the saloon companionway. She pitched forward into the flooded darkness of the interior, and Trent heaved himself after her. Gathering her back into his arms, he unclipped the safety line on her lifejacket and lifted her on to the saloon settee where she was protected from the surging water by his BMW.

Both hulls were flooded, the water driving backwards and

forwards across the saloon deck as the waves lifted first one hull, then the other. The continual slamming of the seas under the bridge-deck beat at them, fountaining up through the manhole Trent had unscrewed in the saloon deck. The sea churned the banalities of his life into flotsam: sheets, shirts, sandals, books, charts, salt cellar . . .

Waves burst over the cockpit into the saloon only to pour out through the manhole each time the bridge-deck broke free for a moment. The wind screeched like a herd of pigs at slaughter. The mast and stays thrashed the cabin top. Thunder exploded, roll after roll after roll, so that there seemed to be no gap between but only an incessant bombardment. The hurricane would drive *Golden Girl* where it willed. There was nothing that Trent could do on deck.

'We'll be all right,' he shouted at Mariana: 'I promise . . . '

They had been perhaps a mile and a half off the river mouth when the hurricane hit. The sea would be rising fast, flooding inland over the mangrove swamps, drowning the coast under ten or twenty or thirty feet of water.

Trent had listened to stories of the 1961 hurricane. Perhaps because of the coral reefs, as now, there had been no tidal wave but the force of the wind had driven the sea inland, thirty feet deep in Belpan City. Rafts of logs, waiting for shipment, had been ripped free of their bindings, smashing through concrete buildings as if they were built of playing cards.

The electrical supply would be cut, all telephone lines would be down, airstrips closed. Soon the road bridges would be torn from the banks by the flood waters spewed raging down from the mountains by the incessant rain. The perpetrators of the coup would be imprisoned by the storm for the next twenty-four hours. Trent had thought, on the way out to the rendezvous with the Baglietto, that the hurricane would be his surest ally. Now he was being proved correct. True, most if not all of the Government ministers were probably taken. But if he survived the storm, there was a chance that he could reach the President ahead of Louis' men.

The wind was still as vicious but the thunder had passed them by and the voice of the seas changed, waves breaking over the catamaran with less force. Trent heard the scratching of branches against the bridge-deck as the wind drove *Golden Girl* inland on the flood tide. Shifting his grip from handhold to handhold, he reached the companionway to the cockpit.

With the rain cutting visibiity to less than a hundred feet, it was as if they were trapped inside a glass tumbler the sides of which held at bay the blackness of the storm. The sea foamed beneath a heaving mat of torn mangrove branches, leaves, reeds, turtle grass and seaweed.

Trent half swam and half wriggled across the cockpit to unblock the drainpipes. *Golden Girl's* stern rose as the water drained, the wind pivoting the catamaran round and driving her stern first. With the companionway protected from the wind, only the waves that broke over the cabin top burst into the saloon. Regaining the companionway, he dragged the doors closed, bolting them. Then he dropped down into the port hull. The bilge pump was on the bulkhead. He pumped steadily for five minutes, crossed to the starboard hull, pumped for a further ten minutes, then back to the port hull for a final five. With the water less than a foot deep in each hull, he squeezed his way round the motor cycle to join Mariana on the settee. From the galley he had brought matches wrapped in cellophane and packed in a screw-top coffee jar. He lit the gimballed oil lamp on the cabinside and, in the soft yellow light, saw that Mariana looked more stunned now than frightened.

'I told you we'd make it,' he said, lips close to her ear. 'We've been washed way inland. The baddies won't move till the storm's over.'

Mariana didn't respond but he hadn't expected her to. Dropping down to the galley, he struck a match to the gimballed stove, put a can of tomato soup, pierced but unopened, into the pressure cooker along with an inch of water, and fastened the lid tight. He gave the soup five minutes to warm, managed to open the can without cutting himself, and split the contents between two pint mugs.

'Haute cuisine, good for you,' he told Mariana, forcing one mug into her hands. She didn't want to take it. She didn't want to move or speak – most of all, she didn't want to think. Trent recognised the symptoms. Fear did that to people. Shut the world out . . .

If he could break her out of it, she'd be all right. And he had to – he needed information.

'You'll have a wonderful story to tell your children. On a small boat in a hurricane and a lunatic asks if you read Jane Austen.'

No reply and not even a hint of a smile.

'The first time your children tell you they've heard the story, remember, I warned you.' He drained his mug, dropping it over his shoulder into the water slushing around in the galley: 'Nothing like a hurricane for washing dishes.'

He cupped his hands round hers, lifting the soup to her lips. He tilted the mug. She could drink or turn her head away. Trent didn't mind which – he wanted a reaction, that was all. She sipped as if on automatic pilot, which wasn't good but it was better than catatonia.

'Damn,' he said, as if something urgent required his attention. 'Hold on, I'll be back.' He took his hand away from hers. She nearly dropped the mug but her brain took over at the last instant. Trent dropped down into the galley and took his time searching out a tin of ginger biscuits.

Mariana had finished the soup. She lowered the mug under her own volition and he took it from her. 'Peek Frean,' he told her, showing the biscuit tin. 'What greater love can man have for woman?'

He forced a biscuit into her hand: 'I know – I'm not funny. People have been telling me that ever since I was a small boy.' He smiled: 'Be grateful. You should hear me sing.'

She looked down at the biscuit, as if surprised by it. Then she brought it to her mouth and nibbled. She looked up at Trent, as if seeing him for the first time: 'I'd have drowned if you'd left me on the Key.'

'Nonsense. The patrol boat would have taken you off.'

'Would that have been better?' So she was seeing the Colombians as the enemy.

'The eye of the storm? With hurricanes it's true. When it reaches us, we'll have calm for half an hour. That's our chance.'

Leaving her in peace so that she could think, he stripped the cover from the BMW. He brushed a few drops of sea water off the top of the carburettor, dabbed the float chamber full and gave Mariana a shrug of apology before kicking the starter. The engine fired on the fourth kick and he flashed her a victorious smile. In the enclosed cabin the noise was unbearable. He shut the engine off and opened the saloon doors to clear the fumes. Nothing had changed outside except that there was more grass and fewer leaves mixed with the foam.

He closed the doors again and stood watching Mariana from the companionway. He was in no hurry. Anyway hurrying would have been unproductive. As with waiting for a hedgehog to uncurl, prodding didn't help.

Mariana finished the biscuit. Trent proffered the tin. She took a minute to make up her mind to accept. He took one himself. He was determined not to lie to her. Talking at all above the screech of the wind was difficult and he had to make his explanation short: 'Mariana, the men running this coup set up roadblocks this morning to pick up any of the Government trying to get into Belpan City. One of their men boasted to me that they intend killing the ministers. I don't think they've got your grandfather.'

129

He wasn't trying to give her false hope but was simply telling her the truth. Though not all the truth. 'There's nothing certain and I don't have all the bits so I can't promise,' he said. 'But I'm certain as I can be that they can't win unless they have your grandfather. If I can reach him, there's a chance I can save the ministers.'

He accepted, as he watched the anger rekindle her eyes, that she felt he was blackmailing her.

'It's your choice,' he said, deliberately increasing the pressure. 'I can't make it for you.'

Swinging down into the port hull, he searched his cabin for dry clothes. His jumpers, unused through the past three months of the hot season, were folded round humidity-absorbent packs and bagged in strong plastic. So were his long trousers, his formal shirts, and what he thought of as his work-clothes: camouflage trousers and combat jackets. He selected a blue cotton shirt and a pair of light wool slacks for Mariana. He took up a sleeping-bag, unzipping it so that she had something dry to sit on. The towels were awash. He dropped back down to his cabin while she changed. He gave her ten minutes.

The dry clothes had given her strength. He sensed that she was judging him. Accepting her inspection, he waited, one hand on the mast support to steady himself. The catamaran heaved beneath his feet, the wind screeched, the stays and mast thrashed the deck.

'You won't hurt him?' she said.

It wasn't a question Trent had expected. But it was the correct question, courageous, and he admired her for it. He gave himself time before answering. She had to know that he had considered and that he was committed by his reply. He looked away, as if studying his own thoughts. Then he deliberately looked back to meet her eyes so that she would know that he had made a decision. With a slight lift of his shoulders, he accepted his decision: 'No, Mariana, I won't hurt him.'

130

He knew what he was asking of her – that she should place her grandfather in his hands. And he was certain that the President had told her not to tell anyone where he had gone.

Mariana's struggle was now internalised, for there was nothing to be read in her face. She looked away as Trent had done. A wave caught the mast, lifting it high and then slamming it down on the cabin roof. She used the noise as camouflage for what she felt to be her betrayal of her grandfather's trust: 'He's up at Pine Ridge.'

Trent swung himself over to the settee so that she wouldn't have to shout. 'Where on Pine Ridge?'

'He has a cabin,' she said, 'up by an abandoned quarry. It's where he goes when he has to write a speech . . . ' She looked away so that Trent wouldn't see her misery: 'He told me not to tell anyone.'

'I know,' Trent said. He unfurled the map of Belpan from the waterproof pouch on the motor cycle. 'Can you show me where the cabin is?'

The catamaran was riding light, the wind driving it further and further inland across the coastal strip. As Trent studied the map, he recalled the topography each side of the Makaa River.

Behind the mangroves lay low scrub, lagoons, and then narrow flats planted with sugar cane. The tide would carry them inland at least two miles and possibly three before they were beached on the first low ridge that had been the coastline a million years before the birth of Christ. Beyond that first ridge came rolling scrubland, the soil impoverished over the centuries by annual burning and the single crop agronomy of the Maya, the land now abandoned. Next came the mountains, their lower slopes cloaked in rain forest which had once covered the coastal plain but was now restricted to tongues licking down the banks of the Belpan and Makaa Rivers.

The highest of the mountain ridges separated the headwaters of the Belpan and Makaa. On the high flanks of the ridge the thick canopy of the rain forest gave way to slender pines where clear streams plunged from pool to pool over granite boulders. From the early days of the Spanish invasion, the ridge had been logged commercially but now the major part of the pine forest had been declared a nature reserve.

Trent pictured the ridge. An American had built a mountain lodge more than five hundred feet below the edge of the reserve where he offered horseback riding along the mountain trails and old logging roads – but that was in the tourist season which wouldn't officially open for a further month. The President's cabin lay three miles into the reserve, four miles to the north and a good eight hundred feet above the lodge, and divided from it by a small tributary of the Makaa so Trent could expect no help there even if the owner was in residence.

Turning off from the north–south highway some twelve miles north of the Makaa, the track leading to the cabin had been made first by loggers and then improved by a quarrying company some forty years ago. For the first miles it led through thick rain forest before climbing along the flank of a long narrowing valley up into the pine-clad highlands. One of the many branches of the Makaa followed the valley but there were no bridges to cross and where the track crossed side-streams, the fords were wide and bottomed with concrete.

Eleven o'clock of a hurricane morning, Trent thought wryly. He'd had no sleep and had been nearly drowned, almost had his throat cut, been shot at and then nearly rammed by a patrol boat. It was going to be a long day.

He said to Mariana, 'I need to try and get us a little further north.'

He gathered six double sheets from the drenched berths, folded them in half and left them by the companionway. First checking his lifeline, he crawled out on his belly to the after locker for the coil of rope Gomez had noosed round his neck.

The wind threatened to pluck him like a ripe orange off a tree. When he turned back into it, waves smashed into his face but the tangled stays had caught round the bow pulpits, holding the thrashing mast sections at bay.

Back in the saloon Trent cut the rope into four lengths and made one fast to each corner of the folded bedsheets. He rolled and tied them so that the wind wouldn't tear them out of his hands while he tried to position them. Then he dragged them out into the cockpit, making one corner fast to the main sheet winch on the cabin roof and one to the starboard jib winch. Every move was hampered by the beating of the elements. The wind screeched in his ears, making consecutive thought almost impossible so that not only did he have to struggle in desperate conflict with the conditions but had also to fight to hold to his concentration. Every move had to be calculated in advance. One error and he would have been torn loose and hurled overboard to be smothered by the driving spray.

Flat on his stomach, he slid across the cockpit to lead the other two lines over the taffrail and back through the portside stern anchor cleat to the portside winch. He winched in hard and let go the lashings round the rolled bedsheets. Their slope and angle up to the cabin top was sufficient to drive the catamaran north. Trent didn't expect the twelve thicknesses of cotton sheet to last but each minute that they held would gain precious distance.

He tumbled back into the saloon. Sprawled on his back on the deck, he lay exhausted under a waterfall of waves breaking over the cabin top. He hadn't the strength to close the doors. He couldn't move. He didn't care. All that mattered to him for the moment was the feel of the bedsheets angling *Golden Girl* northward.

Half past eleven of a hurricane morning. Trent expected

133

the hurricane to last between eight and ten hours. They were close to the eye of the storm. The last of the bedsheets, ripped into ribbons, had been torn away but he believed that they were well north of the Makaa. Mariana had managed to close the doors. Now she watched as he prepared the tools of his trade.

He adjusted the slings on the Greeners' canvas cases so that he could wear one slung across his chest and the other across his back. The yellow silk square that Steve had given him was in his back pocket; eight boxes of buckshot in each saddlebag; binoculars in his combat jacket; two rolls of inch-wide parcel tape; fifty feet of light line; steel hammer and half a dozen steel spikes; spare combat jacket and two pairs of jungle trousers; for night work, black cotton roll-neck, black tracksuit bottoms and black cotton gloves; slacks and a light jumper for Mariana.

She watched as he adjusted the string of red coral beads through the shammy pouch that held his throwing-knife. He fastened the beads round his neck, arranging the knife so that it rested hidden between his shoulder blades. He belted a ten-inch hunting-knife to his right calf. A metre and a half of copper wire with wooden handgrips at each end went in his pocket plus a box of bullets for his Walther in case he should be able to reclaim it from the masthead.

He had become an Untouchable, Trent thought with sudden bitterness as he glanced up to catch a look, almost of horror, on Mariana's face. He was aware of how professional he must appear to her in his preparations for what she saw as killing and which he had been trained to see as protection of the innocent. Even if she could be brought to view his actions in his own light, he would remain for her the instrument of death.

'You'll be safe on *Golden Girl*,' he said. 'Once the wind drops, try and get across the border.'

'In case you fail?'

'I'm not invincible, despite the hardware.'

134

Reaching over her head, he plucked the photograph of his mother from the bulkhead. Mariana watched him slip the picture inside the folded map for protection.

'I'm coming with you,' she said.

It was a statement of fact rather than the opening shot in an argument and Trent accepted it as such. Already he had learnt to recognise the small frown line that drew Mariana's brows together as a signal of immovable stubbornness – or absolute commitment. Which of the two was in the eye of the beholder.

'I'm not useless, you know, and you can't do everything on your own.' Switching from the maternal to the sulky child, she added, 'Anyway you'll need me to back up whatever you tell Gran'pa.'

Trent might have laughed had he not been thrown against the motor cycle as the hurricane drove *Golden Girl* aground. The catamaran's stern slammed on rock and they heard, above the scream of the wind, the rudders shatter. Trent leaped to the portside bilge pump, desperate to clear the remaining water from the hull before its weight broke the vessel apart.

'And don't dare tell me it's going to be too tough for a woman,' Mariana shouted, as she glared down at him from the saloon. She disappeared from view. A minute later he heard the rhythmic thump of the starboard bilge pump uniting with his own pumping.

The sudden stilling of the wind brought with it a silence so total when compared to the continual cacophony of the past hours that the shock of it, for a moment, held Mariana and Trent immobile.

He thrust the doors open. Unlashing the motor cycle, he manhandled it across the saloon and into the cockpit. Only then did he look out across the land. *Golden Girl* had cleared the rocks on which she had first grounded, the wind slithering the lightened catamaran broadside across the sparse grasses sprouting from the leached sandy soil behind the ancient coastline. The rain fell as heavily as ever but was no longer compressed by the wind into a solid curtain. A vast circle of storm clouds hugged the ground and rose towering into the air, so they seemed becalmed on the inside edge of a massive mauve funnel through the swirling walls of which Trent could make out, to the south, a thin line of greater darkness that he knew must be the rain forest bordering the Makaa River. They had been driven far further north than he had expected. To the west lay the highway.

He dropped the gangplank over the stern and wheeled the motor cycle down. He found his Walther safe in the masthead. Tucking it into one of the saddlebags, he looked up to see Mariana with one Greener slung over her shoulders. She held the second shotgun out to him and he slung it across his chest. For a moment he hesitated, nervous of breaking the strange stillness of the deserted landscape. It was as if they had landed on an alien planet, his fear that of awakening the denizens, giant and menacing.

He sensed the same nervousness in Mariana. He smiled at her and, in offering her reassurance, broke the spell that held them. The engine roared into life as he kicked the starter. He swung a leg over, and Mariana settled herself behind him. Already they were close to the middle of the cloud funnel. Ten minutes, fifteen at the most, and the wind would be on them, tearing them from the saddle. Ten, fifteen minutes to gain the shelter of the forest – though even there they would be in danger of being pulped into nothingness by trees ripped from the rain-softened earth.

NINE

The front of the hurricane tore at the lower flanks of the mountains, rending great trees from the rain forest and tossing them aside as if they were little more than sticks. But in the centre of the storm calm prevailed, fifteen miles in radius, a haven in which Trent and Mariana charged towards the north–south highway. They were in a desperate race with the towering, whirling walls of mauve-black cloud. They were safe as long as they remained within the central eye of the storm. On its edge lay chaos and destruction.

Though the big R100 BMW has been designed as much for cross-country work as for the road, the wheels bucked and skidded in the grey waterlogged soil as Trent fought the handlebars, weaving between scrub bush and clumps of hagara grass. Once already he had lost control, the wheels sliding away from under him as he slewed clear of a steep-sided washway. They had lost precious seconds; now they had none left to spare.

Slit-eyed against the blinding rain, he hurled his weight forward as he powered up a ridge, the rear wheel tearing at shale and mud. From the top he could see the highway, a quarter of a mile ahead. It lay across their path, a black snake of tarmac, rain-soaked and unprotected.

Her cheek pressed flat between his shoulders, Mariana

clung to Trent as if it was only her strength that saved them from disintegration. To encourage her, Trent yelled that the road was in sight. With the ribbon of blacktop offering a new perspective, he realised that the vortex within which they fled was turning away from the mountains. They had been fleeing from the pursuing cloud front, but now they were charging to meet its attack. But, in changing direction, the hurricane had given them ten minutes of further respite.

Trent slewed the motorbike over as they hit the highway. Throttle wide, he bowed into the slipstream. Mariana crouched low on the pillion. Spray spun high from the tyres. The speedometer quivered at one hundred and forty kilometres per hour. Clouds towered on every side, and the attacking front was less than a mile to their left.

Trent sought to recall the terrain ahead. He remembered a swamp draining into a lagoon some distance to the right of the highway – the road must have been raised for him to have seen that distance. Given the swamp, there had to be a stream or streams feeding it, which would run through a culvert under the highway.

He knew that he should slow and seek shelter. He began counting to himself as he had always done, even as a child, when under stress. Thirty seconds and he would turn off the road. He sensed the growing tension in Mariana and felt her turn her head so that she could no longer see the wall of cloud less than half a mile to their left. Dark whips flicked at them. The motor cycle shuddered as a squall spat a tongue of rain across the highway. Trent fought to hold the BMW upright. He could see the embankment. He cut power, toe snapping up through the gears. A quick shift of weight, and he angled the bike over the gravel edge, sliding broadside as he struggled for traction. A fresh squall tore the rainwater off the road surface, cascading it down so that they were riding in the inside of a waterfall as Trent powered onward in the lee of the embankment. In the far distance he saw the shadowed mouth of a large culvert angling towards them. The squalls were screeching now over their heads, rain curtains hurtling after each other seaward across the low swampland.

Too late Trent flung the motor cycle into a skid as a steeply-banked riverbed opened before them through the driving rain. Mariana tumbled free as the BMW slid over the edge, dragging Trent with it. Left-booted, he forced the bike upright as he hit the water, which was less than a foot deep. He opened the throttle, blasting the motor cycle broadside into the culvert. Kicking down the side-rest as he jumped clear, he spun round in time to see Mariana slide down the bank. He was about to take her arm and help her into the culvert but she neither needed nor wanted his help. That much was clear as she struck his hand away.

Wading under the highway, Trent found that the riverbed continued the angle of the culvert. It was vertically banked and some thirty metres wide. Water flowed in the centre, shallow and sluggish. Studying the map back at the motor cycle, he saw that it had once carried what was now that branch of the Makaa River which flowed down the valley below the track up to the President's cabin.

A landfall had probably blocked off the river centuries back, forcing it into a fresh path. Now the water ran strongly only when the river overflowed its new bed. With its loss of flow, the river's old mouth had silted up, thus forming the lagoon and swamp. Here, where it cut the highway, the steep bank of the river would give them protection from the full force of the hurricane. Trent was unable to read from the map for what distance the banks remained steep but if a fall had blocked off the riverbed then the banks had to be steep right up to where the new river cut away from it. He checked his watch: twelve noon . . .

Angled away from the path of the hurricane, the concrete tube had become a giant organ pipe across the mouth of which the hurricane moaned and howled as if driven into enraged dementia by their evasion of its savagery. Rainwater, driven off the highway, fell in a solid wall that cut them off from any view of the outside world. Trent looked up from the map to find Mariana watching him. The anger he saw in her eyes was camouflage for the fear she felt. She had been through enough already. She felt safe in the protection of the culvert. But the culvert was a death-trap.

Trent felt her retreat further inside herself as he shouted through the organ howl, 'There's a chance we can make our way upriver.' He didn't want to force her but he had no alternative. Lips close to her ear, he said, 'I'm sorry, but I have to try it.'

He stood on the starter and kicked up the side-rest. Without looking at Mariana, he swung the BMW round to face the mountains. The seconds ticked by. Finally he felt her weight settle on the pillion seat. She didn't touch him, no grip round his waist or leaning of her body into his. He looked back at her and their eyes met. She was about to look away when he grabbed her shoulder. Anger was her only protection and, deliberately feeding it, Trent shouted, 'Don't play games, Mariana. Stay here or co-operate.'

Rage drove life into her eyes. 'I hate you,' she shouted. For a moment, he thought that she would hit him. He let out the clutch. Then both her arms were round his waist as if she wanted to crush his ribs.

As he opened the throttle, the roar of the BMW's engine bit into the moan and howl of the wind across the culvert's mouth. Trent lay flat over the handlebars and bulled the motor cycle clear of the tunnel. He rode with his legs spread wide, boots skimming the riverbed. The rain struck him across the face like a whiplash as he fought to keep the bike upright and driving for the protection of the leeward bank. In seconds his boots were filled with water. He couldn't see. The wind screamed, the hurricane hailed stones and branches. For a moment he thought that he had lost control, and the bank loomed at him. The sudden slackening of the wind shot the BMW forward as if he had released the brakes. He kicked the bike round on his right boot, riding only inches from the bank, the top only four feet above his head. Eyes squinted almost shut, he could see less than ten yards upriver. The bike bucked left as he hit a boulder and the front wheel struck the bank before he could straighten up. Next second they were sprawling in the mud and water, motor cycle on top of them. They had gained less than a hundred yards.

Trent lifted the bike. Mariana beat on his shoulders, screaming at him to go back. To do so was to court death and to surrender, not only to the hurricane, but to surrender a nation, however small, into the hands of killers. Trent knew that Louis' men, if they were able, would strike soon after first light. He had to reach the President's cabin with at least an hour of daylight in which to plan his defence and with time to get through to Caspar on the President's radio.

Thirty feet of high tide dammed the Makaa River. For the past six hours the downpour had been continuous and torrential. The branch of the Makaa had risen fifteen feet and, with no escape, overflowed into its old bed up which Trent and Mariana rode.

As the flow increased, the water nibbled away the downstream face of the hundred yards of landfall that had originally forced the river westward into the Makaa. Minute by minute the flow gained in speed and power, and what had been a trickle became a stream and then a shallow river. Great chunks of earth fell from the face of the landfall; boulders, the restraining earth gouged away, shuddered and rocked and tumbled free.

Over a hundred thousand tons of water pressed on the landfall and each foot eaten away from its face sapped its ability to withstand the massive weight. The density of the landfall was critical to calculating at what moment the dam would capitulate. When it did, a solid wall of water, twenty feet deep, would sweep down the old bed, crushing everything in its way, hitting the highway with the force of an express train. In less than a second it would tear a gap in the highway the width of the riverbed.

As if enraged at its defeat by the mountains, the hurricane once more turned inland. As it howled on to a new course, the river bank no longer protected Trent and Mariana from the worst of its savagery. To the contrary, there was a period in which the riverbed served as a channel for the full ferocity of the storm.

Trent had calculated the distance between the culvert and the junction of the old and new rivers as less than four miles. Half an hour had passed since they had left the shelter of the culvert. He had little idea as to how far they had come and had lost count of how many times they had fallen. He lay sprawled against the foot of the bank with the full weight of the BMW across his legs and pinned between the wind and the growing force of the water like a fly between the pages of a book.

The squall that had flung Trent against the bank had hit them at over one hundred and fifty miles an hour. It had plucked Mariana from the pillion seat, skittering her against the current like a flat stone skipped across a pond. During the occasional moments in which the driven rain lost its solidity, Trent could see Mariana's arms locked round a fallen treetrunk some twenty yards upstream. He imagined her terror. As he was held between the conflicting pressures of wind and water, so he was caught between the desire to reach Mariana and offer her comfort and the need to husband his remaining strength – but he knew that the husbanding of his strength was paramount if they were to survive.

He could feel the swing of the hurricane. Soon the far bank would offer shelter. But what had been no more than a slowly moving stream less than a couple of metres wide now flowed fast and dark with mud across the full thirty metres of the riverbed. In a momentary gap in the rain curtain, he saw that the tree behind which Mariana lay was almost awash. Trent closed his eyes, feeling at the wind, sniffing at it, listening to it. Gathering his strength, he pried his left leg free of the BMW and dragged the bike upright against the bank. Straddling it, he kicked the starter. No response. He kicked twice more. Dear God, he prayed, and leaned his shoulder against the bank while he got his breath. For a moment he thought that he had felt something, an infinitesimal trembling of the earth. He kicked for the fourth time. The engine caught. He rested against the bank, waiting, and this time he was sure that he felt something.

A squall beat him into the bank. It passed and he looked upriver to where Mariana lay hidden upstream of the fallen treetrunk. He could see her plainly and the scream of the wind was softer. The swing of the hurricane was bringing them back into the eye of the storm.

Gunning the engine, Trent slammed into first gear and eased the motor cycle diagonally upriver. The water was two feet deep at the treetrunk. He shouted at Mariana, grabbing at her arms and dragging her upright. 'Move!' he yelled. 'Quick . . . !'

He swung the bike downriver as her weight hit the pillion. Throttle open and keeping to the centre of the stream where there were no obstructions, he powered the BMW in second gear straight back the way they had come. Desperately he looked for a way up the river bank. Twice he had to kick hard against the force of a squall but the wind was dropping fast, the howl gone out of it. And then he heard it – the thick, heavy thud of a big fieldgun far in the distance. But there were no fieldguns . . .

He saw ahead and to their left a wedge of earth fallen from the bank. He rode at it, braked, yanked Mariana off the pillion and yelled at her to climb. 'Run!' he shouted. 'Run for your life!'

He kicked the motor cycle round and gunned it across the river, then swung back to face the spit and the vee-shaped cut in the almost vertical bank. Mariana was halfway up. She looked back. He slammed a fist up at her as if the force of his gesture could throw her the last five feet, and screamed at her although he knew that she couldn't hear. Her head was still a foot from the top. He looked upriver. It was coming. A vast roaring wall of death and destruction. He let go the clutch, lifted the front wheel and drove at the far bank, sand-spit dead ahead. Spray, driven by the wall of water, struck his face. He felt the wind of it and the cold. He hit the spit and threw his weight forward, bulling the BMW up the steep slope and into the vee. Mariana was halfway over the bank. Desperation gave him strength. He grabbed her collar, dragging her clear and across the mud like a life-size rag doll.

The roar of the water deafened them. They heard, like thunder, the explosion of its power as it struck the distant road, and saw the highway break and rise in two sections like two sides of a lifting bridge. Then there was nothing but the river running wide and strong and dark and it was as if the highway had never existed.

For a moment Trent and Mariana were held immobile, stunned by the incredible power from which they had so narrowly escaped. Trent broke the spell. Safe in the central eye of the storm, they had ten or fifteen minutes in which to reach the comparative safety of the track leading up through the rain forest to the President's cabin.

Shrilling overhead, the hurricane clawed at the leaf canopy of the rain forest, tearing great holes in it. The track had become a shallow river: the clay had been eaten away from the broken rock and pebble surface, and the front wheel of the motor cycle kicked continuously against the handlebars. Trent rode in first gear, headlight tunnelling into the forest gloom through which the rain bucketed. Onward and upward the track wound, clinging to the side of the ridge like a pale slippery centipede.

Nature had drawn a demarcation line far more precise

than any national frontier drawn by man and Trent and
Mariana burst free of the rain forest and into the pine-clad
uplands at nineteen hundred feet. They had almost outrun
the hurricane – or the hurricane had dawdled, keen to exact
its full revenge on the mountain flanks that had initially
defeated it. Back on the storm-front, lightning flashed and
thunder exploded in long runs that seemed to envelop the
length of the mountain chain as if spread by a giant paint-
roller.

The pines grew spaced as in a plantation. There was no
shrub and palm cover bound by creepers as there had been
in the rain forest so that the track was little protected from
the squalls that struck up the mountainside, screeching like
banshees, as they bowed the slender treetrunks almost to
the ground. The timber opened as they breasted a ridge
and Trent glimpsed a steeply-sloping meadow up ahead and
a patch of white. The track dipped, weaving into a wooded
hollow. They came to a fork. Mariana pointed Trent to the
left.

Another five minutes and they were at the edge of the
meadow. Trent braked and swung the BMW back into the
shelter of the pine trees. Kicking down the foot-rest, he
dismounted and stretched a little of the stiffness out of his
shoulders. He unslung the gun case from across his chest,
unzipping it as he gave Mariana a grin. 'We made it,' he
said and took the second gun from Mariana's shoulders
without really looking at her.

He checked the actions and pumped a cartridge back into
the breach of each gun before slipping upward through the
trees. The meadow was three hundred yards across and a
little more in length. The cabin stood in the centre. It was
one of those houses children draw: a door in the middle,
matching windows each side, sloping roof and a chimney
sticking up. The roof was thatched with *wano* palm; white
walls, varnished wood – simple, as befitted the reputation
of the President.

He felt Mariana's touch on his shoulder. 'What's wrong?' she asked.

'Probably nothing, but it's like crossing a road,' he told her. 'Look first and you don't get killed.'

He took his binoculars from his breast pocket. Four yemery trees shaded the cabin and a dozen or so pines were scattered across the upper slope. Trent guessed that the meadow had been cleared originally because its soil was richer than the sandy loam common to the ridge. Certainly the trees were massive in comparison with the feathery pines of the forest. The mountainside, climbing steeply from the head of the meadow, was concave so that it formed a natural amphitheatre cupping a quarry face. Trent couldn't see whether the track ran on to the quarry or stopped at the cabin. No vehicle was in sight and the cabin windows were uncurtained and unshuttered. No smoke came from the chimney. Little Red Riding Hood came into Trent's thoughts as he studied the scene.

Thunder rolled as he turned to ask Mariana where the President kept his Land-Rover. A squall screamed through the trees and blasted a curtain of rain up the meadow. Rather than shout, Trent aped driving and raised his eyebrows in enquiry. Mariana mimed a lean-to round the back.

Putting an arm round her shoulder, he crouched down and used a stick to draw the meadow in the dirt. He marked in the cabin, the quarry, and the track up as far as the cabin and back down through the dip to the fork. Pointing to the right fork, he passed her the stick. Mariana hatched the drop to the river to their right and dragged a furrow through it round the side of the meadow and on up the mountain with a branch cutting off at right angles to run along the top of the quarry.

Trent pointed to the quarry road. He scrubbed out the map with his boot before remounting the motor cycle. Mariana swung up behind him. The right fork ran through pine forest well below the level of the meadow before climbing

146

to meet the quarry track, which ran in a slight curve following the concave face of the mountain. The pines on the lower edge fragmented his view of the meadow so that his first clear sight of the cabin's rear came as they reached the quarry top. A steep path cut down from the quarry edge to the meadow.

Again Trent braked in the shadows of the trees and studied the cabin through his binoculars. A County-model Land-Rover had been backed up against a stack of firewood in the shelter of a thatched carport. A sheet of plastic covered the woodpile. A small shield bearing the Presidential arms was stencilled on the vehicle's front door and Trent could see the silver pennant staff on the bonnet. A back door led out to the carport and there were two windows, just as there were in the front. A big storage chest stood to the left of the door. The carport and Land-Rover obstructed Trent's view of the windows.

The quarry was wider than it was deep, perhaps sixty yards across and dropping eighty feet sheer into a small lake, the water dyed red by the mud washed down by the rain. A few rocks showed in the water close in to the quarry face and there was a crescent of sand the meadow side of the water with two giant pines shading the right corner. With the sun out, it would be a wonderful place for a picnic.

Two hundred yards of open grassland stretched between the treeline and the cabin, no cover. Shooting him as he made his approach would be easier than pumping lead into a target. He beckoned Mariana to draw the inside of the cabin.

Large living-room in the front with two doors. One led to the kitchen, the other to the President's bedroom with a bathroom off it. A door connected kitchen with bathroom, with the rear door leading from the kitchen to the carport.

Trent walked back and studied the footpath before remounting the motor cycle. He signalled Mariana to follow on foot and left one of the shotguns with her. First gear, footbrake and handbrake, he slithered down the shale and slippery boulder track that twisted between the pine trees. Twice he nearly lost control and rested, steadying his nerve. He knew fatigue as a temptress capable of leading the unwary into shortcuts that were fatal.

From the meadow edge, he could see the rear windows of the cabin. Nothing moved. He laid the shotgun across his lap. A heavy squall drove up the meadow, bowing the trees before howling away up the mountain face. Lightning struck out of the towering cloudbank. He released the clutch as the thunder broke upon him: the power of its sound smashed him into the saddle as he zig-zagged fast across the smooth grass towards the cabin. He braked and grabbed up the shotgun as he laid the bike over, sliding into the shelter of the woodpile. He crawled on toes and elbows round the Land-Rover. One door, two windows . . .

He had done it so often, yet it got worse rather than easier: pain in the gut, sticky sourness in the back of the throat, thighs trembling with tension but the hands steady. He closed his eyes and waited for the pupils to widen. Up into a crouch, charge. He leapt and took out the window to the President's bedroom with his left shoulder. He hit the floor, rolling, and lay flat, shotgun ready. The President sat at a plain wooden desk to the right of the door through to the front room. He wore Marks and Spencer boxer shorts, a pair of rubber flip-flops, and thirty-six hours of silver bristle on his cheeks. He seemed to take for ever to look down at Trent. Neither surprise nor fear showed in his eyes. He wasn't even focusing. The tumbler in his right hand was almost empty. So was the bottle of Famous Grouse on the desk blotter. Clothes lay on the floor and the bed hadn't been made.

Trent rolled to the living-room door and opened it. Empty. He checked the bathroom and kitchen and only then stood up to look through the windows to be certain that no one had made a run for the trees. He felt no embarrassment. Precautions had kept him alive. He walked round the cabin, checking the ground for tracks. Then he waved for Mariana. He would have preferred holding her back but that couldn't be done without her getting frightened that something bad had happened.

Back in the President's bedroom, he said, 'Good afternoon, sir,' which struck him as a little formal in the circumstances.

The President didn't bother to look up. Instead he reached for the whisky bottle. Trent removed it.

'I've brought Mariana with me,' he said. 'She'll be here in a few minutes.'

Giving the President time to gather himself, Trent straightened the sheets and bedspread. He picked the clothes up off the floor and put them away in the wardrobe, and found the President a clean pair of slacks and a shirt before sweeping up the broken glass.

The President sat studying his tumbler. He didn't seem upset that it was empty and Trent had the feeling that, given the chance, the President would have poured himself another whisky and drunk it for something to do rather than from desire for alcohol. Trent had never heard of the President being a drinker, secret or otherwise, and it was the sort of habit that couldn't stay hidden in a country of Belpan's size.

'I'm sorry, sir,' he said, 'but you have to shower. You can't let your granddaughter see you like this.'

Receiving no response, he went through to the bathroom and turned the cold tap on full. He went back for the President, lifting him from behind by both elbows and walking him into the shower with his boxer shorts and his sandals on. The President walked well enough, no struggle. Trent held him under the cold water, hoping he would make some effort to support himself. Trent was out of luck.

'I'm going to let you go, sir, so you'll have to stand up or you'll fall down.' He thought that was about the stupidest statement he'd ever made. He had no way of knowing what the President thought. He placed the President's hands against the wall, let go, and thanked God when he remained on his feet. Trent checked that there was a towel and said, 'I'll make coffee, sir. I'm sorry, but for your granddaughter's sake, you really do have to straighten up.'

Trent saw Mariana up on the forest edge when he went to fetch wood from the carport. He considered meeting her halfway and warning her but decided that getting coffee into her grandfather had priority. The stove lit easily. He filled the kettle and set it on the hob, then went through to the front room, closed the shutters, and tried radioing on the frequency Caspar had given him for the US Embassy in Belpan City. He didn't expect to receive through the static created by the storm but he broadcast a warning and his position in the hope that the Embassy had equipment that would pick him up.

Back in the kitchen he found a stove-enamel jug. Twelve tablespoons of coffee and a single mug of boiling water struck him as right for the emergency. He poured an inch of condensed milk into the mug plus four spoons of sugar and stirred the coffee before straining it. He carried the kill-or-cure mixture through to the President.

He had hoped to find him attempting to dress but he was still propped up under the shower, hands against the wall.

'Excuse me, sir, I've brought your coffee.'

The President slowly turned his head. The alcohol had sapped the strength out of his jaw muscles so that the skin fell in folds and made him look like a tortoise. He seemed to Trent to have withdrawn so far into himself that there was nothing left in his eyes. That was how he looked, but Trent hoped that part of the dead-eye effect came from the President not wearing his spectacles. He said, 'Coffee, sir,' and offered the mug, though holding it just out of the President's reach. 'You can come out of the shower, sir.'

The President managed to focus on the free hand Trent

150

proffered. Pushing himself off the wall, he grabbed at it, missed, and nearly fell. Trent caught him by the forearm. He swayed as he stepped clear of the shower tray. His knees almost buckled but he fought himself upright and managed to get Trent into focus. Suddenly there was fear in his eyes.

'Who are you?'

'Trent, sir. European Economic Community, Anti-Terrorist Unit. I'm sort of on leave. I'm afraid there's been some sort of coup mounted. I'm trying to help.'

'Who?'

'You, sir. Your Government.' Trent closed the President's fingers round the mug. 'Mariana's coming down the meadow. I'll hold her off as long as I can. Tell her you're not well. I think the coffee would help, sir. And perhaps being sick . . .'

TEN

A light show of billion-ampere strobes blazed across the thick black screen of cloud now burying the mountainside. Dwarfed by the storm and bent almost double, Mariana staggered into the wind and rain. She almost crumpled as the full rage of thunder exploded over the meadow and was still fifty yards short of the cabin when the squall hit. It plucked her from her feet and spun her round, tumbling her back uphill as if playing a game of roll-a-ball.

Trent was already running. His feet seemed hardly to touch the ground as the wind drove him up the slope. He saw Mariana scrabble at the grass, desperate for purchase. Then he was with her, crouching to shelter her with his body. He shouted in her ear that they should crawl but the wind flicked the words from his lips. The only means of communication was sign language. Holding Mariana close to the ground, he turned her into the wind – fifteen minutes to crawl fifty yards . . .

Trent held Mariana tight round the shoulders, blocking her view of her grandfather who knelt at the lavatory bowl as if in prayer. Safe in the kitchen, he shouted at Mariana that her grandfather was resting. The cabin walls shook and the roof trusses bowed as the wind fought to rip the roof free. He looked into the living-room. Despite the shutters, both front windows had imploded, glass powdering the floor. They heard, through the thunder, one of the great yemery trees shatter.

First pouring boiling water over the used coffee grounds, Trent led Mariana through to the living-room, seating her on the sofa. 'Don't move,' he ordered. 'There's glass everywhere. Fall and you'll cut yourself to ribbons.'

He lit the hurricane lamps set in brass wall-brackets and found a pressure lamp for the dining table. Back in the kitchen he poured coffee, adding sweetened condensed milk for instant energy.

Mariana looked up as he returned to the living-room. Wet as a water rat, she sat hugging her knees. The shape of her body hidden, she looked in her mid-teens, defenceless. Her hair had been flattened by the storm so that it made Trent think of a squashed astrakan hat. Bruised shadows of fatigue showed beneath her eyes – eyes in which Trent read gratitude and the beginnings of dependency. He wanted neither. She was part of an equation, nothing more, along for the trip because that was the way of it.

'I'll fetch a broom.' Hurrying through the kitchen, he found the President keeled over on the bathroom floor. He knelt to check the old man's pulse only to discover that the President was uncaring rather than unconscious.

Wiping the old man's mouth on a facecloth, Trent helped him to his feet. 'You'll be better off lying down, sir,' he said, and supported him through to the bedroom. He hesitated before slipping the President's boxer shorts down but it was part of the job. He toppled him forward on to the bed and covered him with a sheet.

Mariana made a move to help as Trent returned to the living-room with broom and pan. Trent waved her back. He wasn't planning to fight indoors but it might happen and sweeping the floor clear of glass was the same as cleaning his guns – not a task to be left to someone else. Anyway, Mariana needed rest.

153

Finished, he tried the radio again. Static crackled and flared through the roar of the storm outside. Trent repeated his broadcast to Caspar and gave Mariana a shrug. He switched the radio off. Fetching the saddlebags from the motor cycle he spread the contents on the table. He knew that Mariana was watching as he stripped the shotguns, oiling them before reloading the magazines. He did the same for the Walther.

The worst of the thunder had passed and there was a softer tone to the storm's rage. Trent crossed to a window, peering out through the heart-shaped decoration cut in the shutter. The terrain was clear in his mind. Ten minutes and he'd try preparing the potential battlefield. He saw Mariana shiver as he went back to the table and slipped the Walther into his belt. She was studying her hands.

'You should change into dry clothes,' he said. 'I'm going to have to go out for a while.'

She looked up at him. For a moment he refused to meet her eyes but she said his name. 'Trent . . . ' Then, 'Is that all you think you can do? Kill people?'

Her choice of phrase had been deliberate. The meaning struck him like smoke touching off a fire alarm. 'What do you want me to do?'

'Hold me. Please . . . ' Then she said, 'Damn,' and her face crumpled. 'Go away, damn you . . . '

Soon after first light, either Caspar's or Louis' men would come for the President. Whoever came, Trent was determined that they should come on foot and across open ground. And he wanted time to ready himself, that most of all.

Slicing pieces of the plastic sheeting covering the wood-pile as extra waterproofing, he had taped his shotguns into the packages that he now carried slung over one shoulder. He had found chainsaw and fuel in the carport storage chest. He had been tempted to use the President's Land-Rover but the tracks would have shown. Now he was on

154

the edge of the pine forest at the bottom of the meadow. He had covered the ground in short dashes between the squalls. With less than an hour of daylight remaining, he carried a flashlight – not that it would be of much help with the rain cascading down as if the Maya Rain God had corralled every raincloud in Central America and pulled the plugs out.

Laying the shotguns well out of danger, he started the chainsaw. The wind, blasting up the valley, decided the direction the trees would fall. One by one, he cut deep wedges out of the trunks each side of the track, watching as the wind snapped them over. He went on cutting until the fallen pines formed a thick overlapping vee across the track on the edge of the meadow.

Carrying on down the ridge, he felled half a dozen pines across the track at the bottom of the dip. He chose small trees because he wanted them cleared. Then he took the right fork of the track, following it for a hundred yards, and blocked it so that clearing the barricade in a hurry would require a bulldozer.

He cut up through the forest to where he'd left the shotguns and followed the treeline round to the left until he hit a shallow ravine almost opposite the cabin. The rain wash-off into the ravine had flushed the goodness out of the soil, so that instead of grass, there was a strip of thin scrub and stunted trees. Trent found a boulder on the edge of the ravine which he prised loose so that a light push would send it crashing down the ridge and he hid one of the shotguns at the foot of a solitary pine.

Crossing the head of the ravine, he headed on up the meadow keeping within the treeline for protection and using the flashlight. He hit the lake at the foot of the quarry. Twice a squall bowled him into the water as he followed the shore round. The chainsaw weighed a ton. He hid the second shotgun under a fallen branch at the foot of one of the pines shading the beach. Resting his back against the tree, he switched off the flashlight and waited for his irises to expand before starting down the meadow.

He had set a pressure lamp on the Land-Rover's hood before leaving the cabin but he couldn't see it through the rain. He was heading straight into the wind and the force of it buffeted him from side to side until his sense of direction became totally confused. He thought of sitting down to wait for a break in the storm but that could have been all night so he struggled on downhill, angling a little to the left, until he met the treeline at the bottom of the meadow. Turning right, he hit the track leading to the cabin and followed it back up. He walked round to the carport and put the chain-saw back in the chest. The lamp had lost most of its pressure. He gave it a few pumps and collected an armful of logs for the stove before going in through the back door. Checking his watch, he found that he'd been out of the cabin for a little over three hours.

He dropped the logs off in the kitchen, adding a couple to the stove, and put the kettle on. He looked in on the President. The old man wasn't in his bedroom. Trent returned to the stove and stood there, warming himself, as he tried to gather his energy. He needed to banish Mariana from his thoughts. She wasn't important . . . not in the scheme of things, whatever that meant.

In reminding himself that his responsibilities were for the President, he recalled the way that Mariana had looked at the old man that first day when he had met them out on the dock, the President casting for bonefish. He had seen pride and admiration in her eyes, and love – and that protec-tiveness of the young for the old that came with love. He thought that she must be feeling a great deal of pain, and that there was nothing he could do about it, and that, if his suspicions were correct, her pain would get a great deal worse . . . Above everything, he wanted to get into dry clothes and sleep, but his clothes were in the living-room – as were Mariana and her grandfather.

He put three mugs on a tray and poured coffee so that he would have something to do when he went into the living-room. It was a lot like hitting a room where there might be terrorists waiting in ambush, he thought as he opened the door.

The President sat at the table. He had put on a fresh pair of boxer shorts or the old pair had dried. And he had found a tumbler and another bottle of Famous Grouse from which he'd taken, at most, two tots. He had the look of an old man waiting outside the doctor's office in a paupers' hospital; sent for, rather than there by choice; content to wait; apathetic as to what the doctor would tell him, because good news no longer existed and bad news was no longer bad, but merely an essential ingredient of his condition.

It was all a flashback to his own childhood and to his father, Trent thought as he looked across at Mariana. She was on the sofa, sitting as he'd left her, arms wrapped round her knees. She had changed into the spare slacks and jersey he'd brought from *Golden Girl*. He had been correct about the pain. What he hadn't considered, or had tried not to consider, was the extent to which he cared.

Mariana said, with a lot of anger in her voice, 'Where have you been?'

The President looked up and Trent was certain that he knew who he was. Careful, with the old man listening, he said, 'Outside . . . walking around.' He handed Mariana a mug and took the tray over to the table. He said, 'Good evening, Mister President,' and, too exhausted to bother with niceties, took him by the elbow. 'You should be in bed, sir. Come along . . . '

In the bathroom, he asked, 'Do you want to brush your teeth, sir?'

The President regarded him for a moment and Trent thought that the old man might rally. But all he said was, 'They're not mine.'

'Then perhaps you should put them in a tumbler,' Trent

157

suggested. 'You'll feel better in the morning . . . or less dreadful.'

The President managed a slight smile that brought a moment of life to his eyes: 'You're most considerate, Mister . . . ?' His esses were a little lax.

'Trent,' Trent said. 'I do my best.'

'No doubt it goes with the territory.'

As should courage in a President, Trent thought. He supported the old man over to his bed and fetched a glass of salted water from the kitchen for his teeth.

The President had got himself into bed and covered himself with the sheet. He looked up as Trent came into the room. 'They'll come in the morning . . . '

'Police or villains, yes, sir,' Trent said. 'Perhaps both. If that happens, it may get messy.' He put the tumbler on the bedside table: 'I've put salt in the water, sir.'

'You are a kind man, Mister Trent.' The President made as if to reach for Trent's hand but the effort was too great, or perhaps the shame. 'You will protect Mariana?'

Trent had expected the demand and understood it. He wasn't prepared to lie. 'My first duty is with you, sir, but I'll do my best.'

'I'm quite sure that your best will be most effective, Mister Trent,' the President said quietly.

Trent felt the knowledge drawn from him as their eyes met.

'Yes, indeed,' the President said. 'Good night, Mister Trent.'

'Good night, sir.'

Trent searched the kitchen. The staples were there and canned vegetables but there were no cans of meat. The President was a keen fisherman and Trent guessed that he hunted – despite the Pine Ridge being a Nature Reserve. Presidential privilege . . .

Chopping onion into a pot, he set it to soften in a little oil and went out to check the Land-Rover. A double-barrelled twelve-gauge stood upright in a gun rack between the two front seats. He found a hacksaw in the storage chest. Back in the kitchen, he stirred rice into the onion, added water and a stock cube and emptied two cans of black-eyed beans into a frying pan, with a half spoonful of chilli, black pepper and garlic purée. He would have preferred fresh garlic but there wasn't any.

In the few minutes that he had been preparing dinner, the water drippng from his clothes had formed a pool round his feet. He was avoiding Mariana and knew it. And he knew that he couldn't continue avoiding her – or not without catching pneumonia, he thought, and smiled at his own joke.

She hadn't moved from the sofa and didn't look up when he pushed open the door. He smiled as if nothing unusual had happened and said, 'Dinner in five minutes. I'll change into dry clothes.' He crossed to the table for his spare trousers and combat jacket.

From behind him Mariana said, 'He's drunk.'

'The bottle's nearly full.' Trent held it up as evidence.

'Don't lie to me.'

'I'm not.'

'You're avoiding the truth, which is the same thing. You do a lot of avoiding. Look at me, damn you. You do, don't you?' She seemed pleased that he didn't have an answer. 'Anyway he doesn't drink.'

'I hadn't heard that he did,' Trent said.

'What did you do to him?'

'Nothing.'

His answer failed to satisfy Mariana: 'You said you wouldn't hurt him.'

'Promised,' Trent corrected quietly. 'I don't break promises.'

'Ever?'

'Mariana, if you have to ask, there's no point in my answering.'

Taking his clothes, Trent checked the President. The old man was asleep and snoring. Satisfied that he was safe, Trent changed in the bathroom. He draped his wet clothes over a chair in front of the stove and ladled rice and beans on to two plates.

Mariana had moved to the table where he had left the map. She had found the photograph. Looking up at Trent, she searched his face for a resemblance. 'She's very beautiful. She's your mother, isn't she?'

'Yes.'

Again she studied the photograph: 'And your father?' There was doubt in her voice.

'The man I work for,' Trent said. 'He and my father were in the army together, friends. It's an old picture,' he added in an incompetent explanation of something she hadn't asked.

She said, 'Oh, I see,' as if it hadn't been obvious to her that the photograph was old. She looked away and Trent thought for a moment that she would leave it alone, but then she looked back and asked quickly, to get it out, 'Did your mother leave him for your father?'

Putting their dinner on the table, Trent reached for the photograph and studied it for the umpteenth time since finding it on Don Roberto's piano – his mother, and the Colonel as a young man. He accepted that the Colonel's look of complacent ownership had prompted Mariana's question, and that his mother, her face unseen by her escort, who lounged at her feet on the grass, projected a sense of distance and of slight embarrassment at the relationship implied by the taking of the picture.

Mistaking Trent's silence for rejection, Mariana said, 'I'm sorry. I was wrong to pry.'

'It's all right.' In part he was relieved that the photograph had prompted Mariana to pose the question in confirmation of his own suspicions. 'I don't know the answer,' he said. 'My parents died when I was twelve. I found the photograph last week in someone's house. Framed,' he added because the framing was important. The contrasting feelings displayed made the picture disturbing; not something to keep for nearly forty years, let alone frame in silver for display in the drawing-room.

He could see in Mariana's eyes that her thoughts mirrored his own. There were no variations of fading between the main body of the photograph and the edges, as there would have been had it been in the frame for years. 'Odd,' he said. And deliberate, he felt sure. A message? A warning? But of what, and why? His relationship with Don Roberto had been strictly business and even that had been in abeyance since Trent's posting to Ireland.

'She was very beautiful, your mother,' Mariana repeated into the silence: 'How did she die?'

'A car crash . . . ' His mother had driven their second-hand Jaguar into a concrete wall six weeks after his father's death. Fifteen years later Trent had visited the spot. The road ran straight across the desert for twenty miles. Then came the corner, the road bending round the walled compound of a Sheikh's racing stables. The wall stood twenty yards back from the road. Possibly his mother had fallen asleep at the wheel. 'She was driving very fast,' he said as he folded the map round the photograph and tucked it into the inner pocket of the waterproof saddlebag. Close to one hundred miles an hour had been the accident investigator's opinion.

'Eat while the food's hot,' he prodded Mariana. 'One day I'll cook properly for you on *Golden Girl*.' In their discussion of the photograph, Trent had forgotten for a moment that *Golden Girl* lay miles inland. 'If I can't get her back to the sea, I'll have to become a farmer,' he said. '*Golden Girl*'s all I've got.'

'Except for your job . . . ' Mariana, too, had spoken without thinking. But it was said and the barrier was back between them, built of suspicions neither of them dared bring to the surface . . . though Trent had intended asking her about her grandfather. Now the moment had passed.

Taking his plate through to the kitchen, he washed it and filled the kettle. Seated at the kitchen table, he began the long, tedious task of hacksawing all but eight inches off the barrels of the President's twelve-gauge. It wasn't a job he enjoyed. The gun had been handbuilt by Holland & Holland of London, perfectly balanced and beautifully engraved. The gunsmith would have murdered him or had a heart attack.

Mariana came to the door. For a moment she just looked, then she said in a strangled gasp, 'That's Gran'pa's gun.'

'I'm trying to protect him,' Trent said. 'Believe me, Mariana. A sawn-off shotgun is the best weapon in an enclosed space . . . other than a grenade,' he added for accuracy, and smiled. 'With grenades you need to be outside the enclosed space.'

She said, 'Oh, I see,' and went through to the bathroom. The partition door was thin and the door was a poor fit.

To give her privacy, Trent said to the door, 'I'll try the radio. Give me a shout when you're finished and we'll have coffee.'

He broadcast his message to the US Embassy, repeating it a dozen times. He wasn't discouraged by the static. Compared to the DEA's sophisticated equipment the President's radio was akin to a man running uphill with a message in a forked stick.

Mariana called him. She was already pouring coffee. He sat down at the kitchen table and picked up the hacksaw. She put a mug in front of him: 'Gran'pa was already drunk when you got here, wasn't he?'

'Yes.' He began sawing.

'Don't,' she said and he stopped. 'Who are you meant to be protecting?'

'The President.'

'But you weren't, were you? You were protecting me.'

'I'm trying to do both.'

'By lying to me?'

'I've never lied to you, Mariana.'

'You haven't told me the truth.'

'I don't know the truth.'

He had bits and pieces of it, and suspicions in which he found difficulty believing, and wished not to believe, despite the growing evidence . . . but not the whole thing. Not yet. Though he sensed that he was getting close – his goal, the gringo brain behind the coup, of whom Miguelito had boasted. He knew that he should discuss her grandfather with Mariana but remained frightened of hurting her, or of being the immediate instrument of her hurt.

'It's complicated . . . ' he began. Which was what adults told children, he thought: *You're too young to understand.* And he'd lost her.

'I don't need your damned protection,' she said. 'I can look after myself. Leave me alone. Do your bloody job. Bloody, that's exactly what it is.' She grabbed up her coffee and slammed the door behind her.

Trent understood her anger. It was born of fear for her grandfather, he thought as he returned to his butchery of the President's shotgun. Finished, he stripped down his Walther. Thumbing the bullets out on to a sheet of old newspaper, he set to work with his knife. He heard the President stumble in the bathroom. Reloading the Walther, he waited for the lavatory to flush before going through to help the old man back to bed. He tucked his Walther under the old man's pillow: 'Just in case, sir . . . ' Then he tried the radio again.

Mariana was asleep on the sofa. He covered her with a blanket and set the alarm clock to ring in an hour, wrapping it in a towel. He slept, sitting at the table, the towel his pillow. Waking, he again broadcast to Caspar. Mariana slept restlessly, curled up like a child. Watching her, Trent recalled sailing towards what he had expected to be his

163

death the previous morning on *Golden Girl* . . . his sense
of deprivation, of having been robbed of his right to a
normal life. By the Colonel. Opening the saddlebag, he
took out the photograph.

ELEVEN

Although the main body of the hurricane had moved north, vicious squalls still tore at the mountainside, flaying the incessant downpour into giant whips of solid water that lashed across the meadow. Trent lay on the roof under a rubber poncho he'd found in the kitchen. He had been there for an hour and a half. The wind and wet had sucked the warmth out of his blood and he shivered constantly. He had wanted rain. If the attack came, the attackers would be confident in their numbers. Their desire to escape the rain might hurry their attack – not much but enough to give him a small advantage.

He had begun his watch half an hour before first light. Now it was the law, sent by Caspar, who were coming. Without binoculars Trent could decipher the POLICE signs on the two Land-Rovers' front doors as the sharp bends in the track forced the drivers broadside to the cabin. They would be at the light barricade at the bottom of the dip in ten minutes. Five minutes to clear the trees. A further five minutes to the vee-shaped barricade where they would be forced to leave the vehicles, then five minutes walk up the meadow.

Sliding down the pitch of the roof, hidden from the track, Trent dropped to the ground. Back in the kitchen, he blew the embers up in the stove, added a couple of logs and put the kettle on. Mariana hadn't moved from the couch. She had slept restlessly but the slim shape under the blankets now lay still. Trent guessed that she was awake.

'The good guys have won. Police,' he said. 'They'll be here in twenty minutes. Kettle's on.'

Returning to the warmth of the kitchen stove, he stripped and pulled on the clothes he'd worn on the motor cycle. They were damp but warm. He slung the twin cartridge belts over his shoulders and tucked a roll of the heavy tape into each of his jacket pockets before making coffee. He carried the pot and three mugs through to the front room.

She was sitting up now. The anger remained in her, hoarded from the previous night when she had slammed the door on him. Sleep had flattened one side of her Afro and a curl had broken free above her forehead. He considered going to her and brushing the curl back, but he wasn't sure how she would react. Probably bite his hand off, he decided and smiled instead.

'You look like a unicorn,' he said.

She pushed at the curl, then reached down for the shoulder-bag that lay at her feet and dug out an ebony hair pick. 'You don't have to stare.'

He crossed to the window. Through the heart-shaped cut-out in the shutter, he saw the Land-Rovers disappear into the dip where he'd felled the small trees.

'You said they were police,' Mariana said.

She referred to his cartridge belts. 'Think of them as a business suit,' Trent said. 'I'll wake your grandfather.'

Taking the third mug of coffee from the tray, he carried it through to the bedroom. The old man looked a wreck. His hands shook as he took the mug. Trent surprised a disconcertingly familiar look in his eyes, a combination of guilt, anger and bitterness that he had learnt to recognise in his own father as the approach of one more milestone in his downward journey. Secretary to the Jockey Club,

166

Secretary to the Polo Club – the clubs ever smaller and in more distant outposts of equestrian society. Trent had gained from that odyssey a mastery of languages and dialects supported by an education shared both with the children of the social élite and with the riff-raff of the stableyard. Captain Hamilton Mahoney, despite his financial disasters, had been a loving, understanding, and exciting father. But prone to lapses of memory after a binge . . .

Unsure of how much the President would remember of the previous day, Trent reintroduced himself. 'Trent, sir. Anti-Terrorist Unit. British.' As an employer, EC lacked punch.

The President fumbled at the bedtable for his glasses. Trent found them on the floor and watched the old man thread the sprung arms over his ears. 'The police are coming up the valley, Mr President,' he warned, as a hint to him that he should tidy himself. 'Looks as if you're safe now, but keep my pistol handy just in case.'

The old man seemed lost for a moment. Then, remembering, he fumbled under the pillows for Trent's Walther. He realised how odd he must look, sitting up in bed, silver bristling his cheeks, coffee mug in one hand, long-barrelled pistol in the other. With a touch of irony, he said, 'Thank you, Mister Trent. I feel better already.'

Politicians were masters of the quick recovery, Trent thought as he went back to the front room. 'He's fine,' he told Mariana and crossed to the window, checking his watch. He had expected the police to have reappeared.

Finally a single Land-Rover ground over the ridge and stopped at the barricade. The second must have got stuck at the first trees – or the driver hadn't bothered to navigate the obstacle. Trent watched the policemen drop down from the vehicle; four of them. He couldn't see their faces. Ponchos, like the one he'd used as protection on the roof, covered their khaki uniforms. One of them waved a greeting at the cabin – the sergeant, Trent presumed. Spreading out a little, they came up the hill, rain and wind pushing them, sometimes staggering under the force of it. They held their automatic rifles across their midriffs, four friends out for a day's sport.

'They're here,' Trent told Mariana and called back to the bedroom: 'Mister President . . . '

Then he remembered another morning. A morning with US Special Forces in South-East Asia. Rangers jumping from a helicopter and spreading out in this same way, a little over-confident as many American soldiers tended to be, hyped up by TV and movie images to believe in their innate superiority. Belpan's police force, if at all, were trained in the British police tradition.

Four down the hill – the others covering the cabin's rear from the mountain. The delay had been to give the second team time to gain position. He was a little surprised to find that he wasn't afraid. But there wasn't much to fear once you could see the enemy. From then on it was just a job of work to be done. You succeeded or failed.

He looked back at Mariana. Since waking, she had hardly moved. Seeing her sitting there, clinging to her anger, Trent was reminded, suddenly, of a mother in a famine-relief camp cradling a dead child – frozen in grief. If she released her grasp, she would have nothing left. Despite any explanations he might offer her, he had to remain the enemy. For the moment, the alternative was too painful to her.

'I'm sorry, Mariana,' he said. 'I made a mistake. The good guys are bad guys in disguise.'

He slid the table into the centre of the room, tipping it on to its side, and dragged over the couch with Mariana still on it, so that the furniture formed a fort. He laid the sawn-off shotgun on the sofa beside her. Her expression hadn't changed. 'Keep down. Don't move. Don't look. If they come in, shoot them . . . if you want to,' he added. The choice was hers.

Forcing open the door against the wind, he waved at the

advancing policeman and stepped clear of the cabin so that they would see he was unarmed. Watching him, they were unable to see each other so could only guess at what warned him.

He ran, neither weaving nor ducking, unarmed and apparently panicked, across the face of the meadow towards the treeline, leaping a low bush, hearing shots. There was little chance of his being hit, but he slipped deliberately, pitching forward, striking the ground with his shoulder and rolling fast for the ravine where he'd hidden the first gun. Once, twice, three times, he rolled, hands scrabbling at the mud, crashing through light scrub for the safety of the trees and the ravine.

He lay there for a moment, getting his breath. Then he was up and levering the round boulder free, not listening to it crash down the mountain, doubting if the attackers would hear or see – and, if they did, whether they would be persuaded that it was his own body tumbling – but it was one extra little chance that cost him only a few seconds. Tearing the wrapping from the pump gun, he unzipped the case and headed uphill fast through the pines. He had planned it carefully, rehearsing every move in his head.

The upper team would have been on the logging track above the natural amphitheatre when he broke for cover. He thought that they would stay there, the track giving them visibility and line of fire. They would have radios.

He crossed the track on his belly and went on up a further hundred yards before starting his circle. He had to take out the man furthest from him first, the man least prepared.

The wind and rain were on his side, masking his movements. It was an old game, familiar from his past, and he was expert in it. His quarry crouched on a rock at the apex of a slight bend in the track from whence he could see in both directions. He held his gun ready – one of the Kalashnikovs which Trent had smuggled ashore. He wore a jungle hat, the brim streaming waterfalls on to his poncho.

169

Trent waited for a squall to hit, then moved fast, dropping to the ground and crawling the last few yards.

'*Ola, amigo mio,*' he whispered, watching the man's shoulder-blades leap as if dragged together by a ten-ton truck. 'No sound, no movement,' he warned. 'The shotgun in your back is loaded with deershot. Even think of being stupid and I'll blow your spine through your navel.'

Against a rifle, the man might have risked diving for the trees. But against a shotgun . . .

'Let me see your face. Slowly, and your hands where I can see them,' Trent cautioned.

Trent was reassured by the absence of hate in the dark, watchful, Latin eyes that faced him. The man was short, slim, mid-thirties. Old enough to have already proved his courage and, like Trent, a professional.

'You and I are peons,' Trent advised, a slight smile of complicity supporting his argument. 'Let the Big Ones die . . . if they have the belly for it. You have a name?'

'José,' the man whispered, his lips hardly moving.

'Good,' Trent said. 'You may look back down the mountain. Up here, how many are you?'

'Three.'

'Positioned?'

José nodded down the track to his right.

'The man closest to you – he also has a name?'

'Juanito.'

'And the third man?'

'We call him the Eel . . . '

'You will use your radio to summon Juanito,' Trent commanded. 'Tell him that you believe there is someone moving below. And be careful in your conversation. I would take no pleasure in killing you.'

With the rain beating at the trees and the wind whistling there was no chance of José using intonation as a warning. Satisfied, Trent ordered him back into the pines. He hit him hard on the neck with the side of his hand, catching him as he fell. Taping the man's mouth, hands, and ankles took less than a minute. Then Trent was up and running – important that he halt Juanito well before José's position or the man would be warned by José's absence.

The track ran along the lip of the natural amphitheatre, no trees guarding it from the eighty-foot drop to the small lake, so Trent could look out from his ambush across the track to the meadow below. The cabin was barely visible in the rain. No shots had come from there. Trent hadn't expected any, but took no pleasure in being proved correct.

Juanito belied the diminutive in his name. Bigger and far heavier than José, broken-nosed, more thug than thinker, dangerous in that his actions would be unpremeditated. Trent took him from the rear. A hard sweep of his right hand, the edge smashing into the big man's neck, should have felled the Latin American, but hidden beneath his poncho he wore a studded leather collar. The studs bit into Trent's hand. Juanito shook his head clear as he rounded on Trent. Trent had to stay in close or be shot down, but in close, the big man had the advantage of weight and strength.

Trent kicked at the man's right knee. Juanito was ready for him, and the Kalashnikov crashed down at Trent's calf. He grabbed at the barrel and fell with it so that the power of the big man was added to his own strength. Trent twisted as he fell, the whole weight of his body tearing the rifle free of the man's hands.

With a roar of fury, Juanito was after him, boot swinging at Trent's head, the rifle loose on the ground between them. Trent rolled again, the boot carving up the side of his skull, the big man thrown off balance again by his own weight. Trent struck up between the man's legs, right hand stiff as a piece of iron. Juanito screamed, falling, hands gouging for Trent's throat. Trent bunched his knees up as a fulcrum and as the man hit them, grasped the big man's trousers at the waist, heaving for his life. The man tumbled on forward and over the edge of the track, a scattering of rocks heard through his scream and the splash as he hit the water eighty feet below. Trent rolled to the other side of the track, grabbing for his pump gun.

'Freeze, Gringo.'

The Eel, Trent thought – tall, thin, small black eyes bright with natural malice, rain drops shimmering on his dark, oily skin, the Kalashnikov in his hands steady as a rock.

'Drop the gun.'

Trent dropped it.

'Hands behind your head.'

Trent obeyed.

The Eel spat over the cliff. 'A pig . . . we are well rid of him. José?'

'Alive,' Trent said. 'In the trees.'

'Take me to him. Walk carefully,' the Eel warned.

A pine tree grew out of the face of the amphitheatre a little ahead of them and fifteen feet below the edge of the track. Then a further sixty-five-foot drop to the water. He would be killed even if he didn't hit a rock – though there had been a far greater profusion of rocks visible the previous evening. Rain had fallen continuously, the mountain spilling waterfalls into the amphitheatre. How deep was the water now, Trent wondered.

Beyond the pine, and a little lower on the cliff, a dozen or so bushes grew from a wide fissure. Below the bushes lay a ledge and then a sheer rock face plunging forty feet to the clay-reddened lake. Or be shot in the back of the head? It wasn't much of a choice.

Trent's thoughts returned to the murdered pilot. At least he retained his sight. And he *must* keep his eyes open, seeing all the way down. A shard of flint on the track marked the point. Seven paces, Trent thought. His mind had become detached from his body so that he was watching himself. This also was familiar to him, the ability, at times

172

of danger, to issue commands to his body as if it were a separate entity. Now! he thought and dived for the tree.

Swing, he screamed at himself as his arms crashed into the pine, not holding, but the weight of his body already carrying him on in the next arc of his trajectory. Don't think, *look*, he screamed against the desire to shut his eyes against the terror of the fall. His right hip struck the rockside above the bushes. Then he was clinging to them, even as he felt them tear loose from the rock. Then the ledge below, the rock edge ripping his hands, and his shoulders almost jerked out of their sockets as he fought his boots flat for a hundredth of a second against the cliff face.

Pushing hard back against the mountain, he spun backwards out from the rock, curling over in the air so slowly that he could watch, in slow motion, first the passing overhead of the dark clouds, then the mountains, the far side of the valley, the meadow, the cabin, and, at last, the lake red with mud. He tucked himself into a tight ball, and, at the last moment, rolled on to his side from terror of the rocks beneath the surface. The breath smashed out of him as he hit. Clay soup filled his mouth, then came the punch of washed-down mud cushioning his body from the final hit of the rock beneath. It smashed into his ribs, forcing his mouth open again, more soup choking into his lungs, his eyes gummed with it as he fought for the surface.

The cliff face protected him from the Eel above. His right leg was numb, his right side ripped and bleeding. He knew that some ribs were broken; it was a matter of how many.

The Eel, on the radio to his four companions, would be running down the path Trent had ridden the previous afternoon on his motor cycle. Trent looked across the lake. Even had he the strength, the swim would take him out from the protection of the cliff. Desperately he hauled himself along the cliff face, right leg dragging over rocks, waterfalls bucketing their charge of stones and gravel on his head.

Fifty yards. He kept on telling himself how short the

173

distance. He counted each fresh handgrip as a half-pace. He encouraged himself with promises that after ten paces he could rest, then demanded of himself that he manage another five and another five until he lost count of how far he'd come and how far he had to go. Through the beating of the rain he thought that he could hear the Eel, feet scrabbling on the gravel path. He imagined being shot in the water and it closing over his head, filling his mouth and lungs, the last moments of life choked out of him. Dying with a whimper, he thought.

The little beach where Mariana had played as a child was to his left. He felt the gravel shelve up under his feet and staggered free of the water. Looking down the meadow to the cabin, he saw no sign yet of the other four but the Eel was very close. Trent fumbled with his right hand behind his neck, then collapsed on the sand where he lay sprawled, his right arm thrown back above his head, clay-sodden hair shading his eyes.

The Eel came round the bushes, saw him and cried his triumph. He walked strangely, swaying at the hips, thin and tall, vicious and deadly. He held his Kalashnikov in both hands, but not aimed at Trent because there was no need. The Gringo was finished. To be certain, he kicked Trent twice on the sole of his right boot. Then he spoke into his radio. 'I have him.'

Now! Trent thought and brought his right arm over fast and smoothly.

The Latino dropped his gun, his hands leaping halfway to his throat before his knees lost their strength. He crumpled quite slowly, the surprise still frozen in his black eyes. Crawling over, Trent pulled his small matt-black throwing-knife out of the man's throat, cleaning the blade before replacing it in the sheath between his shoulder-blades. He thought of taking the man's rifle but knew it was too heavy for him and that he would be incapable of aiming it. He crawled over to the fallen branch by the big pine, found his second shotgun and unwrapped it. The fall had torn one belt from his shoulder, and the cartridges in the other would be too swollen with water to fit the breach. Eight shots, Trent thought, and dragging himself to his feet, he leaned against the big pine, waiting. He wasn't sure if they would all come but thought that they would.

They came: a tight little group, guns in the crooks of their arms, chatting and laughing amongst themselves, like hunters strolling up to view the bag after a fine day in the field.

Trent waited till they were close. He was too tired to care about the morality of it. It was something to be done. He stepped clear of the tree, firing from the hip. The recoil tore at the ripped muscles in his right arm and shoulder. He thought of holding one shell back but he couldn't be bothered. He walked down the hill without looking at the dead men, slowly and with difficulty and pain. In what seemed to him to be the far distance he could see Mariana and the President climbing up the meadow to meet him.

He didn't want to talk. He wanted to sleep – preferably between clean white sheets in his own bed upstairs in his cottage on the Hamble. Then he remembered that the cottage had been sold, the money placed in trust for his father's mother, the income paying the fees of the nursing home where she sat all day rocking herself in a wheelchair – Alzheimer's disease. The sale of the cottage and the setting-up of the trust had been Colonel Smith's doing. Trent had owned and lived in the cottage as Patrick Mahoney, and Patrick Mahoney was dead.

Tired of it all, he sat down on the thin, wet, short grass. Mariana reached him first.

Trent let her take his gun. 'Did they hurt you?' he asked.
'No.'
'No . . . ' Then he added, 'I didn't think they would,' and looked up into the muzzle of his own pistol held steady in the President's hand.

TWELVE

Like a giant steam-iron, a fresh squall flattened the tops of the trees at the bottom of the meadow below the cabin. A momentary gap in the cloud let through the sun. The sunlight struck the almost solid curtain of rain at the head of the squall and the brilliant arc of a rainbow leaped across the mountainside. The cloud gap closed and the yachtsman in Trent watched the curtain of rain drive up the slope, the cabin disappearing behind the curtain.

Trent saw the President's finger tighten on the pistol trigger. Automatically he calculated the strike of the rain-front. The squall would rock the President. At that instant, Trent knew that he could slap the pistol out of the old man's hand. He knew that it would be a kindness. He was too tired . . . tired of caring.

The squall hit.

To Mariana it was a slap in the face, unfreezing her. She jerked the shotgun up at her grandfather's belly. 'Hurt him and I'll kill you. I will,' she insisted like a child threatening to misbehave.

Mariana's rage was so tightly channelled that it struck the old man with the force of a physical blow. The strength went out of him. He gave a slight shrug that accepted his granddaughter's hate, lowered the pistol and turned to walk back down the meadow to the cabin.

The beaten slump of his shoulders was familiar to Trent. He tried to shout after the old man but all that came were memories. Memories of his father, Secretary of the Gulf States Jockey Club. Trent had been twelve years old. His mother had been crying. Frightened of her tears, Trent had ridden his bicycle round to his father's office at the stables. He had opened the door without knocking and found his father at his desk. His father had looked round, and Trent remembered the total emptiness in his eyes – an emptiness that had changed to pleading. Trent had wanted to run to him, to throw himself into his father's arms, to hug and kiss him, to tell him how much he loved him. He had wanted to cry but the tears wouldn't come and his legs wouldn't work. He'd stood there, frozen-faced. The big old-fashioned ceiling fan flup-flupped into the silence between them. Such a short distance between them. And the revolver in his father's hand . . .

Trent had turned on his heel and walked out down the covered verandah, his sandals striking the tiles like the tick of the big grandfather clock in his uncle's house. Honorary uncle. Colonel Smith DSO, MBE, MC, who had retired from the Army and worked in London at something or other that was never clear, at an office in Curzon Street. By the time Colonel Smith made his approach, Trent had read enough espionage books to have made the connection between Curzon Street and Military Intelligence.

Dodging the stable-boys, Trent had hidden at the back of a loose box, his knees hugged tight to his chest. Even now he could recall the feel of the straw and the wet dung and sweat scent of horses . . . and that he had been dry-eyed but filled with fear of what his father might be doing. Not putting a name to it, but knowing that if his father did do it, the fault would be his for not having said or done anything. He had wanted to do something, he had wanted

177

to hug his father and plead with him. But he hadn't had the words or the understanding except to know that his father wanted to leave him and his mother for good, which meant that their love must have been insufficient. Trent's acceptance of this insufficiency had made the distance between the door and the desk too great to bridge because he must have already failed to bridge it for his father to want to leave him. He had heard the shot.

He looked up at Mariana; the rain washing down her cheeks disguised her tears. He considered holding out his hand to the girl – an offer of comfort – but recalled his own terror of disintegrating.

He had sat in the rear of the loose box hugging his knees tight against his chest for fear of falling apart, terrified that someone would find him, because the slightest communication might be the trigger that would slacken his grasp on himself. He had forced himself to slither sideways into the corner so that the angle of the two walls held him from rocking himself. Even now he was unable to recall who had found him or how but he remembered the flight back to London, the packet hung round his neck containing his ticket and passport. At Bahrain airport he had wrapped his arms round himself so that his mother couldn't force on him his stuffed lion cub for company on the flight, knowing that its warmth in his arms would have brought the tears flowing beyond control. And he had fought against her attempt to kiss him. He remembered the threatening kindness of the air stewardess pressing her comfort on him. Colonel Smith's housekeeper had picked him up at Heathrow. He'd been safe at the Colonel's house – no emotion there to threaten his composure.

Easy, Trent thought, for Colonel Smith to instruct him now to build a new persona as if the last fear-filled year in Ireland had been of greater importance than those few moments in his father's office.

He wished the rain would stop. He had no further need

for it, or for the wind. He was too tired to wipe the water out of his eyes.

He said to Mariana, 'There's a man up the mountain. Bound.' He described how to find José. 'Cut his feet free. Leave me the gun.' No need for Mariana to know that the shotgun with which she had threatened her grandfather was empty. 'You won't need it. He's a professional.'

Trent accepted Mariana's disapproval. Picking sides came easily when young. With experience the frontiers melted, judgments were harder to make.

José came first down the mountain. Hands taped behind his back, he walked awkwardly, stumbling on the rocky path. Mariana followed at a safe distance. Part of her anger now directed at the Latino, she had found a heavy stick which she carried two-handed over her shoulder like a base-ball bat. A false move from José and she would club him over the head.

José skirted the bodies of his companions. He glanced back towards the lake and saw the Eel sprawled dead by the water's edge.

Trent nodded at the ground and the Latino sat, facing him. There was a companionship between them. They had gambled their lives, and now the surge of adrenaline was over they were in the familiar physical calm that always followed. Almost an apartness from their bodies, Trent thought.

To Mariana, he said, 'I think we'll get on better if we're left alone. That's if you wouldn't mind . . . '

She did mind. Trent accepted her reluctance to face her grandfather but also knew that to feel she was protecting him gave her a purpose that anchored her in the midst of chaos.

'I may have to threaten,' he said. 'Do things. It's harder with someone watching.' That she was a young woman, delicate of emotion, to be protected from the sight of vio-lence, was there by implication.

Deliberately she looked back at the dead bodies, rain seeping blood down the slope.

'Don't go too far away,' Trent said. 'I may need you.'

Her honour was satisfied. The two men watched her walk away to the protection of a fir tree fifty yards to their left. She sat with her back to the trunk so that she could watch them, cudgel grasped across her knees. Her guardianship of Trent touched both men.

'*Muy peligrosa, la chiquita,*' the Latino said – Very dangerous, the young girl – joking, not to deny his feelings, but to share with Trent their mutual understanding. '*Y tan linda,*' he added. Beautiful . . .

As with the four members of Louis' charter party and the Eel, José spoke with a harsher and less musical accent than that of Mario's Colombian thugs whom Trent had brought ashore from the motor yacht – one more piece of the jigsaw puzzle slipping into place. Miguelito, with his boasting, had set Trent in the right direction. 'You are from Nicaragua?'

'*Si, Señor.*'

'And Louis was a Contra,' Trent suggested as if it was both obvious and unimportant.

José nodded. 'All of us, Señor.'

'Trained by the Americans,' Trent said, again as if it was of no consequence: 'I saw it in the way those others came up the meadow.' Both men found their eyes drawn back for a moment to the men Trent had shot.

So the dead lay sprawled in war and José said, 'Louis was our Commandante, Señor.'

'Life is hard for us peons, and for those we love,' Trent said quietly and glanced across at Mariana. 'You have a daughter?'

'Of fifteen years,' the Latino answered. 'And two sons, eight and two . . . '

'You have luck,' Trent said. He indicated the dead men. 'Friends?'

'Colleagues.' The dead were dead, scores in a match that his team had lost. Perhaps Trent would add him to the body-count – this was Trent's choice. There was nothing that the Latino could do. But it was important to him that he should conduct himself with dignity.

Face, Trent thought. The Arabs of his childhood had placed the same value on it as did Latin Americans and the peoples of Indo-China. Not the Arab city dwellers but the men of the desert. If you must die, you must die, but do so as a man. It was a concept foreign to the Americans, even of Trent's circle, their lack of understanding leading them frequently into mistakes of policy when dealing with the Third World. Trent had tried to explain it once to a Special Forces Major. Think of a Mexican peasant – the local landowner wants his patch of land. He sends his men. The peasant knows they will kill him, and he has nothing to fight with. All he can do is stand straight and spit in the leader's eye. Face . . . 'Goddamned romantic,' had been the Major's comment.

'The girl has been hurt by her grandfather's betrayal,' Trent said now to José.

'Politicians . . . ' The Latino spat between his feet. 'Pigs, all of them.'

'In Africa,' Trent said, 'the Nigerians say of politicians that they are men who say, "Vote for me that I may be of greater importance than you".'

They shared the joke for a moment, a slight smile slipping across José's narrow lips.

A squall drove up the meadow, lashing rain into Trent's face. He shivered. He wanted to be under cover but it was better out here, the Latino unprotected. He mustn't hurry: 'You have cigarettes?'

'In my jacket.'

Leaning forward, Trent felt for and found a tin in the breast pocket. There were matches with the cigarettes. First he took José's hat, shaking the rain from its brim. Then he lit a cigarette and placed it between José's lips. He gave him a minute in which to enjoy the tobacco, then asked: 'You can get out of the country?'

'God willing.' The Latino blinked and coughed as the smoke swirled into his eyes.

Trent took the cigarette, cupping it in his palm in the shelter of his back until the Latino nodded his readiness.

Replacing the cigarette between the man's lips, Trent said, 'When we leave, we will cut you loose.'

It was a promise without strings attached and was accepted as such. 'It will be a kindness.'

Again Trent held the cigarette, fighting against the fatigue that threatened to cloud his thoughts. He returned the cigarette to José so that there could be no hint of bargaining or threat.

Trent looked over at Mariana, knowing that José would do the same. 'To force information from the old man would be hurtful to the girl. Perhaps even harmful,' he added quietly, still studying her. 'The mind of a young woman, her emotions . . .'

'These are delicate,' the Latino agreed.

'We are placed by our work in situations not of our choosing,' Trent said, using the *we* and *our* to underline their alliance. He looked back at José, repeating the Latino's own words: 'It would be a kindness . . .'

Trent struggled to his feet. The feeling had returned to his right leg. The thigh muscles were already stiff, the bruising deep, and he was forced to stand very upright to keep at bay the sharp lances of pain in his side. He exaggerated the extent of his incapacity, determined to show José that, even given information, he would be incapable of action. Looking down, he said with a wry smile of self-mockery, 'I must attempt to release those of the Government who have been taken.'

'They are at a *finca*,' José said.

'With Mario's men?' Trent asked as he helped José to his

182

feet, putting an arm round his shoulders, leaning on him: 'With your permission.'

'It is my pleasure. Yes, with Mario's men. *La Punta del Colonel Ingles*,' José added quietly. 'That is the name of the *finca*.' English Colonel's Point.

Trent thanked him. 'Even should I be captured no one will know from where I got this information.'

'That also will be a kindness.'

'Perhaps you would help me to the cabin?'

Mariana joined them, carrying the shotgun in one arm, supporting Trent with the other. They left José in the shelter of the carport, his feet bound again.

In the cabin Mariana eased up Trent's shirt, binding his ribs with tape. He heard a metallic click from the President's bedroom followed by another and then the harsh thud of solid metal falling on wood. Opening the door, Trent already knew what he would face.

The old man sat at his desk staring at the wall of rough-cut logs. Tears ran down his cheeks – no sobs or whimpers – tears leaking in a slow steady stream down cheeks that seemed to have collapsed in on themselves so that where there had been lines, there were now dark ravines softly powdered with the silver of an old man's beard. Trent's Walther lay on the floor beside the President's chair and two of the bullets from which Trent had removed the powder the previous night were on the rug.

Trent retrieved the automatic, freed the magazine, thumbed out the remaining eight bullets and reloaded with live ammunition from the box in his pocket. 'I'm sorry,' he said, and almost laid a hand on the President's shoulder, but he heard Mariana and looked round to see the self-protective anger back in her eyes. He tried to block Mariana's view of her grandfather, though unsure as to whom he was protecting, and led her back into the living-room and closed the door.

'You loaded your pistol with blanks.'

Trent nodded and watched her as she tried to assess her feelings. A slight frown drew two vertical lines above her nose.

'I didn't save your life,' she said, as if guns rather than her unleashed contempt had driven her grandfather back to the cabin. She looked up at him: 'You knew last night.'

'Suspected,' Trent corrected. 'Whoever's behind this needed a figurehead. The damping-down of the Cold War's changed things here and in Latin America. For a government to be recognised, there has to be a semblance of legitimacy.' All true and easy to say but useless as balm to the bitter disgust and sense of betrayal Mariana was suffering.

He said, 'I'm sorry,' knowing that he was repeating himself. He had a job to do; he had to get moving; but to do so would be an evasion of the more immediate responsibility for Mariana.

His training made him an expert on the emotions that motivated people, his life frequently depending on the accuracy of his analysis. Offering comfort was more difficult, he thought, as he felt the pain behind Mariana's anger, the brittle vulnerability of a twenty-year-old. She needed the release of tears, and he fought against all his training to unguard his eyes to her. Pain had shrunk her physically, her lips were drawn in, her hair was flattened by the rain. He imagined, as he looked into the darkness of her eyes, that she would shatter at any moment into unmendable fragments.

He opened his arms to her, risking rejection. Their eyes held for a moment, Trent suddenly the more vulnerable. Mariana's recognition of the reversal in roles eased the tightness out of her lips, her eyes lightening as she took a half-step forward and buried her face against his chest.

Holding Mariana, Trent looked over the top of her head at the closed door, his thoughts going back to his father – the sense of inadequacy that had made his father buy expensive presents for Trent and his mother, the money borrowed from the Jockey Club or Polo Club bank account to be replaced at the end of the month but not replaced. Trent recalled his own guilt and his mother's at being responsible as recipients of the gifts – guilt spiralling them down, his father into alcoholic desperation, while they waited for the inevitable accounting – nothing said between them – as if silence would make it go away or stop it happening.

Trent's thoughts went to the old man in the next room, President of a bankrupt joke of a nation, despite its vote at the UN, but still a President – the children and grand-children whose expectations he had tried to fulfil, education abroad, jobs, apartments, clothes, cars – too easy simply to condemn the almost inevitable drift into corruption.

'Try not to judge,' he said, gently stroking her hair.

Mariana drew back, looking up at him, eyes wet, nose running. He kissed her forehead. Their lips touched lightly. Easy to kiss, he thought, enfolding her back into his arms – physical love, easy but meaningless without the words which Mariana needed – and other women in his past had needed. Were the words blocked by the years of training in secrecy and in playing a part, he wondered, or had he always been secretive, this secretiveness a quality or malady that had led to his recruitment? The chicken or the egg?

Into the rain-wet softness of her hair he murmured, 'I'm good at writing reports.'

'And killing people.' A slight smile touched Mariana's lips as she freed herself from his arms, the abrupt change in mood a benefit of youth. 'I'm all right now.'

'Sure?'

'I think so.' She sniffed. 'I don't suppose you've got a Kleenex?'

Automatically he felt in the pockets of his drenched combat jacket: bullets, tape, knife. 'I'm sorry . . . '

'I know. It's all right,' she said and wiped her nose on the back of her sleeve.

'I have to talk to him,' Trent said. He looked at his watch. 'Fifteen minutes . . .'

The old man had been President for twenty years. Before that he had been Chief Minister under British colonial rule. Far stronger in character than his own father, Trent thought, as he watched the President almost physically regather the mantle of office about him as he looked up.

'I need to know how it happened,' Trent said with no preamble.

It had begun with money appearing in the President's New York account at the Chase Manhattan, quite small amounts at first. He had been able to pretend to himself that the oversight was his, a mistake in his accounting. He said, 'Perhaps I shouldn't have an account outside the country but it's convenient.' He'd spent the money. The sums got bigger. 'Five thousand dollars, ten thousand.'

'Over what period?' Trent asked.

'The past year . . .'

Faced by the larger amounts, the President had persuaded himself that it was too late to stop, and that somehow it would come out all right. Nothing had been asked of him. No contact had been made. 'You know how it is?'

Then, on a semi-official visit to London, he'd returned to his suite at the Savoy Hotel after a meeting with a junior minister at the Foreign Office. The family photographs he travelled with were missing from his bedside table. One of a pair of large black Samsonite suitcases had been taken from the wardrobe and lay on the valet's bench. The locks were undone. The President opened the case. The photographs were there and the lining slit back to disclose a double bottom packed with neat cellophane packets of powdery white crystal. Despite never having seen cocaine or heroin, he knew the powder was one or the other.

'We've had visits from the US Drug Enforcement Agency,' the President told Trent. 'And you read about it. You know? And watch thrillers on the video recorder.'

One of the packets was open. The President had touched a moistened fingertip to the powder as detectives did in the movies. In the movies the detectives tasted the stuff. He'd been frightened.

'We ran a DRUGS KILL campaign here, posters. That was two years ago,' he told Trent. But detectives always tasted, so finally he'd plucked up his courage. The crystals were bitter and numbed the tip of his tongue.

The President had stood there irresolute, knowing it was his last chance. He knew that he had to call someone but didn't know who to call or how to explain the rest. It would have to come out . . . the money. It was obvious that whoever had set him up had taken photographs of the suitcase showing his family photographs along with the drugs. The President imagined the newspapers, front page.

Trent pictured the scene with understanding and even a little sympathy. The rat caught in the trap. But who had set the trap? Who had walked down the carpeted corridor, package under his arm? A guest of the hotel familiar with its workings. And someone with access to drugs, or to someone else who had.

Though Trent had never stayed at the Savoy, he knew it reasonably well. Each school vacation he had been taken there to tea by the Colonel as a holiday treat. As an adult, he had lunched occasionally in the River Room and at the Buttery and had drinks at the American Bar. And another piece of the jigsaw slipped into place as he visualised the short flight of stairs that led up from the lobby to the Buttery and American Bar. The gift shop was on the left at the top of the stairs, and, opposite it, a big display window of blue tapestry luggage woven with mediaeval animal designs. Steve, the American, had carried one of those bags at Cancun Airport. Now only the linkage was missing, Trent thought as he looked down at the President.

'You flushed the packets down the lavatory?'

187

The President nodded, shamefaced. 'It was the only thing to do,' he said, a slight smile covering his embarrassment.

The Little Boy act, Trent thought, suddenly disgusted but keeping his anger hidden as he thought of fellow Catholics in Northern Ireland excusing themselves for not reporting the IRA: 'They're Catholics, too, boy, ye' know how it is . . . ' Using their Catholicism as an excuse for the cowardice that left the country prey to vicious murderers. The Protestants were no different.

'What did you do with the suitcase?'

Presidents of even the smallest countries were under continual escort for their own safety. The President had spent an hour searcing at Foyle's for books that Mariana would enjoy. On the one free day of his visit, he had taken the train down to Cambridge, where Mariana was attending a summer course, carrying the books in the suitcase. He had told his police escort from the Diplomatic Squad that he would be with Mariana in her rooms all afternoon and that the policeman should take the afternoon off from duty. Pretending to change his mind, the President caught an earlier train back to London and left the suitcase in a locker at Charing Cross station.

'I made sure there were no fingerprints,' he said with another smile. As if expecting to be congratulated for his cleverness, Trent thought.

The President's only instructions had come as anonymously as the money and the suitcase of drugs. Pencilled capital letters: SLEEP SATURDAY NIGHT AT YOUR MOUNTAIN CABIN. REMAIN THERE. YOU WILL BE COLLECTED.

Very careful and very businesslike – as befitted professionals, Trent thought, fighting to control his rage.

The President had told his story. Now he waited.

Trent knew that the old man had never had a chance. If the drug set-up hadn't worked, they would have got to him some other way. He had been stupid, venal, and finally so frightened and desperate that he had reached the point of first considering murder, then attempting to kill himself.

Trent refused to judge. 'I promised Mariana that I wouldn't harm you, sir.' A slight shrug: 'If I live to write it, there'll be nothing in my report. There's nothing to thank me for,' he continued quickly as the President began. 'I'm taking Mariana with me. If you want to walk out in the morning, you'll find the rotor arm to one of the police Land-Rovers tied to a tree ten miles down the track.'

THIRTEEN

Braced in the corner against the police Land-Rover's offside door, Trent watched Mariana fight the steering-wheel. The rain had turned the dirt-track into a quagmire through which the vehicle ground its way in low gear, wheels slithering in mud and kicking up stones, wipers slapping across the windshield.

The jagged white spikes of shattered treetrunks stuck up out of the undergrowth where the hurricane had torn huge rents in the forest. Ripped leaves dipped and surged like fighting kites across the clearings and above the track. Undisguised by the drum of rain on the Land-Rover's aluminium body and by the engine whine and wheel grind, they could hear the roaring of the river in spate and the rumble of boulders and treetrunks tumbled by the foaming water.

The mountain track leading down from the President's cabin crossed a dirt road close in to the foot of the mountains. Prior to the construction of the north–south highway, this road had formed the spine of Belpan's land communications. It ran parallel to the new highway and was connected to it by lesser tracks that came down from the forest logging-camps and from the occasional fertile valley or small plateau such as that on which the President's cabin stood.

Some of these tracks, after crossing the dirt road and highway, threaded their way between Belpan's many lagoons and swamps to the mosquito-ridden fishing villages hidden amongst the mangroves that cloaked the coast. The dirt road had been abandoned in favour of the new highway because of the construction costs involved in straightening the path it wove round the mountain foothills. But, prior to its abandonment, the fifty-mile stretch closest to Belpan City had been tarred. It was from this stretch of tar that the track led off to English Colonel's Point, which lay at the head of a narrow valley some twenty miles north and forty miles inland from the capital.

With one gap already torn in the highway, it was this dirt road that Trent intended taking. In normal circumstances they could have driven the distance in less than three hours. Now there was a good chance that they wouldn't reach the dirt road.

Trent was sure that Louis' men had occupied the telephone exchange to control communications with the outside world, while the hurricane would have wrecked the internal system. He planned sending Mariana on into Belpan City with the Land-Rover in hope of her reaching the British High Commission. With Mariana's help, and despite her arguing that he wasn't fit to ride, he had manhandled the BMW up a plank into the Land-Rover, insisting that it was their insurance should they find the road blocked or impassable.

Miguelito had boasted that they would kill the ministers. 'We goin' put them in one beeg hole,' had been the little cocaine addict's description of their intentions. But José had believed them to be alive. If so, their lives must be essential to the coup because there was always the risk, however slight, of one of them escaping to organise resistance. The gringo brain of whom Miguelito had spoken was a man who never took a risk without reason.

Trent presumed that the absence of the President must

191

delay the coup. Neither the President nor José had known what role the President would play. Trent believed the role central to the coup – a role that would leave him not only in apparent control of the Government but with his reputation enhanced on the world stage.

Trent had never considered intelligence a hallmark of Colombia's drug barons. They had built their huge fortunes by terror, murder, bribery and extortion. All of these were present in the coup but Trent recognised in the concept a sophistication far beyond the norm: the long-term planning of the operation; the acceptance of the need for legitimacy for which the suborning of the President had been essential; taking over the newspapers, planting items in the US Press, questions in the House and in the Senate; sacrificing the aeroplanes and pilots.

Finally there was Trent's own presence in Belpan. Two months had been required to get him on station and he had been here a further seven. Add two months of negotiations and planning before his selection and it became clear Colonel Smith must have had knowledge of the coup almost from its conception.

At the beginning Trent had wondered why he had been chosen. Why an EC operative rather than an American when Belpan was in the US sphere of interest? Now he knew that the choice had been made, not because of the organisation to which he belonged, but because of who he was. Linkage was the secret: the coup, Steve, the Colonel, Caspar, Don Roberto's murder, the photograph, his own posting to Belpan. Linkage and an acceptance of an almost unbelievable ruthlessness . . .

Trent gasped with pain as Mariana braked hard, the Land-Rover slewing sideways into the broken branches of a tall cotton tree barring the track. This was the fourth tree that they had been forced to chop clear. They had developed a routine governed by Trent's injuries. Mariana reversed, swinging the rear end round so that the winch on the front faced down the slope. Stripping to their under-clothes, they pulled on ponchos and struggled out into the rain.

Trent filled the chainsaw with petrol and oil and began slicing side-branches into manageable lengths. Meanwhile Mariana carried a wire belt and pulley downhill. She fastened the belt round the bole of a big cedar tree and returned to the Land-Rover for the winch cable which she led through the pulley and back to the downhill end of the fallen cotton tree blocking the track.

Trent dragged another branch free and turned back to watch Mariana gather the coils of rope from the rear of the Land-Rover and clamber uphill to anchor the vehicle to a tree. Her feet slipped and slithered in the mud, and her hands bled from broken wires in the cable and from the thorns and knife-edged leaves of the undergrowth.

Gallant, he thought – an old-fashioned word but it suited her. Raising the chainsaw, he sliced through another half-dozen branches, switched the saw off and laid it down. As he dragged at one of the branches the pain knifed into his lungs, leaving him breathless. He sat in the mud, unable to move till the pain eased.

Mariana slipped on the hillside and slid the last feet to the track on her backside. The poncho pulled loose on a branch. Trailing it behind, her dark skin slippery with red mud, she walked over and stood looking down at Trent. He suspected that there were tears as well as rain washing down her cheeks – tears of exhaustion.

'Comfortable?' she asked.

Trent managed a smile.

Oblivious of the mud, she sat down beside him and took his right hand in hers, holding it open as if she were reading his palm: 'You're killing yourself.'

'Thanks,' Trent said and found himself imagining Colonel Smith watching . . . like God on a cloud, he thought . . . the punitive God of the Old Testament, but dressed in a Panama hat and carrying an umbrella . . . and wearing dreadful socks. He wanted to laugh but was frightened of the pain. He wondered if Mariana would laugh if he told her . . . but she didn't know Colonel Smith except through the photograph of him as a young man. And she might laugh if he told her that he considered her gallant, so he kept his peace and concentrated on steadying his breathing so that the pain would stop. A gust spun wet leaves round them.

Mariana squeezed his hand. 'I think I'll be a lawyer . . . or an income tax inspector.'

'You'd get bored.'

'I wouldn't.' She leaned her head against his shoulder. 'How much further to the road?'

'About four miles,' Trent calculated. 'Three-quarters of an hour.'

They both knew that there could be a dozen more trees across the track – or a bridge down. Built for logging, the track followed the side of a long ridge. The streams crossing its path were small and the bridges constructed to carry heavy trucks so their luck might hold.

Trent closed his hand over Mariana's and raised it to his lips: 'We'd better get going.'

She helped him to his feet and he restarted the chainsaw. As each branch fell clear, the full weight of the saw rammed the pain into his side. Mariana dragged the branches clear. Half an hour and they were ready to winch the tree over the edge of the track. The tree slid clear and rocked for a moment on the lip before plunging down the slope like a great battering ram, tearing the undergrowth free as it gathered speed, finally plunging into the river.

They wiped the mud from their bodies before clambering into the shelter of the Land-Rover where they towelled themselves dry, awkward in the confined space. Too exhausted to be embarrassed by exposing themselves, they shed their soiled underclothes before dressing.

Mariana drove a further mile before they had to stop and winch a boulder clear of the track. Then another tree and the light was fading fast. Mariana was about to switch on the headlights but Trent stopped her. He was beginning to feel his way into the coup leader's thoughts, not by dissection but by identifying with him as he would with the protagonist in a novel.

It was a familiar process for Trent, uncomfortable in the way it blurred his own identity, as did the slow growth of a cover, possessing him until he had to make a conscious effort to differentiate between his cover personality and the one which he thought of as his own. He sometimes feared that there was no real person left and that he had become a cricket ball, to be continually made and remade by Colonel Smith, reweaving the threads and layers of cork to suit his purposes.

Telling Mariana to stop, he reminded her that with the logging finished, only the President and his guests used the track. Were Trent leader of the coup, he would have set an ambush as insurance down by the junction with the dirt road – a fallen tree and the stationing of two men armed with Kalashnikovs would be sufficient.

Mariana listened without looking at Trent as he rehearsed her in the role he needed her to play.

'Why?' she asked.

'I can't do it on my own.'

'You know that's not what I mean.'

'It's what I do,' he said.

'Get yourself killed?'

Where only this morning he had been the killer . . . odd to consider the change in status an improvement, Trent thought.

Mariana rested her forehead on the wheel. 'You don't even have a proper name. Your mother didn't call you Trent.' She wiped her nose on the back of her wrist and without looking up, felt for his hand. 'I hate you . . . '

Colonel Smith had spent years trying to persuade him to smoke a pipe. '*All that poking around, gives you time to think . . .*'

'If you say you're sorry, I'll scream,' Mariana said.

'It's the situation we're in,' he told her – danger heightened the emotions.

Getting out into the rain, he dragged the motor bike back enough to stop the rear door of the Land-Rover from closing and taped the pressure switch controlling the inside light . . .

Mariana drove with the two spotlights on the roof as well as the headlamps. The rear door swung and crashed at each bump. She turned a sharp corner and saw the tree. She swung downhill then back hard and rammed her foot on the brake so that the Land-Rover slithered broadside to a halt with its tail hanging over the edge and the back door flung wide. Immediately she opened the side door and the inside light came on. If there was anyone watching they would see she was a girl and that she was alone.

'Look vulnerable,' Trent had coached. 'Don't bother about being frightened. You're alone on a mountain track. They'll expect you to be frightened. Leave the headlights on and swing the spotlights to cover the uphill end of the barricade before getting out. Take the torch. If you see someone, put a hand to your mouth as if you're scared out of your wits and scream.'

She swung the spotlights on to the uphill end of the tree, switched on the torch, and got out. She gave them time to see that she was unarmed before draping her poncho over her shoulders. The rain beat into her face. She sniffed and rubbed her nose, then walked over to the tree, waving the torch beam over it. The tree hadn't been sawn but Trent had warned her that, given the option, they would use a tree that had come down in the hurricane. She didn't believe him . . . wouldn't believe him.

She listened through the wind and rain beating at the trees and through the roar of the river below. She couldn't hear anyone moving. She was sure that it wasn't an ambush, but even if it was and they weren't killed, she and Trent would have to strip the tree and winch it clear. There would be another tree, and another, and another. If they ever got to the main road, the bridges would be washed away. Something snapped inside her. She kicked the tree. The pain made her hop. She caught her other foot in a branch, stumbled and sat down in a puddle.

A man laughed.

No need for Mariana to act. She put her hand to her mouth and screamed.

He appeared out of the darkness, silent as a cat stalking a bird. His rubberised poncho glistened in the spotlights – khaki police uniform, jungle boots. He was short and thickset.

Mariana looked up into eyes like smooth black stones at the bottom of a shallow stream Fear had frozen her.

The man put a foot between her breasts, forcing her flat on her back in the mud. He flipped her poncho open with the barrel of his gun. The moustache drooping over his upper lip failed to disguise the sneer.

Mariana lay helpless. The rain beat on her chest, cold so that she could feel her nipples stiffen against the wet cotton.

'There'll be two of them,' Trent had warned. 'One up the hill covering the one on the track. I'll take the one up the hill first. Speak up. I want him straining to hear what you're saying.'

'There's been an accident,' Mariana blurted. 'Up the track. The other Land-Rover . . . my grandfather. Please . . . ' She switched to Spanish. '*Un accidente* . . . ' The words stuck. She swallowed, desperate for saliva.

'Play helpless,' Trent had told her. She wanted to scream his name.

Trent lay where he had rolled ten feet down the bank.

The open door of the Land-Rover had covered him and the lights would have destroyed the night vision of the men in ambush. He kept his own eyes closed. That much he had planned. He hadn't planned to hit a tree with his broken ribs. He smeared mud on the back of his hands and on his face. Mariana screamed. He slipped the dark glasses from his breast pocket, put them on and opened his eyes. The pain had brought tears and he could hardly see. He blinked and looked again. Better. '*Un accidente,*' he heard Mariana say. Then silence. He had to get up the bank and across the track. He eased a hand forward, feeling for dead branches, then dug his fingers into the mud. The pain as he pulled himself up the bank on his belly brought fresh tears. Willing Mariana to keep talking, he found a fresh grip.

'*El Presidente. El Land-Rover secundo. El rio . . .*' Mariana cried through the roar of the river, fear drowning her in whirls of blackness. The man's sneer floated above her – Cheshire Cat, she thought, seeking shelter in childhood memories. She felt the barrel of a gun cold against her thigh, her skirt lifting.

'Little whore,' the man said and spat down into her face. She screamed.

'Don't look,' Trent warned himself. Belly flat, and he was across the track.

'Whore,' the man repeated: 'The truth or you die.'

The gun barrel dug at her. She whimpered like a beaten dog. 'I swear to you. Señor, please, I beg you . . . '

'Beg,' the man sneered. He pried Mariana over on to her belly with the toe of his boot. He shifted his boot to the back of her neck, forcing her face into the mud.

Contemptuously, he poked his gun into her. The hate exploded in her; it was as if he had poked through the coal crust of a fire. Flames of loathing seared through her veins, sour bile in her throat. She fought her cheek flat in the mud so that she could breathe, mud thick on her lips and blocking her nostrils.

She had no need to call for Trent. She could sense him out there in the dark, his revenge a cloak that held the hate hot in her blood as she whimpered at the man and felt his boot rise.

On her knees, she shuffled round to face him, kneeling at his feet, begging him with her eyes. Her fingers plucked at the bottom of her T-shirt, raising it, giving herself to his eyes with whimpered pleas to him to take her, knowing that the other man would be watching; feeling his desire; feeling Trent, feeling Trent . . .

Flat on his belly, Trent searched the hillside for movement. A man rose out of the undergrowth above and beyond the fallen tree. He had known that there would be two of them.

Trent slipped his sunglasses into his pocket, boots digging for purchase as he came to his feet. The man stood there clear as a target on the range. Pain banished, Trent crouched low, feet braced, his Walther in both hands, steady as a rock. The long barrel reached out for the man's chest, trigger-finger squeezing once, and again as the man staggered. Feet still locked, Trent swung from the waist. Smooth and easy, he warned himself as he did on the range. The man on the track leapt into his sight. Trent shot him first in his gun-shoulder, then through the back of the head.

The man collapsed quite slowly and only then did Trent allow himself to see Mariana kneeling, half naked, muddy, her T-shirt clutched in her hands.

He pulled off his combat jacket as he slithered down the bank, draped it over her shoulders and knelt facing her, holding her in his arms, feeling her shivering, her sobs smothered against his chest. He lifted her gently to her feet, holding her, whispering endearments as he would to a nervous foal, stroking the back of her head, easing her towards the protection of the Land-Rover.

But she didn't want to be sheltered. She whispered, 'Please,' and released herself from Trent's arms. She looked

199

back at the man lying dead in the mud. Trent watched as she calmly catalogued the details, imprinting the picture in her memory.

It was something that she had to do. She felt the hate and the fear drain away till finally she was empty. She turned back into Trent's arms, sucking his warmth into the vacuum.

'I'll fetch the chainsaw . . .' he said.

FOURTEEN

The dirt road met the river at right angles. Fallen trees washed down by the current had built up against the bridge like a beaver's dam. Some time after Louis' men had crossed to fetch the President from his cabin, the vast weight of water had torn the bridge free of its mounts. The water tumbled the unsupported span till the concrete shattered, sheets of macadamed road surface flung aside as if light as tarred cardboard. A direct bombing strike would have been less destructive.

Trent had taken the wheel after the ambush. Though potholed, the dirt road was smooth as the top of Don Roberto's Bechstein piano when compared to the track down from the meadow. Mariana lay curled up beside him, asleep, with her head cushioned in his lap. He shone the spotlights upriver to a bend that curved back towards the road. He opened the door to the roar of the water tearing at the remnants of the span supports but the rain had stopped and already the spate had abated somewhat. There was less foam on the surface, and the river flowed in dark smooth rolls of slippery liquorice.

Leaving Mariana asleep, Trent took the torch and walked upstream beyond the bend. A throw of seventy feet, he gauged as he studied a stand of scrub trees on the far bank.

He flung a thick stick out into the middle of the stream and watched the current snatch it. Forty seconds to the centre of the bend. Dangerous but possible.

Returning to the Land-Rover he found tyre-irons, foot-pump, jack, and a cruciform wheel wrench in the toolbox. He unbolted the spare wheel, let out the air and levered the tyre free from the rim so that he could pull out the inner tube. He pumped the tube full, leaving it in the Land-Rover. First loosening the nuts on the rear off-side wheel, he bound the rope-end to the wheel brace and shouldered the rope back upstream.

Gathering half a dozen rocks, he practised the throw into the scrub trees on the far bank. Once he was confident of the distance, he recoiled the rope carefully so that it would run and hefted the wheel brace. His first throw was too high, the brace catching in the treetops and pulling loose. The second attempt fell short; the third landed in the fork of a treetrunk. Trent put his full weight on the rope. The brace held. He jerked the rope up and down and still it held. Satisfied, he took a turn round a tree on the bank his side of the river, hauled the rope taut so it wouldn't catch on anything floating by and made fast with a looped double-hitch. Coiling down the rest of the rope, he watched the river for a while. The flotsam was mostly dead branches and light shrub.

He thought about Mariana as he walked back to the road. She would be safer staying with the Land-Rover but he thought that she'd be happier with the turn-off to English Colonel's Point behind her. Her emotions had taken a beating and waiting was always tough on the nerves.

He woke her gently and held her in his arms while she regained her bearings. She listened in silence while he explained how he planned to cross the river. Then she pushed herself free and looked out at the swirling current.

'It's up to me,' she said. She looked at him but he couldn't see her face. 'It always will be. I mean, between us . . . '

He thought how easy it would be to take her back into his arms. It wasn't his way and it wouldn't be fair to her. 'I believe the ministers are alive,' he said, 'and I think I can free them.'

'I'll come with you.'

'Across the river but not to the farm. I have to do it on my own.'

'I know. It's your job.' She was too exhausted to project anger or even bitterness into her voice.

'I'm sorry,' he said, and started the engine. Swinging across the road, he drove through the ditch and up the river bank to the bend. He jacked up the Land-Rover while Mariana squatted on the bank, watching the water. Removing the already loosened rear wheel, he let out the air, freed the inner tube and pumped it up again. He cut the rope in two at the looped double-hitch round the tree and tied the end to the inner tube. He tied one end of the spare rope to the tree to keep it from being blown away and the other to the second inner tube. He squatted down beside Mariana. He didn't touch her. 'Ready?'

She nodded.

'Jump as far out as you can,' he said. 'The rope will act as a pendulum with the current forcing you over to the far bank.'

'I know.'

He wanted to leave it at that but she'd been watching the flotsam wash by for the past five minutes and she wasn't a fool. He fetched the two ponchos from the Land-Rover, folding them into a pad.

A dead branch raced past, thick, heavy and sharp-ended.

Trent held the inner tube and Mariana stepped into it. She wouldn't look at him.

'Ride as high in the tube as you can,' he instructed. 'Use the ponchos to protect your face.'

She grabbed them and jumped before Trent could tell her to wait. He watched the current take her. Her rope snagged on something out in mid-river. He looked upstream. The Land-Rover's spotlights lit the butt-end of a tree two-thirds of the way over to the far bank. The jagged ends of the tree looked like a bunch of white butcher's knives.

The tree would catch on Mariana's rope and she would be dragged into the jagged battering ram. Trent imagined the knife-ponts gouging into Mariana's face, into her eyes. No point in yelling – the roar of the water would have drowned a foghorn.

He grabbed the second tube and hurled himself out into the river, his legs already kicking as he hit the water. He didn't think that he would make it but the current was pushing the tree towards him. The first branch hit his arm. He grabbed, heaving himself forward, and managed to hook the inner tube over the jagged points of the shattered trunk, expecting the tube to rip or the rope to snap. He scrabbled up through the branches, dragging the last few metres of slack, and looped a half-hitch over the stub-end of a broken branch. Another branch whipped across his face, forcing him under. In a moment the tree would begin to swing broadside across the river, and the branches would sweep Mariana deep down to the riverbed with no possibility of escape.

He dragged himself out against the current, trapping himself between the branches, and fighting to hold his body stiff so that he acted as a rudder that drove the stump towards the far bank. The current whipped the top of the tree round towards the Land-Rover. The water surged over Trent as the rope took the weight of the tree, acting as the arm of a pendulum. The butt-end sliced back away from the far bank and the river was open for Mariana. As suddenly as it had come the pressure slackened as the rope snapped. But already the tree was into its swing, the current ramming the leaved top branches back towards the centre of the river. A branch caught on the riverbed, rolling Trent under.

He fought up the branches towards the trunk. He didn't know why he was fighting. Then the tree rolled again and lifted his head clear of the water.

For a second he could see the far bank. Mariana clung to a tree root. Her mouth was wide open, and Trent knew that she was yelling his name. Then he was past her, the tree racing at the remnants of the bridge.

He wanted to scream against the terror of the steel framework ripping into his body. The tree caught and rolled him higher out of the water, then the river tore it loose. Another twenty yards and Trent saw a tree blown over but not fully into the river. The water surged up and over it, smooth as oil. He thought there would be broken stumps waiting to impale him and let go of the branches, letting the current sweep him up. The fallen tree slammed into his belly, the pain in his ribs driving into his lungs. He scrabbled desperately for a handhold, feeling his nails tear. For a second his feet were on the trunk. He dived for the bank, the current pulling at his legs as he grabbed at a stand of saplings. Pain blinded him and he almost surrendered. The current swung his legs parallel to the bank and his feet struck mud. With his last strength, he fought his way into the protection of the saplings and lay there with nothing happening except the pain.

Mariana's despairing calls summoned Trent back from oblivion. Searching the river bank, she had crossed the main road. Rather than use his name, she called, 'Where are you?' repeating the words over and over again as if, by repeating them, she ensured that he was alive, only questioning his position.

The insistent threat of the river roared beside him, waves slapping the fallen tree, spray whipping his face where he lay in the saplings. He rolled on to his knees and tried to crawl away from the bank before answering her but the burning agony in his right hand forced him to his feet.

'Here,' he called. His feet squelched in the marshy grass-land as he hobbled towards her. About a mile to the turn-off to English Colonel's Point – he wasn't sure if he could make it.

Mariana halted with a metre between them. The darkness hid her expression. Trent didn't want her to be emotional. He thought that if she were, he would hold on to her and not be able to move. And he thought that he was too old to be close to tears. He tried to remember when he had last cried: not when he had hidden in the loose box after discovering his father – not even after hearing the shot. Nor had he cried when Colonel Smith had told him of his mother's death; there had been no pain, merely the arid emptiness of desolation. And he was sure that he hadn't cried since – so he must have been quite young. Exhaustion played funny tricks, he thought.

'Hello,' he said.

Mariana didn't answer so he added, 'Good, you're all right,' and checked his watch. 'We ought to keep moving. Dawn in a couple of hours and I want to come out of the dark at them.'

'Don't,' she said.

He nearly said, 'Don't what?' but stopped himself.

As if he had said it, she said, 'You know . . . play games.'

She stepped forward. Standing close to him, she reached up and held on to the front of his combat jacket. Trent knew that she was about to tell him that she loved him.

He said quietly, 'I've been Trent, the off-beat yachtsman, for the past eight months. Next month I may be Ibrahim Mohammed with three wives and two dozen children . . . or Pepe the Gay Barman in silk shirts and a midnight swish.'

'I feel safe,' Mariana said with a tiny giggle that she cut off almost as it began, as if frightened of giving way to hysteria.

'Safe?' Trent asked. It was a remarkably incongruous description of the two days they had spent together.

'With you,' she said. 'You know what I mean.' She rested her cheek against his chest: 'You're such a coward.'

He turned her towards the road, supporting part of his weight on her shoulders. 'You're going to have to help me over the rough ground,' he said. 'I should be all right on the tarmac.'

They took nearly an hour to cover the mile to the turn-off up to English Colonel's Point. Twice they had to wait while Trent fought to bring the pain under control. There were moments when he thought that he would have to give up. The clouds were breaking to show patches of stars and the wind had dropped to no more than a light breeze. It was this that kept Trent going.

They halted a hundred yards short of the turn-off.

'I don't know how you get to the city,' Trent told Mariana, 'but you don't take risks. You're a peasant girl. A tree fell across your husband's leg. You set the leg in clay. That's how it's done up-country – clay reinforced with strips of mosquito net. You're going to the hospital to fetch antibiotics.'

Kneeling on the roadside, he took Mariana's trainers and cut the toes out, fraying the edges. Using a rough stone, he sawed off the metal tips from one of her laces, chopped the lace in two and knotted the halves so that the knot showed and the lace looked as if it had been in the shoe a year. Her other lace he replaced with a brown length from one of his combat boots. He worked slowly because of his injured hand, fingertips caked with blood.

'That's what the pros look at – shoes. And no sneaking around,' he warned. 'Keep to the middle of the road so people have plenty of time to see you. And you speak Creole – nothing else.' He grinned at her: 'So much for the London School of Economics. If you reach the British High Commission, tell them what's happened. If you can't make it, don't bother. Most important is that you don't get hurt.'

He knew that he should have said, 'I don't want you to get hurt.' He couldn't read her expression in the dim starlight. He wanted to touch her but was nervous of what would happen.

'If you fail . . . ' she said.

'I won't. I'm going to talk to them – that's all. The shooting's over . . . '

He watched her walk on down the road. She looked small and vulnerable.

Where the track leading to the President's cabin had followed the ridge, the road up to English Colonel's Point ran up the floor of the valley. A roadblock similar to that on the mountain would be at the foot of the valley. No point in Trent trying to avoid it – he hadn't the strength left. And if he did circumvent the roadblock, he hadn't the strength to reach the farm. His only hope was to bluff. It wasn't much of a hope but he had to try.

The valley was nearly a mile wide where it opened on to the main road. Two trees lay across the track, their ends extending into the fields on each side of the drainage ditches. Trent held his arms above his head and hobbled slowly forward.

A torch beam struck his face and he halted with his eyes shut against the light. He heard footsteps, and kept his hands up.

A man said in the soft lilting Spanish of Colombia: '*Oye*, it's the gringo.'

'That's what you called me last time,' Trent said. He thought he might as well get it over with. 'What I am is a cop.'

He heard the slight hiss of the man's breath. He knew that there were guns pointing at him, and how easily a nervous man could fire without thinking.

'I walked in here of my own free will,' he said as casually as if they had met on a Sunday-morning stroll to church along the Hamble River: 'I may be a cop but I'm not a fool. I want to talk with your boss.' Contemptuously, he added, 'Not the gringo boss. And I'm not talking about Louis, the boss of the Contras or whatever they're calling themselves now. It's your boss I want to talk to – Mario, *El Jefe de Los Colombianos*.'

He could hear two men whispering on the other side of the barricade, so there were at least three including the man with the torch.

'Listen to me,' he warned, voice held deliberately flat; they were the ones whose lives were at risk. 'Listen to me or you will make pet food for the vultures. You have been set up . . .'

As the President had been set up with cocaine in the Savoy Hotel, as the pilots of the two aeroplanes had been set up. As Trent had been set up, both with the murder of Don Roberto and as the apparent gun-runner for the coup. And, before that, he had been set up in Ireland to be killed as a terrorist by British soldiers waiting in ambush. The same *modus operandi*. The same mind plotting the moves, Trent was sure, as he recalled receiving his instructions, Colonel Smith's tall erect figure outlined against the window at the Rena Victoria Hotel. And he was sure now that the coup itself was a set-up.

From the beginnng Trent had believed that the coup could only succeed with international approval. That the planner of the operation had put the President under his control through blackmail was proof that the President had a future role as head of Government. For that to happen, the coup must fail. And, if it was designed to fail, what could be more perfect than the President as the tool of its downfall? The President, a hero on the world stage, would be the master of his country . . .

FIFTEEN

Two men stayed to guard the barricade. The third drove
Trent up the valley in a four-by-four blue Toyota station
wagon. They had tied his hands behind his back, one of
them whistling as he saw the torn fingernails. Trent leant
against the door of the vehicle, his body twisted halfway
round to keep his weight off his hands.

The valley narrowed to a point, the track zig-zagging up
the final climb to end in a gravel yard, open barns on each
side, a drystone wall at the head. Trent catalogued a tractor,
ploughs, harrows.

A sentry appeared out of the shadows, gun trained on
the Toyota. Trent recognised the man as one of the party
he had brought up the river, and knew that there would be
a second man ready to give covering fire from the barn.

His driver greeted the sentry. 'I have the gringo from the
sailing boat. He came of his own will. He wishes to speak
with Mario.'

'Take him,' the man said with a jerk of his gun.

Stone steps led up from the yard through a wrought-iron
gate which the hurricane had dragged off its top hinge.
There was little wind now, few clouds, and more stars.
Three hours to first light, Trent guessed.

The driver pulled him out of the Toyota and held him by

the arm as they climbed the steps. Trent was unsure whether the man was helping him or showing his dominance.

The house known as English Colonel's Point stood at the back of a grassed terrace. The head of the valley protected it from the wind on both sides and from the rear. It was a long bungalow built of whitewashed adobe and roofed with red corrugated iron. A covered verandah ran the full length of the house-front. The pillars supporting the verandah were lengths of palm tree from which the leaf stubs had been adzed, after which the smoothed trunks had been oiled and polished.

Vines had grown up the pillars but the wind had ripped them free and they writhed now in the light breeze like bundles of thin young snakes across the clay tiles flooring the verandah. Six sets of double french windows opened on to the verandah with arched double doors of mahogany in the centre. Curtains of bleached jute draped the windows, the yellow light of kerosene lamps leaking round their sides.

Two men stood on the verandah, Kalashnikovs at the ready. Again Trent recognised them from the gun-smuggling expedition. Colombians, so he was corect – so far, at any rate.

'The gringo from the boat,' his escort called to the men.

'Wait,' one of them ordered. He part-opened one side of the double door, light darting across the tiles like a lizard's tongue.

The slight form of their leader, Mario, appeared and the door closed behind him. 'So, you have returned to us,' he said, the slight lisp both menacing and oddly effeminate. 'Like a pigeon.'

'Like a cop,' Trent corrected quietly. Drenched, muddy and haggard, his hands lashed behind his back, it was difficult to project authority into his bearing but his life depended on it. 'You Colombians have been tricked,' he said, voice calm and direct. 'You are sacrifices in a gringo's conspiracy.'

211

'You lie,' the man lisped.

Trent shrugged. 'Why would I bother?'

'To save them.' Mario spat at the door behind which Belpan's ministers were imprisoned.

'I save them . . . without weapons? With broken ribs?' mocked Trent. 'With my hands torn? You believe that I am Batman that you expect such miracles? Then where is Robin? Perhaps he is already behind you.' Trent's laugh was soft and teasing: 'Consider, Señor Mario. Consider carefully . . . '

'What should I consider?' Though the Colombian had attempted to sound dismissive, there was an edge of doubt to his voice that his men recognised.

Trent felt his escort's hand tighten on his arm, the silence thick with tension. He knew the men below were listening and he pitched his voice so that they would hear. 'Why have you Colombians been kept separate from those the Americans trained?' he asked. 'The Fascisti from Nicaragua? Contras, they were called once, but now their war is over. And for what will the President be used if he can be rescued from the mountain where we left him?'

'Left him?'

'Left him,' Trent pressed. 'And with nine dead men for company. Contras, all of them. But there are many more. While you . . . '

Dismissive of the small band of Colombians, Trent indicated the valley below with a slight jerk of his head: 'In the morning the Contras will come in the uniform of the police. You will welcome them. Then they will kill you. They will kill your prisoners. They will call the journalists to take pictures for the foreign newspapers. They will show the blood still running from the bodies of the politicians. They will name you as the murderers and they will explain, naturally with humility, how they were helped by God to save Belpan from Colombia's drug smugglers. The President will be there with his politician's smile and they will relate how

212

he directed their attack. The world will believe him a hero and the saviour of democracy.'

Trent knew that it was true and he knew that the Colombians must believe him. They would talk amongst themselves, but, in the end, they must believe.

'The President alone will have power,' he said. 'He will declare an emergency and rule by decree while promising new elections that will be delayed once world attention shifts to the next famine or coup d'état or football competition. Those who were once called Contras will control the country for the American gringo who trained them,' Trent continued calmly. 'Your employers, who financed the gringo, will complain, not that you and your men are dead, Señor Mario – you are of less importance to them than mosquitoes – but that the gringo cheated them. Nevertheless they will pay the fees he will demand for use of the airfields and in a year, perhaps two, the gringo will vanish to enjoy his millions hidden in secret bank accounts.'

He felt rather than saw the man from the barricade and the two gunmen from below the terrace edging closer, the better to hear. Three plus the two on the terrace made five out of twenty – with Mario added, six. A minority, but sufficient, and Trent knew that he had them. His smile was deliberately mocking: 'Do you perhaps think that, before he departs, the gringo will buy marble for your graves, Señor Mario? Who knows? Perhaps you even believed that there was honour to be found amongst thieves?' Trent shook his head in wonder at the Colombian's naïveté.

'You should be imprisoned because you are killers,' he said. 'But given such innocence, perhaps I should forgive you. Peons are of no interest to me. It is the other I want. The Gringo Boss . . . '

It was enough. One of the gunmen swore and a second began to argue, only for Mario to order him to hold his tongue. The man protested.

Listening, Trent felt the last of the strength drain from his legs. 'You must excuse me,' he said: 'I am a little tired . . . '

The darkness was absolute, and there was a great deal of pain. Trent lay on a bed, belly down. His hands remained tied and now his feet too were bound. He had no memory of it, but the Colombians must have carried him into the house. He hadn't heard the door open and he couldn't hear breathing, but he knew that there was someone in the room. It wasn't something over which he made mistakes.

A spring clicked into position to hold a knifeblade open. It was a solid knife, probably a Buck. The knife found and cut the rope between Trent's feet. A moment later his hands were free. The door opened and closed without sound. He was alone.

He clenched and unclenched his hands, waiting in trepidation for the agony that would strike beneath his torn fingernails with returning circulation. The pain came and he sat on the bed, his hands under his armpits, rocking himself. He bit on his lip to stop crying out. Tears ran down his cheeks. Finally it was bearable. He fumbled along to the bedhead and found a wall behind it. Following it round to his left, he discovered a window, with shutters held closed by a flat iron bar. He inched the bar free and eased the shutters back.

Stars shone and the first faint touch of dawn softened the shadows. Freedom lay outside . . . or death. As death had awaited the pilot on Key Canaka, the Good Ol' Boy. Trent struggled on to the window ledge. He hesitated for less than a second before dropping to the ground. No lead pipe waited to beat his brains in. He attempted to run but his right leg refused to carry his weight and his ribs felt as if they were churning his lungs into blood pudding.

He tried to think. Whoever had cut him loose had done so because they believed his account of the conspiracy. And whoever it was had acted on their own initiative or there would have been no reason for secrecy. When the others discovered Trent's absence, they would come looking for him. They would expect him to escape down the valley, or they might calculate that he would count on them expecting him to do that.

And how would Caspar play it?

He found himself in a small citrus orchard. Using the trunks for purchase, he dragged himself up the beginnings of the valley head. The rains had left the ground soft and his boots found purchase. He came to a fence and a gate. The hillside steepened, rocks, light scrub and, still higher, secondary forest. Hearing movement to his left, he froze, waiting. A cicada stuttered for a moment before breaking into full pitch; it was answered by a second and a third and a fourth, the spreading siren shrilling its guarantee of the storm's end.

Mist floated across the hillside. Hidden in the grey, Trent limped through the thin cover, boots feeling for broken branches and loose stones. Chachalacas brayed at each other as if they were donkeys rather than birds, their strange ee-unh-ahh, ee-unh-ahh echoing through the trees. An Aztec parrot chuckled through the squeaks and cheeps of flycatchers, sparrows and kiscadees and, over to his right, a woodpecker beat at a dead treetrunk.

A slight breeze split the mist into cloudlets that clung briefly to the hillside before parting under the soft grey light of the new day. Men shouted behind and below him. His escape had been discovered, he knew as he focused his binoculars on the verandah of English Colonel's Point. Mario was there, arms waving as he dispatched a man up each side of the valley head. The men obeyed with reluctance, boots dragging, shoulders hunched. Trent was certain that they had been arguing through the last of the night and that his account had sapped their determination.

The mist had cleared, and he swept the valley through his binoculars, mapping every detail of the terrain: first the house in its patch of citrus, then the broad lower yard with its barn and tractor shed from which the track zig-zagged down to run between narrow paddocks planted with guinea grass, where a dozen or so Brahma cattle grazed.

The paddock below Trent was sheltered from the sea wind by a steep promontory jutting out from the hillside. The track cornered sharply round the tip of the promontory before bending to the left round a banana plantation. Some eighty yards long on the track front, the plantation had been whipped by the hurricane into a grotesque tangle of shredded leaves and shattered trunks. A further paddock lay behind the plantation. Beyond the promontory a long, sail-shaped field of flattened corn spread to the right of the track – fifty acres or more. Next came a line of trees, then more corn on both sides leading into open ranchland that stretched to the highway far in the distance.

By the time a truck, approaching up the valley, came within accurate small-arms range from the house and terrace, it would be hidden, first by the plantation, then by the promontory. In Mario's shoes, Trent would have positioned a marksman high on the down-valley side of the promontory to cover the dead ground.

The two men Mario had ordered up the hillsides had made little progress. Trent wasn't bothered by them. Threading his way between bush and trees, he searched for a position from which to view the downhill slope and the dead ground. Reaching the head of the promontory he found that it curved. The only position from which to view the complete slope was out of cover and high on the promontory ridge. Slithering on his belly, he wormed his way out on to the open crest from which he could see both back to the house and down the slope.

Camouflaged by the shade of a rock, he carefully quartered the slope with his binoculars. No sentry, Mario had been lax or stupid. Twenty yards to Trent's left a humming-bird had found a bush in flower. The bird was a mere three inches long, slim as a bullet. Its back feathers were emerald green, its crown an iridescent blue. It darted, flower to flower, hovering as it dipped its long beak into the nectar.

Louis, Trent thought . . . Louis, the psychopath, with his endless supply of clean handkerchiefs.

Ten minutes passed before he saw a movement away in the distance. Another five minutes and he could make out the shape of a big American four-wheel-drive station wagon, a couple of Land-Rovers, and half a dozen army trucks. The convoy approached slowly up the valley, station wagon leading, and disappeared behind the banana plantation.

A further five minutes and the station wagon reappeared, nosing its way down the track like a fat shiny dung beetle. Caspar was at the wheel. Through his binoculars, Trent could see the cigar jutting from between his ruddy lips. He wore one of those caps Americans wear to advertise which resort they can afford to patronise – this one quartered in red and blue. Mariana sat beside him.

Trent slithered out of the shade of the rock and moved downhill so that he would be hidden from the house. In a minute the roof of the station wagon would hide him from Caspar so he hurried to his feet, waving like a bookie's tic-tac man at the racecourse. The extra height showed him the tip of a rifle barrel sticking out from below what he now recognised as an overhang thirty feet down the slope. He had sixty seconds at the most. And he was tired, desperately tired – and stupid. It was his stupidity that hurt the most.

He took a step to the right so that he was directly above the overhang. A stone shifted under his right boot and his leg gave. He tried to save himself. Half blinded by the pain in his torn fingers, he slid helplessly over the edge. Miguelito rose in his path. It had to be Miguelito. Trent hit him with his shoulder, tumbling the small man out of the tiny scoop of a depression in which he had been hiding, and the rifle spun out of his hands. Trent saw it break as it hit a rock

217

way below. They were in each other's arms, slipping, sliding, falling. He saw or felt the pistol in Miguelito's hand, then his own hand was round the butt, clinging to it as if there was nothing else left in the universe that could save him.

A bush parted him from Miguelito, the little man holding to the branches as Trent slid on down. The rainwater in the ditch saved him. He hit it broadside, water fountaining, crawled to his feet, swayed, nearly fell, caught at the hood of the parked station wagon and steadied himself.

He saw the horror in Mariana's eyes. Caspar slid across the bench seat, opening her door. One-armed, he lifted her on to his lap and dropped with her to the roadway. He held his pistol to her head, left arm locked round her throat. Looking into her eyes, Trent felt her pain almost as a physical blow. Pain that she had failed him, if only through error. Trent knew that he would win. Dive, pistol up, his first shot taking Caspar in the chest, the second through his head. Mariana would die but she would die whatever Trent did. Caspar had no further use for her and she knew too much . . .

'Drop the gun,' Caspar ordered, cigar hardly moving.

The sun caught a single tear swelling on Mariana's lower lid. Deep brown eyes filled with anguish for him. Love, Trent thought. He had always known that there was no place for it in his profession. His dive had to be to the right, Mariana's head giving him cover from Caspar's pistol. His sense of physical emptiness was so profound as to almost choke him. Now! Trent ordered himself. He smiled at Mariana and dropped Miguelito's automatic. The barrel struck a pebble and the tiny sound crashed into the silence.

There was viciousness as well as victory in Caspar's smile. 'You're a pig-ignorant Irishman, Mahoney,' he said. 'You should've stayed in the bogs.'

The demented cocaine addict giggled his delight: 'Hey, Boss, you let Miguelito keel the son o' beetch?'

Caspar grinned as he glanced quickly at the Colombian standing above them on the hillside: 'Sure, have yourself a party.'

Face, Trent thought. He couldn't spit in Caspar's eye. The American was upwind and Mariana was in the way. And he couldn't stand the fear and pain for him that filled Mariana's eyes. So he grinned as Miguelito slithered down the hill to retrieve his automatic which Trent had dropped on the track. It was a stupid grin, he thought, but it was all that he had to offer Mariana, so that she would know that he was unafraid and she should be too. It wouldn't be for long now. One minute, two, and it would be over. But it had to be played right.

Despite his exhaustion, he kept on grinning straight into Caspar's face as Miguelito raised the pistol. He said, 'You're bright, Caspar, but you're scum.'

'Yeah, and you lost your guts back in Ireland,' the American sneered round the butt of his cigar and that was the last piece of the jigsaw confirmed.

Trent fought to hold down his rage.

Miguelito was behind him. 'Hey, leetle dog,' he giggled, 'you step a leetle to the lef' so the nice lady don' get blood on her pants.'

Trent obeyed – two steps. Smile, he ordered himself, smile and keep on smiling.

'I do it now, Boss?' Miguelito pleaded, his mad giggle echoing off the rocks.

'Do it when you goddamned please,' Caspar said. 'Nothing worse than a dumb Mick,' he said and lowered his pistol. 'Yeah, kill him.'

'And you thought you were setting up your pension fund,' Trent said. It was too late for pensions. Caspar looked utterly surprised. His mouth opened and the cigar fell. Then Miguelito fired and there was a hole in Caspar's forehead, dead centre. He spun like a student at a beginner's class for weekend ballet dancers.

219

Trent leapt at Mariana, plucking her up and hurling her into the ditch. He dived after her, sheltering her with his body. Miguelito landed facing them, a few metres away. He had scooped up Caspar's pistol. He chucked it to Trent and they lay there, Miguelito covering the track down from the house, Trent the approach up the valley. The drug craziness had vanished from the Colombian's eyes, replaced by a cool professionalism Trent recognised from his own training. And it was training that had positioned Miguelito in the ditch so that the two men covered each other.

Miguelito had cut him free up at the house. Nor had it been accident or carelessness that had enabled Trent to escape from Miguelito on the river bank after the arms smuggling. That, too, had been deliberate, Trent knew, as had been the initial confrontation on *Golden Girl*. He eased his weight off Mariana, using his elbows to push himself backwards down the ditch.

'Keep low,' he ordered as she raised her head to look back at him. Tears streaked the mud on her cheeks. 'Are you all right?' he whispered.

Miguelito sniffed his amusement at the incongruousness of Trent's question. 'Sure she's all right.' The madness flashed back into his eyes, his lips parted, sloppy with drugs, drooling. 'Gringo, we in Latin America,' he hissed. 'You lie on a girl, you marry her or her brothers carve you in leetle pieces.'

Brilliant, Trent thought of the man's acting. Miguelito? But he knew now, with certainty, that those wide cheekbones, black eyes and black hair came from a very different heritage. Their eyes held, Miguelito accepting Trent's knowledge with a sheepish grin and apologetic shrug of his shoulders.

'Who sent you?' Trent asked in Russian of the Tartar KGB Agent.

'Personal initiative,' Miguelito answered in the same language. 'The rules are changing and you can't trust politicians. We young ones need each other. Remember, friend, you owe me one.'

'Two,' Trent corrected: 'Thanks, Tovarishch.'

'My pleasure.' Miguelito's eyes narrowed against the sun. Trent saw a movement where the track rounded the stand of trees below them. He squeezed off a shot by way of discouragement rather than in hope of hitting one of the Contras and looked back at Miguelito.

The Russian had slid out the magazine from his pistol. He showed Trent six fingers. Trent had seven shots in Caspar's automatic. Not that the numbers mattered. If they stayed in the ditch they'd be picked off by the Colombians from one hillside or the other. If they left the ditch, the Contras would shoot them from the plantation.

In Russian, Trent said, 'Let's get the girl out of it.'

Miguelito nodded.

'Then into the plantation,' Trent suggested. 'The cover's thick and there's too many of the Contras for them to be sure who's moving.'

Trent felt Mariana's muscles jump as he rested his free hand on her leg. 'Listen, I'm going to fire the station wagon's petrol tank. When it blows up, get into the corn-field. Keep flat on your belly,' he warned. 'Once you're in the centre of the field, crawl in under the stalks and don't move till we call.'

Without waiting for her reply, he put two bullets low through the station wagon's rear sidepanel. Miguelito ripped the sleeve off his shirt, tore the cotton into strips and bound them round a stone.

'Ready,' Trent told Mariana as the Russian held his lighter to the bundle. The Russian's arm arced and the three of them flattened themselves deep in the ditch. For a moment Trent thought that he had missed. Then the hot roaring swush of the petrol explosion blasted the air above their heads.

'Go,' Trent snapped at Mariana and was already rolling

for the ditch the other side of the track. He lay there exhausted by the pain in his ribs and hands but the Russian was on the move and pride forced Trent to follow. Two hundred yards, the snake crawl, pull and push, toes and elbows supplying the power, rock and stone cutting through his jacket and the blood running before they were halfway. But at least he had his combat jacket. The Russian wore only a cotton shirt with one sleeve missing.

Miguelito was ahead of him by thirty yards, only twenty from the trees – it was time. '*Oye!*' Trent shouted in Spanish. 'It is the Englishman. Let me surrender to you. The gringo is dead.'

He threw his pistol high so that the Contras would see it fall in the middle of the track. 'Listen to me,' he shouted. 'Listen, let me surrender. You can use me to bargain with the authorities.' Ten yards between Miguelito and the trees. Now, Trent thought. Do it, he told himself. Lying in the ditch, he raised his hands high above his head waiting for the stream of bullets that would tear them from his wrists. Don't stumble, he warned himself, no sudden movement. He stood, hands high, and stepped clear of the ditch into the centre of the track.

'Walk towards us,' a voice called.

Gomez, Trent thought as he obeyed. He didn't look towards the trees where the Contras waited and he didn't look at the ditch. The Contras would be watching him, all of them. He counted his steps, the slow, short, dragging steps of an exhausted man. He lowered his hands as far as the back of his neck, too tired to hold them up.

There had never been any hope of their both escaping and he knew that Miguelito would understand. The Russian had to get past the plantation. There was even a remote chance that he could steal a truck or a Land-Rover. Trent imagined, with each step he took, the inches that Miguelito would have gained. He knew that Mariana would be listening, and he imagined her lying in the cornfield. Fear would have sucked her belly empty and he could almost taste the sour burning of the bile clogging her throat.

'Run!' Gomez yelled.

So the Colombians had got round the hillside.

Trent tried to run but his right leg folded. A Kalashnikov hosed the banana trees, the bullets shredding the leaves and tearing chunks out of the soft wood. At least one of the Colombians had believed his story.

The Contras returned the fire as if they had sufficient ammunition to stage a minor war. A second Colombian opened up from the crest of the promontory. Bullets kicked flint from the road surface as Trent rolled back into the ditch on the plantation side of the track.

'Crawl,' Gomez urged, voice cracking with anxiety. Out of gratitude for Trent having saved his life? Or because he saw Trent as insurance?

Trent pinpointed Gomez's position, twenty yards down the edge of the plantation by the track. Once past the corner of the trees, he was safe from the Colombian on the far hillside. But the moment he left the ditch he would be open to the man or men on the crest of the promontory. He crawled a further ten yards and called to Gomez to give him covering fire.

As the gunman fired, Trent rolled out of the ditch. Rolling again, he heard Gomez curse viciously and two heavy pistol shots slammed through the lighter fire of the automatic rifles.

Belly flat, Trent wriggled into the protection of the tangled trees. There he saw Louis. The Nicaraguan held a ·45 revolver. Slim and deadly, he swayed like a snake as he peered between the trees, searching. Four shots in the revolver . . . He spotted Trent and smiled. Trent struggled into a sitting position, hands behind his head, eyes pleading for mercy. Louis sniffled his pleasure into a clean handkerchief. Bleak eyes were exposed as the pink lids lifted. His smile broadened, his tongue-tip flicking out across thin lips.

He raised the revolver slowly to extend the pleasure of killing. A truck's diesel engine roared. The Latino lost his concentration for less than a second. Then he fired. Twice.

The first bullet hit inches short, blasting a little fountain of mud over Trent's jungle boots. The second struck the wet soil between Louis' feet, and the revolver fell from his hand. His knees gave, and he fell sideways against a tree, arms strengthless as he tried to embrace the trunk with one hand, the other clawing at the small flat handle of the throwing-knife protruding from his throat. He slipped to his knees, rocked a moment, and tumbled forward on to his face.

The truck's engine screamed as the driver charged the trees. Both Colombians and Contras were firing wildly. Trent retrieved his knife and found Gomez. The gunman lay on his side, frothy blood on his lips. Louis had shot him in the back. He forced a piece of paper into Trent's hands, dying eyes pleading. With a stick dipped in his own blood Gomez had written numbers above five crosses interlinked round a Z.

'Union Banque, Zurich?'

Gomez tried to speak but blood drowned the words. His lungs were haemorrhaging. Suffocating, he fought to speak with his eyes, the desperate demand not for himself but for his family. Three sons, three daughters: 'I'll see they're cared for,' Trent promised. 'But I need my eight thousand dollars back.' He slipped the gunman's billfold out of his back pocket and into his own.

The truck smashed through the banana trees to his left, turned short of the plantation's edge and charged back. Trent risked standing and Miguelito saw him. And there was another noise now – the whine of jet engines linked to the swush-swush of helicopter blades.

Trent grabbed at the truck door, dragging himself on to the front seat. 'Crazy idiot,' he shouted as Miguelito floored the throttle.

The little Tartar giggled: 'Hey, leetle dog, all part of the service. Your guys?'

'Probably.'

'Let's get out of here before they shoot our arses off.' The banana trees fell like spillikins as the Russian bulled the army truck at full revs in first gear. Two Contras rose out of the greenery, less than ten yards in front. Their Kalashnikovs were up, ready to fire. The Russian hit the klaxon and dragged the wheel hard over. The tail-end of the truck swung and Trent saw the Contras dive clear of the spinning wheels.

The vehicle bounced clear of the trees and across the track into the cornfield, Trent flapping out of the window the yellow silken square which the American had given him in Cancun. A helicopter hovered directly overhead, down-draught slapping the corn flat. A further four were herding the Contras out of the plantation while two more dipped over the promontory towards English Colonel's Point.

Trent dropped to the ground, the yellow handkerchief above his head. He felt foolish waving it.

Miguelito giggled: 'Man, and I was just starting to have myself a little fun.'

'Dumb idiot,' Trent said. 'Thanks.'

'My pleasure. I'll send you a postcard . . . '

Trent sat on the truck's running-board in the sun. For some reason that he didn't understand he had spread the yellow handkerchief on his lap, and his hands rested on it. Mariana stood beside him. They were close but not touching and they weren't looking at each other. The crew of the helicopter stood a little away from the truck, talking quietly amongst themselves and deliberately not looking towards him. They reminded Trent of doctors on ward-round going into a huddle over a terminal patient's case. He wondered if he was beginning to smell of death. He'd known a Special Forces Major who did. Not of death, Trent corrected himself, but of killing. The smell of a killer. He had never understood the desire of fighter-pilots to paint their kills on their planes. Perhaps the speed and distance in aerial combat made the killing less immediate and personal – more abstract. Less bloody . . .

That was it, Trent thought as he looked down at his hands caked in blood. His own blood, Louis' blood, Gomez's blood. And it wasn't over. Not yet . . .

Little wonder that he didn't dare touch Mariana.

'I'm sorry,' she said. 'There was a police car. They offered me a lift and I told them I wanted to go to the British High Commission.'

'They took you to Caspar?'

Mariana nodded.

'It doesn't matter now.'

A tall soldier, older than the helicopter crew, walked down the track towards the truck. The crew didn't salute and they didn't quite come to attention but there was a stiffening to their posture. The absence of badges of rank told Trent that the man was SAS. The soldier didn't introduce himself but merely nodded a friendly greeting: 'Trent? We've been standing by in Belize. Sorry we're late. Weather held us up.'

'That's all right. Who got word to you?'

'The President via the High Commissioner. Gutsy old boy,' the soldier said admiringly. 'Late sixties, and got himself across a river and twenty miles over the mountains in the tail-end of a hurricane to an American's riding camp. Used the radio.'

Trent heard Mariana sniff. Of all the pains of the last days, he thought that this was the worst . . . the pain of sitting quietly in the sun unable to take her hand. She pulled the yellow handkerchief out from beneath his hands and blew her nose.

'Who was your chum?' the soldier asked with a nod towards the acres of flat and tangled cornfield.

'What chum?' Trent asked.

The soldier grinned: 'The one in the cornfield who doesn't exist.'

'Not even in your report,' Trent said.

'Your party.' The soldier inspected Trent much as a vet would a horse that had taken a fall at Becher's Brook: 'We'd better get you to hospital. Civil or Military?'

'Military,' Trent said. 'Mérida, in Mexico. You'll need clearance.' Trent gave him the frequency and looked up at Mariana. He thought that he must do it quickly – quickly and cleanly. But the words wouldn't come.

She laid a hand lightly on his forearm. Her eyes were a very deep brown. 'It's all right, Trent. I know. You're sorry . . . '

'Yes,' he said, 'I mean . . . '

She kissed him on the cheek, more of a peck: 'Go on.'

He said, 'Right,' and tried to stand but his right leg wouldn't work.

The soldier beckoned two of the helicopter crew over to support him under the shoulders. One of them was young, hardly into his twenties.

'I'm sorry about the blood,' Trent said.

'That's all right, sir. Part of the job . . . '

SIXTEEN

Colonel Smith was in a vile temper as he strode down the main corridor of Mérida's military hospital. The strike of his leather heels on the tiled floor sent the young orderly scurrying ahead as if a Rottweiler was after him.

The Colonel hated hospitals. He hated their smell of disinfectant and yesterday's boiled fish. He hated the way everyone spoke with the hushed authority of a Papist priest hearing confession. He hated the simpering female nurses who thought themselves superior because they knew how to wipe a man's behind or shave round the front bit. And he hated the pansy walk of the male hospital staff – the young orderly was typical of the breed, smooth cheeks needing a shave only once a week.

Most of all, the Colonel hated doctors.

Illness of any kind was either malingering nonsense or proof of feeble will – usually both. Hospitals supplied the malingerer's support system and doctors were their allies, becoming disgracefully rich on the proceeds. Added to which every last one of them was a damn liar pretending to knowledge he didn't have and to secrets to which he had no right.

The orderly opened a door for the Colonel and cringed back, half bowing. The Colonel glared at him and stalked into the Senior Surgeon's consulting-room. The surgeon was a giant of a man, mid-thirties, neat in a white coat with pen and stainless-steel torch in his breast pocket . . . as if he were a poodle and cat vet, the Colonel thought.

The surgeon wore his black hair oiled back. His wristwatch was one of those vulgar affairs on a heavy bracelet in two tones of gold and he wore square rimless spectacles. He was sitting in a high-backed tilt-and-swivel armchair upholstered in imitation black leather behind a big desk of fake black wood with a marble top which was designed to impress the fools who put their trust in his knives.

The two chairs on the other side of the desk were of the same fake black wood. They were small, armless, upright, and deliberately uncomfortable to emphasise the social gulf between patient and doctor.

The single window on the right of the room looked out over a patch of lawn shaded by a frangipani tree. A screen for displaying X-rays stretched the width of the rear wall behind the desk. It was turned off. There were paintings on the other walls, framed in chrome and mounted on matt black to match the desk and chairs. The paintings were of overlapping shapes of nondescript colour.

So-called modern art was another of the Colonel's hates. The speckled carpet reminded him of mouse droppings.

'Smith, Colonel. You're Gonzalez,' the Colonel barked.

The surgeon said, 'Major Gonzalez,' from habit rather than to correct the Englishman. He half rose from his chair, huge hand outstretched across the desk: 'Delighted to meet you, Colonel Smith.'

The Colonel ignored the hand so the surgeon changed his gesture to an invitation to one of the upright chairs: 'Won't you please sit down?'

His voice was a deep rumble and his accent Californian, which further irritated the Colonel. Why on earth did foreigners adopt the accent and vocabulary of a nation of immigrants?

229

'Prefer to stand,' the Colonel told him. 'Been sitting on a damn aeroplane for the past twenty-four hours.'

'Perhaps a cup of tea?'

'Tea!' The Mexican doctor was insane! 'Good God, man, it's two o'clock in the afternoon. I want to know what's wrong with the Englishman you've got here.'

The surgeon spread tanned, massively muscular hands: 'I thought that I had explained, Colonel, over the telephone – '

'I don't want medical gibberish. I want the truth, properly explained in layman's terms. The man works for me. His father was an old friend. I brought him up.'

The surgeon sighed and, in need of its authority, reseated himself in his executive chair. The chair groaned under his weight.

'The patient suffered four broken ribs on the right side of the body,' he said carefully, elbows on the desk, thick fingers steepled. 'Though uncomfortable, this should not have been dangerous to a man of the patient's physique and fitness, Colonel. Unfortunately the patient appears to have continued an extremely active role for some time after the initial incident. Without doubt there were further falls.'

The Colonel grunted his irritation: 'Get on with it, man.'

Fresh protests came from the chair as the surgeon swivelled to face the screen. He switched it on to display three chest X-rays, and pointed with a white conductor's baton to the broken ribs: 'Note, Colonel, that, on first impact, the ribs pierced the right lung.'

The surgeon's baton pointed now to a series of darker sections in the right lung: 'You see here, Colonel, the extensive damage done to the lung by the ribs in subsequent falls and while the patient took what the evidence suggests to have been consistently violent exercise.'

With the point of the baton, the surgeon encircled a dark mass that filled the right side of the chest in each of the X-rays: 'Severe haemorrhaging, Colonel.' He switched off the screen, laid down the baton, and swivelled back to face Colonel Smith. 'We are transfusing fresh blood, Colonel.'

The Colonel's eyebrows rose like the wings of a hawk: 'Are you telling me that this haemorrhaging is still going on?'

'I would prefer to say that we have been unable to halt the haemorrhaging.' The surgeon's tone was frosty.

'What's the difference?' Colonel Smith snapped back.

'One implies incompetence, Colonel. The second, that we have been unsuccessful despite skill and the best of equipment. The heart is our main difficulty. The patient suffered shock compounded by intense fatigue. The heart-beat is feeble. At this time the patient is unable to withstand a further operation.'

'What are you doing?'

'Waiting, Colonel.'

'Can he speak?'

'Not at this time, Colonel.'

Four words when a simple 'No' would have done. 'Presumably I can sit with him for a while. Fond of the boy,' the Colonel added, and was immediately irritated with himself for stepping out of character. 'You have his belongings?' The surgeon handed him Trent's wad of dollar bills together with a receipt to sign.

To the layman, Trent looked like a three-dimensional map of London's underground transport network with the control system thrown in for good measure. The Colonel watched the heart signal trickle weakly across the screen. He knew about that. He'd seen it on television. And he recognised the plasma sachets.

Despite the beard, not a bad face, the Colonel thought as he looked down at Trent, but too much of his mother in him. Beautiful woman, and a wonderful seat on a horse. But a terrible spender. He'd had the money for her. Believing they had an understanding, he'd bought a mare for her

231

to ride to hounds with the Quorn the year before he'd
made Captain and been permitted to marry by regimental
tradition. He'd paid her dressmaker and even given
her an egg-blue MG. Then he'd asked her to marry him
and she'd turned him down. Said she was fond of
him but . . . Everyone knew. Laughing stock of the regiment. He'd transferred to the Ministry. A year later she'd
married his best friend. Wonderful man, Mahoney.
Marvellously loyal, warm, and fun to be with. But a bit
of a scamp, no money sense, and not a penny to his name
beyond his pay.

The Colonel had warned Mahoney that no good would
come of the marriage. The fellow had laughed and insisted
he be Best Man. Six months and the Colonel had to bail
him out of a mess with the Squadron accounts.

How old had the boy been when he'd agreed to care
for him? Twelve? The damn woman had called him from
Bahrain, telling him of Mahoney's suicide, wanting help,
and not for the first time since the scandal with the accounts.
Driven poor Mahoney to it with her spending, he'd thought,
and told her to go to hell. But he'd agreed to take the
boy.

He'd been ready with comfort. He'd prepared himself,
rehearsed the words, even practised in front of the mirror
in his bedroom how he would hold the boy. He'd known
that to be important because he was bad at physical contact.

The Colonel remembered the tightly-controlled set of the
boy's face as he walked into the hall with his one small
suitcase of summer clothes. He had stood there as if nothing
had happened, blank-faced, freezing him out. Same as his
mother, shuddering when the Colonel had tried to put an
arm round his shoulders.

The Colonel had been angry, of course, natural given the
circumstances. And, though he'd tried, he never could stand
the boy. Secretive, unemotional; but good at his books.
Perhaps he'd made a mistake in stopping him going to

university but the boy had the makings of a first-rate agent and the Colonel had wanted him out of society before his face got too well known.

He thought of the times he'd used him, moulded him into a fine weapon. But he'd gone soft. Questioning things.

Promising the boy's mother to send him to a school run by those damn monks in frocks had been his first mistake. And posting him to Ireland, the Colonel thought irritably. Damned Catholics. Continually re-infected by matters that were past history and better forgotten. Talking of the potato famines and the land clearances as if they'd happened after the Second War rather than before the First. Asking for understanding when there wasn't anything to understand other than that a terrorist was a rabid dog and needed to be put down by a bullet in the head.

But he'd made something useful of the boy for a while. Though always disobedient, of course . . .

The Colonel brushed a hand through his short grey hair. He was tired. Too much travelling. Backwards and forwards to Brussels as if an aeroplane were a bus and now out here again. And he still had things to do before he got to his bed at the hotel . . .

Colonel Smith slept well despite the change in time zones. He breakfasted in bed on coffee and toast with butter and a Mexican honey from the Yucatan which he found surprisingly good. Having bathed, he shaved with his usual concentration, using a Wilkinson Sword blade fresh from its wrapper fitted to a solid-silver razor given to him by his father the year he entered Sandhurst. He was pleased but not surprised to find his hand steady as a rock.

He dressed carefully in a cream linen suit pressed for him by the room valet, who had also polished the Colonel's brown brogues to a suitable perfection. He wore his regimental tie, one of his favourites despite his having transferred to the Ministry with his military rank gained as necessary cover for his job rather than through service with the Regiment. The package was waiting for him at the front desk. Briefcases were not something a gentleman carried, but today he needed one. Panama hat suitably straight on his head, he hailed a taxi and directed the driver to the military hospital.

There was no change in the patient's condition. The Colonel said that he would sit with the boy for an hour. The surgeon said that he had ordered a more comfortable chair put in the patient's room and called for an orderly to escort the Colonel.

The Colonel inspected the boy but there was no more to see than there had been the previous day. Dismissing the orderly, he hung his hat on a hook on the door and seated himself. He thought it would be sensible to wait a while so as to get the feel of the hospital and become accustomed to the sounds of feet in the corridor outside.

Watching Trent, he thought again that he'd done well with the boy. All his men had done well. They had brought the Communists to their knees. Now there were committees investigating the methods they'd used. Americans, of course.

He'd pretended to like the Americans and trained the boy to do their dirty work. Now he'd be damned if he'd let them pull him down. How dared they summon a British officer before one of their wretched committees? Disgraced, ostracised, unable to show his face in his club. Let that happen and he might as well be dead.

But it wouldn't happen.

He'd been prepared from the beginning, always working the boy through Bob French as his cut-out. And French had called himself Don Roberto at the end! French's father had been nothing but a jumped-up clerk. And French had done well out of it, the Colonel thought as he remembered the big beach house at Cancun; servants, gardeners, chauffeured Mercedes.

It had been a long time since he'd had to do this sort of thing, he thought, as he took his reading spectacles from their case and threaded the sprung half-loops over his ears. He took a sachet of blood plasma treated with anti-coagulant from his briefcase and crossed to the Christmas tree of hanging tubes suspended above the bed.

Less than thirty seconds and he was back in his chair, the sachets safely exchanged. He'd practised, of course. With twenty minutes to wait, he took the *Sunday Times* from his briefcase.

From beneath shuttered eyelids, Trent watched the Colonel read his newspaper. He had thought that he might mind but he had grown used to the idea while lying in bed. Before that he had been too busy staying alive. He hadn't spoken for three days, other than whispering instructions to Pepito, and he coughed to clear his throat.

The Colonel glanced over the top of his newspaper and Trent said, 'I'm afraid you've made a mistake, Colonel.'

The Colonel moved fast for a man of his age but Trent warned, 'Don't be a fool, I've got a gun. And you're on video. The window's barred and half the Mexican army's outside.' He sat up in bed and rolled the bandage down his right arm, freeing the tubes. There weren't any needles.

The Colonel sank back into his chair. He had gone pale. But he sat bolt upright, grey eyes cold and watchful.

Trent imagined, for a moment, that he could hear the Colonel's brain racing as he sought for a way out. 'You never were any good in the field, Colonel. You're a desk man – too busy manipulating to notice when you're being manipulated.'

'Manipulated? What the devil do you mean?'

'Right from the start,' Trent said quietly. 'Delusions of kingly grandeur. In fact, you've been a pawn. You were set up, you and Caspar. You've made the case for clearing out

235

the old guard at Langley – your friends, Colonel. That's what this is about.'

'Don't talk damned nonsense,' the Colonel barked. 'Who the devil do you think you are? I trained you, boy. You're mine. I'll break you like that.' The snap of his fingers was as loud in the small room as a pistol shot. 'You and whoever put you up to this. Don't think you've finished with me yet. I've got every job you've ever done on file and who you did them for. I go, the whole damn lot of you go.' By God, they'd learn . . .

'You're not listening,' Trent said: 'It's over, Colonel. You tried to murder me. That's on film and we're in Mexico. The big man you thought was the Senior Surgeon is Mexican Intelligence Service and a friend of mine.'

For a fraction of a second doubt showed in the Colonel's eyes.

'I'm not seeking revenge,' Trent continued. 'I'm still in your debt, Colonel, despite what you've done. That's why I chose Mexico. I thought you could make a better deal here than you could back home or in the States. They'll hold you for attempted murder until the deal's struck.' He shrugged: 'It may not sound much but you'll be safe and reasonably comfortable. You've got half the Intelligence community after you like bees after honey, which means the honey's worth something – negotiate before the other half of the Intelligence community cuts your tongue out.'

It was the best he could do. And he owed the Colonel that much for the love the Colonel had shown his mother in rescuing his father from the first scandal and for giving him a home and schooling. It couldn't have been easy, having him in the house as a continual reminder of the love the Colonel had lost.

'Down here,' he said, 'I could have you put away for the rest of your life.'

A slight tic marked the Colonel's cheek.

'I'm sorry,' Trent said, because, despite everything, he

was sorry for the old man. But he remained watchful. And there were matters from his past that needed clarifying. His throat hurt and he reached for the glass of water on the side table before asking quietly: 'I never was transferred to the EC? I suppose I'm dead?'

The Colonel was unable to quite hide his relish: 'Yes, my boy, I'm afraid you are.'

'That's what I presumed,' Trent said. 'But you did sell the cottage? My grandmother's financially all right?'

'Of course she is. Odd job, this . . . ' The old man shook his head again, as if desperately tired. 'Not good for a man.'

Born with less money and from a different background he'd have made a fine actor, Trent thought. He said, 'You must have believed that you'd covered yourself and the Department. All those favours you did for your American friends at Langley filed away as freelance operations done by me without your authority, and my fee handled by Don Roberto Fleming or whatever his name was.'

'French,' the Colonel said with disdain: 'Robert Charles Richard French. Not one of us.'

Not a gentleman was what he meant. Trent knew the old man well: 'You had him killed.'

'Said he was going to Washington for some wretched Congressional Committee. They'd been pressuring him for months. It would have been the Philby affair all over again, turning everything upside down. Politicians poking their noses where they had no right. They'd already asked for you, but I'd tucked you away in Ireland. I'd have been next on their damned list.'

Trent saw the hate in the Colonel's eyes, unguarded for a moment. He had guessed as much but had wanted proof. French's death would have been laid at his door; his knife, the rogue field agent with an 'immediate' issued, shoot on sight, one more part of the package neatly tied.

'You paid for the catamaran from a fund traceable back to me?'

'Yes.'

'Controlled by French?'

A slight sneer curled the Colonel's upper lip: 'French understood that sort of thing.'

Money was what French had understood but it was a word a gentleman never used. 'The records will show that I faked my own death in Ireland?'

They had walked across the field in light rain towards the farmhouse, Trent and five members of the terrorist cell which he had infiltrated; corduroys tucked into gumboots, thick jumpers, tweed jackets; shotguns under their arms; two rabbits and a hare in their game-bags; a half-breed Labrador and an Irish setter at their heels as proof that they were innocent of evil intent. A low plump ridge ran the length of the field, the green of the grass a little richer than the rest.

He had sensed, in the terrorists, an extra friendliness that day; they had slapped him on the back and laughed a little too loudly, and he'd suspected that he had been betrayed to them. The adrenaline, already pumping, had saved him. Prepared for violence, he had dived almost before the first volleys smashed at them from the dry-stone wall to their left and from the barn ahead.

One bullet hit Trent in the shoulder, a second in the thigh but the adrenaline gave him that extra strength and speed to reach the ditch below the wall. He remembered his terror as he lay there in the mud, certain that he had been betrayed by someone on his own side and not knowing why.

He knew that he was trapped in a shoot-to-kill operation – no prisoners. He was reluctant to shout his passcode for fear that it had been cancelled. At any moment a grenade would drop on him from the other side of the wall. He could feel the soldier counting, and he said it quietly, his passcode, so as not to startle him.

He heard the man swear and the grenade curled way over his head, exploding on the plump low ridge in the field that

238

marked where three hundred and something people, an entire community, had been laid to rest during the famines by one man with hardly the strength left to wield a spade so that he had shovelled the dirt over the dead rather than bury them deep.

He heard the soldier speak into his radio, a soft Northumbrian accent, and the man in command of the ambush shouted at Trent to come out with his hands up.

To the soldier the other side of the wall, Trent said in his own voice and accent which he hadn't used in two years, 'Tell the damn fool I can't move. One of you got me in the leg. My shoulder's smashed and I'm bleeding like a stuck pig.'

The soldier said, 'Yes, sir,' and Trent remembered the wave of guilt that had drawn him down towards loss of consciousness, guilt for the separatist voice of the British upper class that held him apart from the five young men dead in the field.

Looking across at the Colonel, he said, 'You betrayed me to the IRA and to the Army. That's over-kill.' Little wonder that he had been obsessed by paranoia those last months.

The Colonel's chin jutted, eyes pale, white showing on his cheekbones: 'I read your reports. Lot of sentimental slop. Halfway to becoming a turncoat.'

'Nonsense,' Trent said. 'You wanted me dead so I couldn't be called before the Congressional Committee. You must have got one hell of a shock when I survived.'

The Colonel sneered.

'You backed Caspar,' Trent continued, 'to make sure his operation got off the ground with me implicated as the gun-runner and French's killer. That got rid of the two of us. The curtain was meant to come down with you wearing a crown of laurels for sending the SAS in from Belize to save Democracy. Brilliant! There's no political mileage for a Congressional Committee in giving a hero a hard time. But you made one mistake. Don Roberto left me a warning and you didn't spot it.' Trent took the photograph from under his pillow and flicked it across the room. It fell at the Colonel's feet and he picked it up. 'You must have loved her a lot – and hated my father,' Trent said, then he saw the look on the Colonel's face and knew that he'd got it wrong.

'I couldn't stand the damn woman,' the Colonel said, glowering at Trent, hands clasped, knuckles white. 'And you're your mother's son. Your father killed himself and you didn't shed a tear.' Bitterness thickened his voice: 'You're a cold fish. That's why I trained you. You had the makings right from the start.'

So all the remindings of his mother had been one more of the Colonel's manipulations. 'I saw Dad,' Trent said, 'just before he killed himself. I couldn't help him.'

'Good God!' For the only time in Trent's experience, the Colonel seemed genuinely shocked. He shook his head as if trying to clear his thoughts: 'You should have told me. I told your mother I'd give you a home for your father's sake. Only man I could ever talk to . . . '

'I'm sorry,' Trent said. And he was sorry.

'Damn you, I don't want your sympathy,' the Colonel snapped, furious at having lowered his guard.

Trent swung his feet to the floor. His right leg ached, there was a good deal of pain in his side despite the strapping, and the fingers of his right hand were bandaged. 'May I have your wallet?' he asked.

The Colonel took it from his inside breast pocket – pigskin, one of the gold corners missing, polished by decades of use. From it the Colonel had taken Trent's school pocket-money, the value of the single crisp new note keeping pace, year by year, both with inflation and Trent's seniority.

'You always put me on the school train yourself,' Trent said.

'Duty,' the Colonel said.

'Pleased I was leaving,' Trent corrected, knowing it was true. He had felt it as they stood side by side on the platform at King's Cross station.

He checked the wallet. His eight thousand dollars were there in a separate compartment to the Colonel's private funds. Trent showed the bills to the video camera above the door, scrawled with difficulty because of his fingers a receipt on the slim notepad in the wallet with the Colonel's miniature gold pencil, and handed the wallet back.

The Colonel said, 'Thank you,' and slipped it back into his pocket as he had done after handing Trent his pocket-money. He fumbled for the cigarette-case Trent's father had given him.

Trent pointed to the No Smoking sign above the bed and limped to the door in his hospital pyjamas. But he found that he couldn't simply walk out. Turning back, he said, 'Don't do anything stupid.'

'What do you think I am?' the Colonel growled. 'A damn fool? Get out.'

Three men waited in the corridor. The Mexican wore uniform; the tweed suit with a razor rash had to be British; the American looked as if he had come up in the world fast and wasn't sure how to act. Trent nodded to them and said, 'He's yours. Take care of him.'

Dressed in his white surgeon's coat, Pepito beckoned from a door down the corridor.

EPILOGUE

Trent's clothes had been washed, patched and pressed. The orderly, who had helped him dress after Pepito had strapped on the equipment, led him down the corridor to the Hospital Commandant's ofice as if he were important. Trent didn't feel all that important. He was sick of it all, and considered walking straight on past the Commandant's office and out of the hospital but he owed the Colonel one last service and he owed the same service to himself and to the world, not that it would make much difference to the world.

They met the American hurrying down the corridor. He had been Robert at Frankfurt in a grey flannel suit, Steve in Cancun. Now he wore a linen suit, button-down shirt, and a club tie. The only thing that didn't change was the smile. 'Great to see you,' he said. 'I just flew in from Washington.'

Trent wouldn't have been surprised to learn that the American had been circling over Merida for the past two hours waiting, before touching down, for radio confirmation that there'd been no last-minute disaster at the hospital.

The American had his hand out.

Trent showed him his bandaged fingers.

The American said, 'Hey, that's too bad,' and put his arm round Trent's shoulders instead. 'Hear you did a really great job,' he continued, thrusting Trent into the Hospital Commandant's office. His smile beamed total friendship and absolute support: 'Great. I mean really great. Great. Just great.' Shaking his head in admiration of the unbelievable, he said to the two men already in the room, 'Can you believe this man? I mean, Jesus Christ . . . '

Trent got the message. Washington was pleased.

Trent knew one of the men in the office by sight: British, twenty years younger than the Colonel, but of the same breeding and education. Because he was younger, he was probably more liberal in his opinions – or less given to prejudice, which wasn't quite the same thing. The man said, 'Well done.'

'Thanks.'

The second man was a Mexican dressed in an expensive dark blue suit. He was smoking a thin cigar and wore too much gold on his wrists. He smiled and there was more gold: 'We are delighted to have been of service, Señor.'

'I'm sorry,' Trent said. 'I should have asked first,' but the Mexican and the American were already fully occupied with shaking hands and exchanging luncheon invitations with the warmth of old schoolfriends.

The American led the Mexican outside – though, with their arms around each other's shoulders, it could have been the other way round.

Infected by the mood, the Englishman held out his hand: 'Charles Benson, we've never really met.'

Trent showed his bandages and Benson looked embarrassed: 'Yes, of course. Sorry about that.' He waved a surprisingly calloused and muscular hand at one of the two armchairs facing the Commandant's desk: 'Do sit down. Couldn't have been very pleasant upstairs. You look all in.'

'Thank you,' Trent said. He hadn't expected understanding and looked at Benson properly for the first time. Brown eyes, brown hair, slim face, slight of figure. His forelock, threatening to fall forward over his forehead, gave him a

243

boyish look at variance with his age, and, though tired, he was obviously fit.

Trent presumed that he'd flown via Washington. 'Do you play polo?' he asked.

Benson said, 'What?' Then he looked at his hands and smiled: 'Yes. Yes, actually I do. Clever of you.'

'I'd like to talk to the American alone, is that all right?'

'I expect you would.' Benson thought for a moment: 'I'd rather you were on leave. You could do that now, go on leave, I mean. It's within my authority.'

Trent hadn't realised that he was employed.

'No one's called you anything,' Benson said. 'Do you mind sticking with the name Trent?'

Which again struck Trent as unusually understanding. He'd been wondering who he was.

'Good,' Benson said as the American came back into the office. 'John, I've given Trent a couple of months' leave. He'd like a word with you before he goes.' He looked at his watch, old and on a plain leather strap: 'I ought to get back to the airport.' He smiled at Trent, a trace of mischief in his eyes: 'Perhaps your friends outside will give me a lift once you're through.'

The American swung the second armchair round to face Trent and sat down, at ease and relaxed.

'John Volkstadt,' he said with a smile that told Trent that the American was out from cover: a named variety rather than one of the nameless or multi-named flock. 'Nice fellow, Benson. You'll enjoy working with him. On the ball and has the right ideas.'

'The yellow handkerchief . . . ' Trent said, and shrugged his embarrassment: 'I mean . . . '

Volkstadt knew what Trent meant. With a slight gesture, he dismissed the need for thanks.

But Trent continued: 'You saved my life. I don't know how you did it.' He still hadn't said enough. Afraid of office politics, Trent had been reticent at their meeting in Cancun. He had to come out in the open now: 'We won, didn't we?'

'We certainly did.' A job well done, the smile said.

'And I'm safe . . . ' It had been so long since he'd been safe.

'Hell, yes,' Volkstadt said, his patronage confirmed, the smile generating power.

Trent moistened his lips: 'I'd like to say . . . You know? At any time . . . '

There it was, the offer of his services . . .

Volkstadt's smile vanished, eyes cool, calculating, as he waited to assess the depth of Trent's commitment.

'Belpan's President,' Trent said, but he was shy of going too far: 'You know. At the Savoy . . . '

Volkstadt knew.

'That sort of thing,' Trent said.

The American said, 'I'll bear that in mind.'

God, but it was difficult. 'I didn't understand,' Trent said. 'I knew the Colonel hadn't done it. He wouldn't. Not in England. And he would have had difficulty getting hold of the drugs. Caspar hadn't the power . . . '

A slight lightening in Volkstadt's eyes told Trent that he was on the right line. Power was a word the American loved, particularly when applied to himself.

'It must have taken a lot of courage,' Trent said. A field agent's admiration was serious praise and the American smiled – not the big, bright, practised smile but a slight lift of the corners of the mouth.

Trent shook his head in admiration. 'And putting Caspar and the Colombians together.'

'That son of a bitch. He jumped at the chance.' Volkstadt grinned, no acting now: 'If I hadn't dreamt it up, he'd have come up with it himself.'

'He hadn't the brains,' Trent said. 'He was tough, but that's not the same thing.'

'Tough – and he'd been around.' Volkstadt was unable to hide his pride entirely.

'But I still say he hadn't the brains. I'm not saying he was stupid. But the concept . . . ' He looked Volkstadt directly in the eyes: 'That's why I'd like working with you. Most people just aren't that bright.' He knew he'd said it right.

Volkstadt smiled, not exactly embarrassed at the compliment, but acting a little shy. He'd given it a lot of thought. 'It's kind of a knack more than being bright,' he said: 'I think about a problem and I can see the pressure-points as if they were on a map. You push a little, give a couple of tugs, add a few ingredients, and next thing all the pieces fall into place.'

'But to put Caspar in with the Colonel,' Trent said, again shaking his head. 'The Colonel's really been around.'

'Too damn long. Without you running errands for the Agency, he'd have been out to grass goddamned years ago.' Volkstadt was confident, basking in Trent's admiration and wanting more. 'You're what kept him alive, you were his channel into the Langley Establishment.'

'The Cold War warriors must have got one hell of a fright when you pressured French to give evidence,' Trent said.

'Fright! You should have seen them.' Volkstadt laughed: 'They were already burying stuff you did for them over the past fifteen years as if they were dealing with an anthrax outbreak and I bring them the news on French.'

He looked over at Trent to make sure he understood the perfection in the way it worked. 'I was in this meeting and they're panicking and I say, *Jesus, that's bad. Maybe you should take him out.* Next thing they're sending this fruit-cake down from the States. Your prissy Colonel let him into French's house. The Colonel didn't have the guts for it himself. We got it on film. A knife like the one you hang down your back.'

'The Colonel will talk . . . '

246

'Talk? He'll sing any damn tune I choose. Accessory to murder and attempted murder – this is Mexico. He comes through or I'll crucify the son of a bitch.'

'Poor old man,' Trent said.

'He tried to kill you!' Volkstadt protested, eyes suddenly watchful, the practised smile back in place. 'Whose side are you on?'

'I'm not on anybody's side. I do my job.'

The smile vanished. 'The hell you do. I've got stuff on you that'd make your hair stand on end.' Volkstadt stood up. His eyes were hard and flat and for a moment Trent thought of Louis, the psychopath. 'Play games with me and you'd better watch your back.'

Trent pushed himself out of his chair. He hadn't a lot of strength but he thought that he probably had enough. 'I have watched my back,' he said: 'I'm wired and you're dead.' He hit Volkstadt as hard as he could straight in the face and felt the American's nose shatter.

Trent said, 'Damn,' and put his hand under his armpit.

Unlike Volkstadt, he hadn't got any baggage. He walked out of the hospital.

A white Cherokee jeep stood in the shade of an acacia tree. Benson leant against the hood. Pepito lay beside the jeep on a Guatemalan blanket. He had his head in the lap of a dark, good-looking woman in her early thirties. The woman wore jeans, a sleeveless T-shirt, two good rings and an expensive wristwatch. A second woman sat a little to one side, reading a book. Wrap-around skirt and a white blouse that left her midriff bare. Short hair, short nose, wide mouth and horn-rimmed spectacles.

Figaro played on the jeep's sound system. The Mexican appeared to be asleep. Trent walked over. His hand hurt. The woman closed her book. *Of Love and Shadows* by Isabel Allende, which might mean that she was on the right side, Trent thought.

'Manuella Fuentes,' she said.

'Trent,' Trent said: '*Muy cantado, Señorita.*'

Pepito yawned and opened one eye: 'Hit him?'

Trent showed his hand. Blood was leaking through the bandages.

The Mexican said, 'With snakes you should always use your boot.' He pointed back over his head at the woman whose lap he was using. 'Tina's an engineer, Venezuela. We thought we'd drive down and work out how to get your boat back in the sea.'

'Sounds okay,' Trent said.

Pepito yawned, stretched, and stood up: 'We invited Benson. Crazy gringo, says he has to get back to the office.'

Despite his suit, Benson looked very much at ease and one of the gang. 'Perhaps next time,' he said.

'Thanks for waiting,' Trent said to him. 'I've got the whole thing on tape,' and to Pepito, 'Are you going to get this recorder off me, or do I have to wear it for the rest of my life?'